MORE PRAISE FOR

UNDERBURN

"A POIGNANT, FUNNY, AND TIMELY FAMILY DRAMA FOLLOWING THE OFTEN-TWISTED PATHS WE NAVIGATE TOWARD UNDERSTANDING, RECONCILIATION, AND FORGIVENESS. IRIS FLYNN IS OLIVE KITTREDGE IN GO-GO BOOTS." -- CHRISTOPHER CASTELLANI, AUTHOR OF LEADING MEN

"A WITTY, HEARTFELT NOVEL WITH ENDEARING, IMPERFECT CHARACTERS WHO ARE IMPOSSIBLE TO RESIST, A DEFT EXAMINATION OF A FAMILY IN FLUX."— KRISTYN KUSEK LEWIS, CONTRIBUTING BOOKS EDITOR, REAL SIMPLE

"BILL GAYTHWAITE HAS WRITTEN THE RARE NOVEL THAT IS AS GENTLY TOUCHING AS IT IS SHARPLY HILARIOUS. THE CHARACTERS IN THIS BOOK LEAPT OFF THE PAGE AND INTO MY HEART, THEIR EVERY MESSY MOVE CAPTURED WITH EMOTIONAL PRECISION. UNDERBURN IS A BOOK TO CHERISH." - ABDI NAZEMIAN, STONEWALL AND LAMBDA LITERARY AWARD-WINNING AUTHOR OF LIKE A LOVE STORY AND ONLY THIS BEAUTIFUL MOMENT

UNDERBURN

A NOVEL BY

BILL GAYTHWAITE

Delphinium Books

UNDERBURN

Printed in the United States of America

For information, address DELPHINIUM BOOKS, INC.,
1250 Fourth Street, 5th Floor
Santa Monica, CA 90401

Library of Congress Cataloguing-in-Publication Data is available on request.
ISBN 978-1-953002-44-0

First paperback edition, November 2024

Jacket and interior design by Colin Dockrill, AIGA

For Tommy, of course, and for my son, Zach

CHAPTER ONE

Frank was eating his Chicken Marsala in a desultory fashion. The lavish meal was a bad choice. Iris wondered if they shouldn't even be eating here in the dining room, with its stuffy formality, its place settings and linen napkins. Frank and his boyfriend had been staying with her since the home they rented had been destroyed in the wildfires. Perhaps Frank, as he sat at the table, was contemplating the furniture and dishes and everything else he needed to replace. Iris sighed, thinking of this. They'd been taking all their meals here since they arrived. She might have just ordered pizza tonight and had them eat at the kitchen island. A kinder option, she imagined.

"Isn't the rice lovely?" she said, switching gears.

Iris was making an effort. That's how she thought of it: *making an effort in this atmosphere of loss*. Though Iris hadn't lost anything personally, she still felt bereft on her son's behalf. Frank looked exhausted. His face was puffy and creased and there were dark half-moons under his eyes, like smudges of soot. Iris's home was in an area near the beach that was unaffected by the fires. The charred devastation she observed on the news, the underburn, as she'd heard it described, was almost impossible to contemplate. It reminded her of war zones and lost years and even her own vanquished youth. This was a grim parallel, she realized, and attributed it to the realities of aging and to the increasing challenges she faced due to the arthritis in her spine. Her body, at seventy-three, was, she imagined, its own version of scorched earth.

"What exactly do you mean by 'lovely'?" Logan, the boyfriend, asked now.

He fixed her with a curious gaze. He kept her slightly off balance with questions like that. They had been with her only a short time, but Iris could already tell that Logan enjoyed challenging her, toying with her in a silly cat-and-mouse fashion. The truth was she didn't know what she meant about the rice. It was simply something to say, something to keep the conversation flowing, but no matter what she said, he'd have some *witty* comeback for her, so Iris ignored the question entirely, picked up her napkin, and dabbed at her lips. It was obvious to her that her son's boyfriend thought she was a ridiculous old lady. She had a strong desire to fling a plate at him. But part of the effort she was making was to be pleasant to Frank's *much younger* boyfriend.

She'd known about Logan, in theory at least, for a while. Frank had mentioned he was seeing someone, but he hadn't told her his name and she'd been unaware they were living together, not until three days earlier when they'd been evacuated and both shown up on her doorstep. The first thing she noticed about Logan was his flashy, insistent youth. He couldn't have been more than twenty-six or twenty-seven. He was wearing baby blue tailored shorts and a tight navy blue shirt that accentuated his gym-toned physique. His sneakers were also an unsubtle shade of blue. Even in a life-or-death crisis Logan had managed to arrive color coordinated. He was bluntly, unapologetically handsome, with the casual air of someone whom people made too many allowances for. Beauty had its privileges, of course. Iris had been beautiful once, too, when she was that age and for a while after, and it had afforded her some opportunities as well (she'd had a minor Hollywood career), but in her case there weren't enough opportunities or there wasn't a sufficient amount of luck attached to them to really transform her existence. Her youth, however, was difficult to evaluate from this distance and there was certainly no point in looking back.

"Did you call FEMA today?" she asked now.

There were emergency funds available from the government, but as Frank's home was rented and he had no rental insurance, it was still unclear about any amounts available to him and the procedures ahead.

"No," said Frank. "I need to go down there and talk to someone in person."

"Well, you should," Iris said with some force.

"Yes, Mother," said Frank.

"Yes, Mother," Logan repeated. Frank shot him a glance.

Frank usually just called her Iris or occasionally Ma. *Mother* was his way of telling her to lay off. He had a position of some authority at a rehab facility in Thousand Oaks that had a celebrity clientele—pop stars and A-list actors in freefall. Though he'd just lost everything he owned and was in full crisis mode, Frank's responsibilities there as the chief intake administrator made it impossible for him to take even a day off—or so he said. Of course, Iris was pleased that Frank could immerse himself in his work. Her son hadn't always been so gainfully employed. Things hadn't been easy for Frank in that department. His music career had never taken off and there had been a long stretch of dead-end jobs while he was pursuing it. In addition, he'd had his own struggles with painkillers, which had, curiously enough, led him to this current career. He and Iris had not always gotten on well and been rather estranged when he lived on the East Coast. But at least now that he was back in California, it seemed like he had found his niche in the recovery world and their relationship was strong enough that he'd chosen to show up here after the fire.

Iris wanted to ask if he'd heard anything more from his landlord. It was the landlord who had called Frank to tell him that there was nothing left of the little house in the Malibu Hills he'd been renting. Iris wondered if, when he was allowed back to the property, Frank might recover a few items. Perhaps something had survived after all. They could sift through the rubble together. She would volunteer to help. But Iris decided not to mention the landlord or the salvage idea because she didn't know much about what might actually survive a fire and Frank was not someone who appreciated false hope in any form. And any further discussion of the lost house would surely remind him of Bertram.

Bertram was Frank's twelve-year-old orange tomcat whom Frank hadn't been able to save. The fires had spread quickly, and word of the neighborhood evacuations got to Frank while he was still at work. When he tried to drive to the property to rescue the cat, he hadn't gotten within three miles of the house. His neighborhood was beyond the anchor point, where a fireline had been constructed. Iris knew that her son had been extremely attached to that animal. Bertram had belonged to an old boyfriend in New York, a man Iris had never met. Keith had been killed in an accident. There were numerous photos of Bertram on Frank's Facebook page, posed on a chair or sofa displaying a fed-up look in his eyes. It was best not to remind him of Bertram. She didn't want to watch her son crying at the dining room table about a cat. Iris herself had never been sentimental about animals. She had grown up on a potato farm in Maine, where sentiment of any kind was decidedly frowned upon. Her parents forbade her and her sister from even naming the barn cats, who were only allowed on the farm to keep the mouse population in check and were never permitted in the house.

Thinking of poor Bertram somehow reminded Iris of the last scene in *Breakfast at Tiffany's*, when Audrey Hepburn tosses her cat out of a cab in the middle of a rainstorm, to prove some point about how she wasn't attached to anything. That's when George Peppard rattles off a long speech about how everybody belongs to everybody else, which brings Audrey to her senses and then they both go looking for the cat, which they find in an abandoned lot as they embrace and the rain comes down and *Moon River* swells over the closing credits. Iris had seen this movie as a teenager at the one theater within a thirty-mile radius of her family's farm. She'd had mixed feelings about the film. Even then she was disturbed by Mickey Rooney's racist impersonation of the Japanese photographer, not to mention that feel-good take on high-class prostitution. But she had still wept at the ending, not because of the cat, but because of hunky George Peppard and his heartfelt speech and Audrey Hepburn's waiflike beauty in the rain.

Iris drifted back to the conversation at the dinner table. Logan was going on about how Kylie Jenner was the world's youngest self-made billionaire. A questionable subject after losing everything in a wildfire, but Logan seemed like the type to travel light and he might not have lost anything except more tight T-shirts and tailored shorts. He could afford to talk about ridiculous people, people who had no real claim to fame, but had hijacked it nonetheless.

"I don't see how you can call that girl self-made," said Iris. "She's from a rich, privileged family. She was part of that horrible television show. Everything has been handed to her. She's the poster child for someone born on third base."

"Wow! " said Logan, raising his hand up like a traffic

cop and laughing. "She knows who Kylie Jenner is? I'm impressed."

Logan directed his comment at Frank, as if Iris weren't sitting directly across from them.

"Yes," said Iris, "*she* knows all about the Kardashians and Childish Gambino and Chance the Rapper and how to create an Instagram account, too. *She's* a fucking genius."

So much for her efforts to be pleasant to her son's boyfriend.

Logan was struck silent for a change. Frank was staring out the window into the backyard, toward the pool, as it shimmered in the last, shifting light of the day. Iris wondered if her son was thinking of the houses and apartments he'd grown up in, which were nothing like this one at all. Those former residences didn't have pools, for instance, or lush backyards or even enough property to toss a ball around, but considering the present circumstances, Frank might have been thinking about anything.

Iris got up, cleared the table, and then crossed into the kitchen. The kitchen was large and bright, with an abundance of countertops and built-in cabinets. Several of the cabinets were completely empty, but the emptiness pleased her. Sometimes Iris would open them and stand there, simply admiring the bare spaces. Her life was pared down these days and she liked it that way. Marie Kondo was her hero. She was rinsing off the dishes in the sink when Frank came in with the water glasses.

"Thank you," said Frank as he placed the glasses next to her.

Iris looked up at him, not certain for a moment if he was being sarcastic.

"Thank you," he repeated. "You know, for feeding us."

"It's no trouble," said Iris, but of course, this wasn't true. It *was* trouble to prepare a large meal for people, to put it out and to clear it away. If she were eating alone, she might have just fixed herself a couple of hard-boiled eggs. But how many things, she wondered, did people say during the day that were complete and utter lies? After thirty years selling real estate, her career after Hollywood, Iris knew that truth was often an elusive concept.

"Don't let Logan get under your skin," Frank said now.

Iris looked back into the sink. "Who says that he is?" she said.

"He has an unusual sense of humor."

Is that what we're calling it? she wanted to say, but instead she only muttered, "I see."

"And he's very young," Frank then said, which seemed like an entirely unnecessary observation. And also a bit dismissive.

Iris took some bowls down from the cabinet over the sink. She moved to the refrigerator to retrieve a container of rice pudding she'd made earlier in the day and then began to spoon it into the bowls. She hoped if she looked busy enough, it would prevent Frank from trying to explain the nooks and crannies of Logan's personality, at least if that's where he was headed. This might not have been Frank's intention. Her son had never been one to *overshare*, but perhaps after the fire, the basic tenets of his personality had become unmoored and she distrusted her ability to remain quiet if he tried to make excuses for Logan or explain away the young man's presence in his life. Explanations were clearly unnecessary. You only had to take one look at Logan to see what the initial attraction was, and if the boy possessed less subtle charms, Iris wasn't in the mood to hear about them.

Frank helped Iris bring the bowls of pudding into the dining room. Logan was standing in front of the sideboard with a framed photo in his hands.

"Was this your headshot or something?" Logan asked Iris. "Frank told me you were sort of in show biz back in the day."

"No," Iris answered, "that's just . . . a photo."

She had, in fact, used that particular image as a headshot when she was new to Hollywood, but why should she admit that to Logan? In the photo, Iris wore an expression of brisk sincerity and confidence. There was a look of quiet amusement in her eyes, and her hair, quite long then and the color of amber, cascaded beautifully to her bare shoulders. It was the best photo of her ever taken. The photographer had been so pleased with it, he used it afterward as an advertisement for his studio.

"Wow," Logan said while staring down at the photo. "That's really you!"

Iris flinched at the thoughtless comment, as her youthful vanity sometimes still rose up and clung to her like a wet towel.

"Yes. Can you imagine?" Iris said coolly, but Logan didn't seem to notice.

He put Iris's photo down and pointed at the picture next to it—Erik rappelling down a rock ledge, bearded and wild-eyed, grinning at the camera.

"This your dad?" he asked Frank.

"Yep," Frank answered.

"Cool-looking dude," said Logan.

Iris hated that Logan, this accidental interloper, was offering up his unsolicited commentary as he waltzed around her home, as if wandering through a museum exhibit.

"That he was," Frank replied, "among other things."

Iris coughed uneasily. Erik was great, great fun and the love of her life, but he'd been so incessantly undependable during their marriage, with his lost jobs and stupid infidelities, that occasionally when she thought of these things, she wanted to stash his picture in the hall closet. Her husband had been dead for three years now, but memories of their complicated relationship remained persistent and vivid.

Logan moved on to the photos of Frank next, various candid shots from infancy through his teenage years.

"Would a smile have killed you?" Logan asked now, as he glanced at the pictures.

"What can I tell you?" said Frank as he sat down to his pudding. "I owned moody adolescence."

"Looks like you were leasing a miserable childhood, too." Logan laughed.

"He wasn't as unhappy as those photos imply," Iris blurted out, surprised by the defensive tone in her voice. "He just froze up whenever anyone pointed a camera at him."

"Don't worry, Mother Gessemoni," Logan said. "No one's bringing you up on any charges."

Frank scoffed at Logan's use of their surname.

"One thing's for sure," he said, "if you keep calling her *that*, you'll be wearing your pudding on your head. Now get over here and have your dessert."

Logan left the sideboard and ambled over to the table, parking himself down like a sullen teenager.

"You know I've been off Keto ever since we got here," he said. "Who knows what I'll weigh by the time we leave."

Logan said this as he picked up a spoon and began to shovel pudding into his mouth.

"I'm not sure that fad diets help anyone in the long run," Iris observed disparagingly, though she herself had been devoted to Atkins in the nineties, and from what she'd read about this Keto thing, it was only some repurposed version of that.

"Not a fad," Logan mumbled with his mouth full. "Just logic."

He tapped the side of his head for emphasis.

"Well, dear, you certainly don't need to eat a blessed thing I put in front of you. No one is forcing you."

But by this time, he had almost polished off the pudding and was practically licking the bowl.

"I hear you," Logan grinned. "No worries."

Later, Iris couldn't sleep. She'd been exhausted when she went to bed and had even drifted off for a few minutes, before being jolted awake. When she woke up, she remembered the hazy beginnings of a dream—Erik racing up some steep stairs in front of her, climbing, climbing, turning around every few moments to grin and beckon her along. There was no mystery in this dream, as Erik was always on the move, in more ways than one, hatching career plans that never really added up or throwing himself into every passing California craze, from EST to Karma yoga. One month he was a club promoter, the next he'd be selling speedboats or working security at the Hollywood Bowl. This was part of Erik's charm, his great excitement for the world and everything in it, his overwhelming optimism about life and opportunity. It's what attracted Iris originally, but after a while she sometimes needed a break from the colossal challenge of him, his vast and bustling energy. So when he'd decide to take off for a month of hiking in the Grand Canyon, it wasn't always unwelcome news. Erik had charmed and cajoled his way through endless failings as a husband and he'd also been scrupulously honest with Iris from the start, even about his occasional and fleeting affairs.

"I will always be faithful to you in my fashion," he'd told her early on, sometime between the *Summer of Love* and *The Me Decade,* "but I could never promise monogamy and I won't lie to you about it or be a hypocrite either."

That *faithful* line was from some old Ronald Colman movie.

"You think that bullshit gets you special points somewhere?" Iris had replied.

She had thought of her parents back in Maine, who had been utterly committed to each other in all things; her father a solid and steadfast provider. The chores and rituals of the farm were as enduring as the sun. But where had all that devotion really gotten them? They had both been miserable people, pinched and monosyllabic, breathtakingly judgmental with everyone they encountered. Erik, on the other hand, was ceaselessly upbeat and extroverted. He never pretended to be anyone other than who he was, which was a strong selling point in the make-believe world of Southern California. Not for one instant did Iris ever doubt Erik's love for her or his sincerity. His love was like a heat-seeking missile, in fact. He'd dote on her and Frank whenever he was in their orbit. He was an engaged and loving father and wildly supportive of Iris's career, too, of her *great artistry*, as he often referred to it, in his wishful enthusiasm.

The occasional infidelity was not going to be her line in the sand.

As she lay there in the dark, she wondered, not for the first time, about which personality traits got passed on, specifically how much of her husband's freewheeling nature had been imprinted on Frank. Her son certainly didn't possess Erik's chatty, gregarious nature, but he'd bounced around in a similar fashion. It was only now, at forty-two, with his demanding job at the rehab, that Frank was showing signs of real responsibility. It was because he'd hung on too long in the music business, Iris thought. After dropping out of college, he'd played guitar and sung backup for years in an Indie Folk band called *Unsung Hero*, which mostly covered the music of similar, more successful groups—*Bright Eyes, The Mountain Goats, Lullaby of the Working Class*. Iris still remembered their names. Frank's band was just starting to find its footing and they were about to be signed to a label, when he was kicked to the curb by the homophobic lead singer. He'd fled for New York City after that. He was already thirty years old by then and it didn't help that he arrived in New York embittered, with his spirit crushed, which was usually how people left that town. He threw himself into the starving artist life, trying to get some traction as a solo act, playing in downtown bars and clubs, sometimes working in the kitchen afterward as part of the gig. He became a busker in New York, performing on the city streets and in the subways, with variable success. He did better around the holidays, he said, when people tended to be reminded of generous impulses. Frank lived in bombed-out sublets in lousy neighborhoods or tiny makeshift apartments with crazy roommates. This all seemed like needless waste to Iris. Her son once accused her of not believing in his talent, and there might have been some truth to that. He was a good musician (she'd paid for all those lessons!) and a fluid, interesting singer, but success involved too many other variables. Iris wasn't sure if he had enough grit and determination.

Getting kicked out of the band had obviously set him back. Frank often had a wistful tone in his voice after that, whenever he called home, a cadence of diminished expectations. This was probably why he had settled for singing on the streets of New York, where he could retain some semblance of control. Iris remembered how happily supportive Erik had been of Frank back then, pleased that he was *following his dream*. This wasn't so surprising, considering Erik had had his own musical ambitions when he was young (he'd once contributed some lyrics to a forgotten song by

The Turtles), and after those dreams had played out, he had followed an assortment of other ones, right off cliffs and down rabbit holes.

Iris wasn't sure what had woken her up. Perhaps it was some noise from the guest room across the hall. Maybe it was Frank and Logan making love. She didn't feel embarrassed or squeamish thinking about her son messing around with his boyfriend. If anything, she hoped Frank was able to find some comfort in Logan's strapping arms. Frank had come out to his parents at nineteen, somewhat crossly, as if he was looking for an argument. Iris's matter-of-fact reaction seemed to annoy him more than anything else. It was Erik who took longer to come around. This was a surprise to her, as her husband usually flaunted a *Free to Be You and Me* vibe. To his credit, he didn't let Frank see any of those mixed feelings. He had said all the right things at the time and held his son close. But privately, he'd groused about it, slammed things around for days.

"I just didn't plan on this," he'd told Iris.

"In my experience," she had responded, "it doesn't make sense to put much faith in plans. They have a way of changing on you."

Iris had said this rather pointedly, given that she and Frank had always adjusted to Erik's various whims, changes of direction, and financial disregard. Iris thought he might have attempted to be a little less thrown by something as fixed and undebatable as their son's sexual orientation.

Iris got up, grabbed her robe, and left the bedroom. The guest room, as she passed it, was completely quiet. When she reached the kitchen, all the lights were on and Logan was sitting at the cooking island, scrolling through his phone with another bowl of pudding in front of him. He didn't notice her at first, and as Iris watched him, it occurred to her that at this hour he might be on some sex app, in search of a hookup. She wasn't stupid. She knew what young men got up to in the middle of the night. And then when he finally saw Iris standing there, his face didn't look entirely innocent either.

"Just trying to get some more news on the fires," he said, putting his phone down. "They're still raging to the north."

"Terrible," said Iris as she filled a water glass at the sink.

"True," he said.

She debated with herself whether she should just walk back with the water to her bedroom, but she ended up sitting across from Logan at the island instead.

"I hope you don't mind me getting more pudding," he said.

"Why should I mind? I'm glad you've decided the Keto police won't barge in and drag you away."

"It's more that I have a weakness for rice pudding, but I know you must think I'm being ridiculous," said Logan, pointing to his muscular torso.

He was in gym shorts and a sleeveless T-shirt.

"I work out like a fiend, of course, but on the show they really watch our appearance. An extra five pounds could get me canned."

"Oh. That can't be good," said Iris.

She wondered if she should reach over and take the pudding away from him. The last thing Frank needed was for this kid to lose his job and then he'd have something else to worry about. Logan was a background artist on *Windsor Valley High*, a show that sounded like it was designed for angst-ridden teens. He had explained that he was in most of the classroom shots, where he played one of the overaged students. He was called a featured extra. Sometimes they threw him a line and sometimes there were locker room scenes where he had to take off his shirt. Hence, his carb concerns.

"And where does this show air?" asked Iris.

"It's on the Neptune Network."

"I'm afraid I don't know it," she said, more snootily than she'd intended.

"That's totally fine," Logan said cheerfully. "I just figured since you have that pop culture thing going for you, then you might have heard of it."

"Well, there are limits to what one can retain in one's head," said Iris.

"It's a very popular show. There's a huge following on Insta," Logan said.

"I'll have to take your word for it," replied Iris. "It's hard to keep track of all the TV shows these days. There are so many platforms. I'm surprised my microwave hasn't started handing out development deals."

"That's funny," Logan said, but without actually laughing.

"When I was acting," said Iris in a tone of tired explanation, "there were only three television channels."

"Yes. I've heard about that," said Logan, as if they were discussing something from the Industrial Revolution.

It was the sixties when Iris had arrived in Hollywood and she'd found television work quickly. She kept working for a long time. Making a living was more challenging, of course, once she married Erik, with his irregular paychecks, and then later, when Frank came along. She had loved acting. She knew what it was like to give her all to something, only to get so little in return. This attitude had played into her worries for Frank when he was trying to scrape a music career together. Recently, though, she had begun to wonder—if she were just starting out again, would her career maybe amount to something, given all the increased opportunities, all the new venues and original programming? Or maybe, like Logan, she'd be playing an invisible high school student on some brainless TV show for snarky teens. This was probably unfair, as Logan was still so young, it remained to be seen where his career might take him.

"So have you had any training?" she asked him, suddenly interested.

Logan shook his head.

"It's not that way anymore," he answered. "I don't think you really need an acting school. Acting is, like, instinctive. You're, like, born with it, more or less. That's how I see it anyway, from my perspective."

Which would be from the back row of a fake history class on the Neptune Network, Iris felt like saying.

"By the way," Logan was telling her now, "Frank says I owe you an apology."

"For what?" said Iris. She could think of a few possibilities.

"Earlier tonight when I said, 'That's really you!' when I was holding your photograph. As though it was unexpected. Frank tells me you're a little touchy about your looks."

"Did he now?" said Iris.

The apology wasn't really necessary, and yet it somehow made her feel worse than the original remark.

"Frank's barely told me anything about your old showbiz career," said Logan. "How did that come about?"

There was some flicker of interest in Logan's eyes that prompted her to answer.

"Well, I guess my real start was winning a beauty contest back home in Maine. First prize was some cash, a free plane ticket to Los Angeles, and a screen test in Hollywood."

"Wow. That's like something out of a movie," said Logan. "It was sort of the same thing with me. A casting agent came into a Starbucks where I was hanging out. He walked around and around staring at everybody, but in the end, he only handed out two business cards, one to me and one to this girl who looked like Zendaya. He said we each had the right look for a show he was casting. That's how I landed *Windsor Valley High*."

"That doesn't sound like the same thing at all," Iris said glumly. "I actually *won* a contest."

"I know," said Logan. "So did I, basically anyway."

Iris made a real effort to let this subject go. Partly because she realized she'd been telling the same lie for over fifty years. Erik had never even known the truth and neither did Frank—that she hadn't actually won that contest. She'd been second runner-up. Afterward, Iris had bought a bus ticket with her own savings and headed to California the following week. She crashed thirty or forty agents' offices as soon as she got off the bus, until she was signed. Later she found out the winner of that contest hadn't gone to Hollywood at all. She had stayed in Maine and ended up marrying one of the contest judges.

"So what movies were you in?" said Logan, pushing away his pudding and fixing her with a blissful gaze.

"A few forgettable ones," she answered, "but mostly I had small parts on television, shows you've never even heard of, I'm sure."

"Like what?"

"Oh, I don't know, *The Beverly Hillbillies*, *Bewitched*, *I Dream of Jeannie*. A bunch of others."

It was unclear if Logan had heard of any of these programs, but since he was watching her with such happy expectancy, she went on.

"When I first got out here, I was a go-go dancer at a club on Sunset."

"No shit," said Logan.

"Yes," said Iris. "And one day somebody saw me there

and I got called in to be a backup dancer for a promotional film they were doing. It's what they call a music video these days. Anyway, it was for the song 'These Boots Are Made for Walkin'.'"

"Get the fuck out of town!" said Logan, almost jumping up from the cooking island. "You're in that? With Nancy Sinatra? I've seen that video like a thousand times on YouTube. It's one of my favorite things on the planet!"

Iris laughed out loud.

"Yeah, right," she said.

"No, it's true. I love it. It's the campiest thing ever made, which doesn't mean that it's not also really great. But why wouldn't your son tell me this like right off? He should have led with that, right after he introduced himself. 'My mom's in the video for "These Boots Are Made for Walkin'."' I would have slept with him right away, instead of making him wait a week!"

Iris sipped some water. She assumed this comment required no response.

"Oops," Logan said. "Sorry. That was probably inappropriate. People tell me I have boundary issues."

"Don't worry about it. I feel like that was a genuine compliment."

"Absolutely," said Logan. "That's just how it was meant. Seriously, though, I would have retired after doing that video. You didn't need to accomplish anything else!"

Iris could see that the kid was half serious, but that's not exactly how the job had felt to Iris at the time. It was just another gig. The song was already a hit by then and she'd spent a day shooting the short film on a mostly bare set in a studio in Burbank with Nancy Sinatra and five other girls in go-go boots and long fuzzy sweaters barely covering their panties. It was unclear at the time where this fledgling music video would even be shown, and the director/choreographer was sour and miserable for most of the shoot. Iris wasn't one of the strongest dancers. She had no real training. She hadn't even auditioned for that club on Sunset, where the owner had just taken one look at her and given her the job. After she started there, she'd taken to wearing a fake wedding ring and telling everybody her husband was fighting in Vietnam to keep the boss and the other creeps at bay

"In the Quang Tri province," she'd tell these men gravely, with downcast eyes.

After shooting the video, Nancy Sinatra, who was sweet and professional, invited everyone to a wrap party at Ciro's, a famous dance club in West Hollywood. Iris didn't go out much. She already worked long hours in a busy nightspot, after all, but she couldn't exactly say no to Nancy Sinatra. Ciro's was upscale and crowded, the walls painted a slick fire engine red, and the ceiling was covered with iridescent tiles. The clientele appeared to be a mix of flower children of studio executives and real-life celebrities. A tall, rugged-looking guy, who didn't fall into either category, approached Iris as soon as she walked in and pulled her onto the dance floor. His moves were terrible, which didn't seem to dull his enthusiasm in the slightest. He just pointed to his feet and laughed at himself, raising his hands up in the air in a funny, apologetic gesture. Iris was so immediately disarmed by his happy, buzzing goofiness that she quickly slipped the fake wedding ring off her finger.

This, of course, was Erik.

"Did you ever dance in an Elvis movie?" Logan was asking excitedly.

"No," Iris laughed. "I wasn't really a dancer for very long. I married Frank's father shortly after that shoot. And he didn't want me dancing in the club anymore."

"That seems a bit controlling," Logan frowned.

"Not really. He just had a protective side and the club was pretty skeevy. I wore a bikini and danced in a cage. It was grim."

This was probably the reason Frank hadn't told Logan the "Boots" story. He'd always been a bit embarrassed hearing about his mother's early dance *career*, her modeling for trade shows (she had to smile seductively while demonstrating refrigerators), and her television roles where she had often played some sexy girl strutting around in a mini skirt or low-cut blouse. She'd have only a scene or two (these were always small parts), but who wants to think about their mother flirting in a swimsuit or tossing out saucy lines to the camera? As she'd gotten older, the roles were less overtly sexy, but still adhered to a general theme—the drunken ex-stripper, a loopy showgirl. These were not anyone's idea of *artistic opportunities*. Her good looks had opened the door for her in the business, but then quite quickly she had been typed, for which she partly blamed her longtime agent. She'd been happy enough to sign with the guy when she arrived in Hollywood, but he wasn't powerful enough to get her seen for prestige movies or a meeting with Norman Lear. As the years passed, her career felt driven by the law of diminishing returns.

"Don't you miss it?" Logan was asking her now.

She stared at him across the cooking island, confused.

"Performing," he explained. "You know, giving something back to the world."

"I think you're overstating what I was doing back then."

She didn't think falling into a pool on *Green Acres* had contributed to much of anything.

"But no," she answered simply. "I don't miss it. Life carries on."

If she missed anything, it was the kind of career she

never had in the first place. The truth was she had grown tired of the scramble for work, the scrimping required to support her family, not to mention the fake cheer and the whistling past the graveyard and those leering casting agents. Then the parts, as flimsy as they were, had begun to dry up, which was the natural by-product of Hollywood's cruel and arbitrary obsession with youth. Prices were skyrocketing all around them in those days and so she and Erik were always on the lookout for cheaper housing—something closer to the studios, because if you got on the 101 at the wrong time of day, it could take you three hours to travel five miles.

They had bounced around too much when Frank was little, lived in too many places. Iris often had to park Frank with actress friends or babysitters for long stretches if she was auditioning or filming and if Erik was out of town, which was not exactly a rare event. Her young son would carp bitterly about all this, about her neglect and distractions. Even now, in his forties, Frank could still make some weary comment about those early days. "My so-called childhood," he might say. He had been a lot more forgiving of Erik. Frank accepted his father's absences as if they were entirely natural occurrences. Erik had worked his magic on the kid, of course, and sometimes he even took Frank with him on those golden camping trips. They'd come home joking and boastful after a week or two away, like a couple of army buddies, and Iris was so filled with gratitude for her son's happiness (he'd never been a lighthearted kid) that she stifled her own complaints. But there was nothing new in that story as far as mothers were concerned.

She had moved on to real estate when Frank was twelve, through a connection with a publicist she knew, someone else who had left the business. Selling real estate required a different kind of hustling than Iris was used to, and it took a long while to find her footing. She possessed an eager, pleasant style selling houses and she also had a thick skin when it came to rejection, qualities honed after several thousand auditions. Her middle-aged beauty, faded by Hollywood standards, was still attention grabbing out in the real world and this didn't hurt either. Sometimes she'd even be recognized by a client and then she'd find herself regaling them with stories about what it was like on the set of *Barnaby Jones* or *The Rockford Files*. But things didn't really click for her in terms of financial success until the California housing boom of the late nineties. By that time, Frank had already left home and was touring with his band.

"Iris," Logan was saying now. "I should tell you something."

His tone was suddenly bleak and hesitant, and his face had clouded up. Christ, Iris thought, does the kid think we've bonded over Nancy Sinatra? She wasn't in the mood for any of his confessions right now. But he kept talking anyway.

"I wasn't just looking at the news when you came in here." he said. "The thing is, I'm worried about Frank. I know his troubles were before my time, but I was Googling some stuff about relapse."

"Frank has relapsed!" Iris shouted.

"No, I don't think so. I mean, not yet."

"Not yet? What would make you say something like that? My son is sober! He's been through rehab. He *works* in a rehab, for Christ's sake!"

"Yes," Logan answered, "I know. But he's also been through something terribly traumatic. He's lost so much, everything from his past, his guitars and music, his vinyl collection—all the stuff that belonged to Keith, including poor Bertram. Losses can be like triggers, Iris. That's what I was reading about."

"Why would he start using again?" Iris replied. "That would only make everything worse. He knows that. My son is not stupid!"

"It's not a question of stupidity, I'm afraid," said Logan. "I know Frank isn't stupid, but he *is* an addict and he's just been through something traumatic."

"Will you please stop using that word?" Iris snapped. "I know what's he's been through. He's staying here, isn't he? Along with you!"

"Yes, of course." said Logan. "And we appreciate it. But I thought we might be allies in this. I thought you and I might *need* to be allies, so I felt I should tell you my concerns."

If that didn't sum up Logan's generation in a nutshell, thought Iris, the need to share every little notion that came into their heads on any platform imaginable, even while seated at her cooking island.

"Well, thanks for sharing," she said sadly.

Then she sat there, slumped on the kitchen stool, absorbing what he'd said, as the truth rained down on her. Why hadn't this terrible thought occurred to her immediately and why was she so annoyed with this boy for bringing it to her attention? It was certainly true: Her son *had* lost everything. He'd lost more than she could ever know or even imagine. *Of course* he was vulnerable and at risk. Frank had been clean for nearly three years, but that wasn't really so long in the scheme of things. Was it simple denial on her part or was it just too hard to remember those days—as the memories of Frank's addiction were also attached to Erik being in the final stages of lymphoma? In fact, they had only found out about Frank because he'd flown home to see his father one last time. Iris had been pleading with her son for months to make the trip, but Frank kept putting it off. It was finally Erik who had gotten on the phone with him and said flatly, "I need to see my boy. Get your ass on a plane. There will be a ticket waiting for you at the airport."

Iris had met him at LAX two days later. Frank was edgy and disheveled, skinny as a pipe cleaner, and when she looked into his face, she noticed his eyes were unfocused and bloodshot. When she asked him about his appearance, he'd blamed the long flight.

"What?" she said. "You lost thirty pounds on the plane?"

Iris dropped the subject when Frank asked about his father's condition. Erik didn't have much longer, she'd told him. The chemo had completely failed, and he wasn't a candidate for a bone marrow transplant either. He was at home but getting weaker by the day. A hospice nurse came by in the afternoons. Frank had put his head against the car window after hearing this news and turned his face away from her. They had driven on in silence after that. When they got back to the house, Erik took one look at his son and practically sat straight up in bed, as sick as he was.

"What the hell is wrong with *you*!?" he had shouted.

Erik pointed his finger at Frank and said that he recognized somebody who was strung out when he saw it. Erik had been an active participant in the sixties drug culture before he met Iris (and for a while afterward, too) and he had remained savvier than she was in that department. Iris was floored. Frank had never been a druggy kid, not even while touring with his band. Maybe because his father was in such rough shape, Frank's defenses were weak, because after some probing questions, he broke down and told them about the painkillers. He cited a string of setbacks in the city, starting with the shocking death of a boyfriend they didn't even know about. Keith had died in a bike crash near Central Park. Frank had inherited the guy's cat.

"Well," Erik told his son, in the most serious and resolute

voice Iris could ever remember him using. "We're going to get you into a rehab as soon as possible and you are going to get the help that you need and you are going to get healthy. You won't fight it either, because this is your Pop's *Make-A-Wish* moment and you're going to be man enough to grant it to him."

Three days later, Frank checked himself into Harmony West, which Iris and Erik paid for. They took some comfort in knowing Frank would not have acquiesced so easily if he hadn't wanted to get sober in the first place. Erik had rallied some, while his son was away in treatment, waiting for him to come home. When he did return, after sixty days, Frank looked a little shaky, but he'd put on some weight, his eyes were clear, and he was embracing his recovery. Once again, he resembled their sweet-faced boy.

Erik had died soon after that, at peace, Iris liked to believe, and then Frank had packed up his things in New York and moved back to California, with Bertram in tow. He rented a tiny home in the hills and got a job at the rehab facility where he had been a client, working his way up to his present position.

Iris sat up very straight.

"I should have been thinking about relapse, too," she said quietly. "I'm not someone who likes to imagine the worst. I apologize to you."

"No worries," said Logan, gazing from his empty pudding bowl into Iris's eyes. "But I need to tell you something else. I'm not sure what you've been thinking about Frank and me, but I need you to know that I really care for him—like a hundred percent. He's been super kind to me . . . and kindness has sort of been missing from my life."

There was something in the way the kid said this. Iris had no trouble believing him.

"Frank has a big heart," she said, "though he tends to hide it."

"Not with me," said Logan. "I won't let him."

The boy's voice cracked with emotion. She stared into Logan's handsome, flushed face and realized she had probably misread him from the start. The dopey hunk she thought she knew was just some facade for this other, more substantial person sitting across from her now.

Something occurred to her then and she got up from the stool and rushed over to the cabinets.

"What is it?" asked Logan.

Iris rarely took anything stronger than aspirin for her arthritis, but her doctor had given her a prescription for Percocet. *For the rougher days*, he had said. She reached into the cabinet now, picked up the bottle, and turned around to show Logan.

"It's okay," she said. "Not even opened."

They shared a sad smile before she put it in the pocket of her robe.

"I guess I should get back to bed now," said Iris. "We'll discuss this some more tomorrow. And regarding your ally question—sure, you can count on me."

"Good to know," said Logan.

She picked up her water glass and Logan's bowl and brought them to the sink.

"So do you ever look at that music video anymore?" he asked. "It's such a hoot."

"Not for ages," she replied over her shoulder.

But this wasn't true. She'd found it on YouTube just a few months earlier, when she was in a nostalgic mood, a weakness for nostalgia being the natural consequence, she supposed, of her advancing age. She had marveled at her youth and effortless beauty while watching the video, and she remembered quite clearly the very real feeling of being terrified she'd screw up the dance steps and be responsible for causing another take. And while she watched, she couldn't stop thinking about how the girl in the film was only a few hours away from meeting Erik and from her life changing forever. She thought of this again now as she crossed the kitchen, how shooting that video had led her to this very moment. Otherwise, she'd be in some other house and Logan wouldn't be here at all. She thought Logan might be amused by this idea, his cosmic connection to Nancy Sinatra, but when she turned around to tell him, he was back to scowling into his phone. Iris left the kitchen then and walked down the hall. The guest room was still quiet. She reached out and placed her palm on the door, making a silent wish for her sleeping son and for all the others out there who were navigating a world on fire.

CHAPTER TWO

Frank had no idea where he was. He'd woken up with a start. A dim, hazy light was spilling into the room, reflected from the pool in the backyard, creating some flickering shadows on the ceiling. At first, the flickering aspect reminded him of flames, so he had a moment or two of real panic and was about to bolt from the bed, but then he remembered that he was in his mother's guest room and her place was away from the danger zone, which was why he and Logan had landed here in the first place. Frank thought he must still be in shock after losing everything in the wildfire, if shock felt anything like the droning electrical current coursing through his limbs right now or the dull relentless throb behind his eyes. He turned on his side to look at the clock and saw that he was alone in the bed. It was 2:07 a.m. Perhaps Logan had gone to jerk off in the bathroom. Frank wasn't sure why this particular notion should cross his mind or why the idea of Logan in a solo act of pleasure saddened him so much, except it was easier than contemplating the loss of all his possessions. This got him thinking of Bertram again, whom he already missed tremendously. The cat was the last real connection Frank had to Keith and his life on the East Coast, a fact he wished right now he could push from his mind. But it was nearly impossible to control his thoughts. Earlier, at the dinner table, he had stared out the window and suddenly remembered a documentary he'd seen about volcanoes. Volcanic ash was said to travel thousands of miles in the air. It must be true of wildfires, too, thought Frank. As he looked outside, he had imagined everything he owned reduced to ashes, drifting to unknown destinations. If he hadn't been so distracted by his mother's subtle surveillance from across the table and the familiar edge to her voice, this terrible idea might have led him to a panic attack. He'd heard on the news that fires were still burning on both sides of the Pacific Coast Highway, hundreds of homes destroyed, over ninety thousand acres engulfed. The third worst October fire on record in Southern California. He knew he shouldn't be asking the question "Why me?" when these horrible, deadly circumstances were impacting so many others. But the heartache was overwhelming.

Liam, his NA sponsor, liked to say the second act of Frank's life had begun with his sobriety and his move back to California, but it was technically his third. The second act had been years earlier, when he was thirty and he had fled for New York City, after getting booted from the cover band where he'd been a guitarist and sung backup since dropping out of USC. *Unsung Hero* played a lot of local gigs and toured some around the Pacific Northwest. He'd been with the band for years, his involvement fixed and uneventful, until a cute keyboardist came on board. Frank had developed a blazing little crush. The keyboardist was either an all-purpose flirt or liked to give some seriously mixed messages, because nothing ever happened between them—except that the homophobic lead singer, who had always been blandly tolerant of Frank in a *Don't Ask, Don't Tell* fashion, got so unnerved by the infatuation taking place right under his nose that he bounced Frank out of the band. The split happened as the group was finally getting some attention from a label. Frank made sure to remind people of that fact when he told the story. It heightened the devastation aspect.

In New York, Frank had tried to make a go of it on his own. He was done navigating the internal politics of crappy cover bands and homo-panicking lead singers. Legit gigs were few and far between when he got to the city and he couldn't land any representation either, so he'd eventually become a busker, playing on the city streets and in subway stations. There was a fairly organized process for the subway work, and you didn't need a permit. After a while, Frank auditioned for the Music Underground Program, sponsored by the transit authority, which acted as a sort of manager for the city's underground musicians, assigning locations and schedules, providing a professional gloss to the busker experience. Frank had always auditioned well and so he had landed a spot. Some buskers looked down on the bourgeois aspect of all this. Sam Razio, a cranky saxophonist Frank knew from when he first arrived in the city, used to say, "We're fucking street musicians, dude, not Josh Groban!"

But Frank enjoyed living within some of these set parameters. He could still choose his own repertoire, which pleased him. He liked slowing down the arrangements to classic Jim Croce or Joni Mitchell ballads, because it gave him the illusion that he was creating something original. He enjoyed repeating numbers, too, five or six times in a row to a constantly changing audience, like an artist painting a tree again and again, trying to get it exactly right. He still dealt with the usual headaches of performing in public, the overheated stations in summer and the crowded platforms, when trains were delayed or broken down—not exactly an infrequent occurrence. Crazy people would sometimes sidle up next to him to sing along, drowning him out, or teenagers would fling pennies at him and tell him he sucked. One time a homeless guy pissed into his open guitar case, soaking the day's earnings. But for the most part, Frank's shift would pass uneventfully, and he'd collect a decent amount of tax-free cash, grateful for a certain amount of autonomy and a smattering of genuine applause.

Once when Frank was performing on a subway platform at Times Square, he noticed a cute guy with glasses, who was about his age, standing a few feet in front of him with a pensive look on his face. It was difficult to know whether the guy liked what he was listening to or not, because he let a few trains go by, as he watched, but then he boarded an Uptown Number 1 without dropping anything into the guitar case. When he was there again the following week, Frank realized he'd been on the lookout for him. Frank worked his way through three or four Tracy Chapman songs, before taking a break, reaching in his backpack for a bottle of water. The guy stepped up to him then, amid the mad swarm of people. This was rush hour. "You're very talented," he said. "But I bet you're just playing for the sake of it, aren't you? You'd be here, even if nobody was contributing a cent."

You mean in the way that you're not contributing a cent? Frank wanted to say, but he did not say this. He simply said, "Maybe you're right," and sipped some more water.

Frank had a policy of agreeing with the public, knowing that they could easily turn into an angry mob. He did not think Keith's comment (for this was Keith) was particularly original. Most of the buskers he knew, most real musicians, played for their own sake or their own sanity or because they felt like they couldn't *not* play. It surprised Frank when Keith remained on the platform and began asking him more questions, about acoustics in the subway and the brand of his guitar. He seemed very eager for the information, and Frank wondered at first if he might be writing an article for a website or making a report of some kind, but it turned out it was only Keith's natural curiosity. He worked as an archivist at Columbia University, organizing and cataloging old letters and historical documents, trying to put some order to the past.

Later, when they went out to eat, it seemed Keith was trying to make sense of Frank, too. Keith had never known a busker before, or anyone who sang or played guitar or even anyone from California. He acted as if Frank were an important new discovery found in a lost box in some attic. This was not an assessment Frank had ever experienced before and so it was rather intoxicating. They had gone to a narrow, unclean diner on West 46th Street. Photos of old Broadway actors lined the walls. Jerry Orbach was hanging above their booth, wearing a caustic expression on his face.

"Is it always your job to be this inquisitive?" Frank asked, after they had placed their orders and the food had arrived and the questions kept on coming.

"Yes and no," said Keith. "Archivists are a bit like detectives. That part is true. But I don't invite everyone I meet out to dinner or ask this many questions usually. I only do that with people who really pique my interest . . . or have pretty blue eyes."

It was a cheesy line, but Frank found himself blushing anyway. They sat silently for a minute.

"You know, your face looks different when you perform," Keith then said, motioning at him with a French fry.

Frank wasn't sure how to respond to that, so he didn't say anything at all. He glanced up at Jerry Orbach.

"There's a happy tranquility that comes over you," said Keith, "a sort of captured joy."

"And what about now," asked Frank, turning back to Keith, meeting his gaze, "out here in the real world?"

"It's still a very nice face, only a less joyful one," Keith had replied.

This was the moment Frank had begun to fall in love. It was probably the notion of being seen, of finally being revealed. Frank had grown used to flying under the radar. He was thirty-eight years old. He'd been in the city for eight of those years, *shoveling shit against the tide*, which was how he usually thought of his existence. Ever since coming out, he'd been awkward and bashful around guys. He'd barely even slept around. He liked to hide behind his guitar. Whatever romantic optimism Frank possessed had been worn down over the years like the finish of a car. He had pretty much given up on ever finding anyone. His love life felt like a book out of print. Then Keith had appeared, with his direct little queries and heated glances.

Keith was essentially a shy, bookish person. The bookish part was no surprise, given his profession. Like Frank, he didn't have a slew of dating experience either—which was a kind of comfort to them both. Keith told Frank that he had never approached anyone so confidently before, but he had simply grown bold after watching Frank perform.

"Blame Tracy Chapman," said Frank after they had slept together for the first time.

Given their *meet cute* beginnings and compatible romantic histories, Frank believed destiny had played a part in bringing them together. He was totally smitten, but he chose to keep the relationship under wraps at first. He didn't mention Keith to his parents when he called home. His mother in particular had often fretted about his solitary state, like something might be broken in him. He was sure that putting words to this strange new miracle would have somehow jinxed it. He just wanted some time to pull this new happiness around him and revel in it.

In the spring, Frank moved into Keith's sunny, cluttered apartment on West 106th Street, with its cramped bookcases, crowded surfaces, and the conspicuous, glowering Bertram, who stalked around the space with weary indignation, like a dethroned monarch. This was five months after they had met on the subway platform. Frank was grateful to the universe for the first time in his entire life—but then not six weeks later, while riding his bike to work, a garbage truck made an illegal turn and Keith was struck and killed instantly. Frank had received the call from the emergency room. When had Keith added him as the emergency contact on his phone? He had to go identify Keith's body in a hospital on Amsterdam Avenue. A nurse gave him directions to the morgue, but then he got lost in the bowels of the place. An orderly found him wandering the hallways, acting as if he'd been clubbed over the head. When he got home that night, he sat on the sofa, half believing Keith would walk through the door at any minute. He was silently pleading for it to somehow be true. The grief must have temporarily short-circuited the rational area of his brain. Everyone had been so kind, the nurse and the orderly and even a tough-looking cop who'd given him the details of the accident in a calm, compassionate voice. It was perhaps the unexpected kindness that had undone him. He'd gotten up from the sofa finally, grabbed his best guitar, an expensive Gibson J-35, and paced around the apartment before smashing it to pieces against the kitchen sink.

The driver of the garbage truck was given a traffic citation and other cyclists created a memorial at the scene of the crash, leaving notes and flowers and bike locks. The cruelty of Keith's death felt as preordained as their first meeting. Frank felt as if a power line had been cut within him. He gave up music afterward, dropping it like a bad habit. Without Keith's encouragement, he had no interest in kidding himself about any relevance he might have as a performer, and was overcome when he even tried to hold a guitar; his singing voice smothered and lost. And then, after that, came the painkillers and that blurry, miserable year of addiction.

Logan was coming through the guest room door now, attempting to be very, very quiet. His movements were so slow and exaggerated that he reminded Frank of a cartoon character.

"It's okay. I'm awake," said Frank.

"You are?"

"So it would appear."

Frank leaned over and turned on the bedside lamp. His mother's spacious guest room, with its stark furnishings and bare, coral-colored walls, was suddenly bathed in a warm glow, as was Logan dressed in his running shorts and sleeveless T. He stood over the bed and tilted his head at Frank, like a quizzical dog.

"How long have you been awake?" asked Logan. "Did I disturb you when I got up?"

"I don't know."

"Sorry," said Logan.

"Why are you apologizing?"

"Well, just the same," said Logan.

"*Just the same* what?" said Frank. "Never mind. Where were you?"

"In the kitchen, with Iris."

"What's everybody doing up?" asked Frank.

"These are troubling times," said Logan.

His tone was grave—or since this was Logan, his tone was less grave than earnest.

"True enough," Frank smiled.

His mother always had a touch of insomnia. When he was a kid and got up in the middle of the night to go to the bathroom, he might encounter her roaming around, going over her lines if she was filming the next day. Once, he remembered now, she had even let him stay up with her to run a scene—though this was a vague and solitary recollection, so Frank wondered if it was even true or perhaps his memories were something else that had been impacted by the fire and they were now dislodged and floating along with the ashes. Then again, sometimes he had a surprising propensity for wishful thinking (perhaps what remained of the hopeful artist in him) that extended to the past and sometimes blurred things retroactively. He wanted the memory of that time with his mother to be real.

"We were talking about her acting days," Logan said now. "She did pretty well for herself, you know. Lots of guest appearances. Why didn't you tell me?"

"I didn't *not* tell you," said Frank.

"You made it seem like she barely worked."

"I did nothing of the sort," Frank responded, though he wasn't sure what his silence on the subject might have implied.

In truth, Iris *had* worked . . . a lot. She had been the bread winner actually, his father being rather unreliable in that department. Iris had played a bunch of small roles, modeled a bit, and done commercials, but she'd never been a star in her own right or even a series regular. She'd been a blond bombshell type. Some of her parts required her to deliver her lines in a breathy Marilyn Monroe fashion. Iris's real-life voice had been nothing like that at all, not even accidentally. As a child, Frank never knew how to express the confusion he felt about these very different versions of his mother, which essentially boiled down to two—the ditzy blonde who spouted wisecracks on the screen and the rather solemn woman who ran the show at home, with her chilly aplomb. Frank's father, a happy, jack-of-all-trades type, always insisted the family sit in front of the television together whenever Iris was going to be making one of her TV appearances. Erik was a terrific audience. He'd laugh out loud if Iris was spouting double entendres on some tired sitcom or praise a subtle acting moment (so subtle, Frank never noticed them) if she was playing a nurse in an emergency room and the role required a more serious interpretation. Erik would insist they watch the program all the way through, so he could bellow the name his wife used professionally (her maiden name) as it scrolled by in the closing credits. *Iris Flynn!* he'd shout jubilantly. His father's infectious cheer was hard to resist. Frank wasn't sure why he hadn't mentioned Iris's past glories to Logan, such as they were. Maybe it was because Logan was an actor, too, technically at least, and the comparison felt a bit awkward. Logan playing a background teen on a show set in a high school was disconcerting enough, but at least all the students were being played by glossy actors pushing thirty. Logan himself had just turned twenty-five.

"She danced, too, like a go-go dancer in a cage." Logan said excitedly. "And she was with Nancy Sinatra in that 'Boots Are Made for Walkin' video. That definitely seems like crucial information that should *not* have been left out."

"What exactly was she doing out there? Reading to you from her résumé?"

"No. We were sort of comparing notes, you know, about our careers."

Oh brother, thought Frank.

He tried to imagine Iris listening to Logan as he discussed the plot of his teen soap opera and the show's social media presence, with its fan podcasts and loyal Insta followers, but given his mother's utter disdain for most aspects of pop culture, he just couldn't picture it. Over dinner, she'd practically done a spit-take when Logan started making affectionate observations about the Kardashians.

"She was quite successful, your mother," Logan stated conclusively.

"Well, I wouldn't go that far," said Frank. "She never won any Oscars."

"Wow! Oscars? Is that really your definition of success?" Logan laughed. "Don't hold it against me if I only win an Emmy or two."

Frank hoped Logan was joking. Peer recognition seemed like quite a leap from where he was currently, getting a few minutes of screen time each week, so far in the background he couldn't have been picked out of a lineup. Logan was difficult to figure out. People always said you had to be careful about the questions you asked unless you really wanted the answers. It was like how Frank refused to decipher the cursive lettering above the scorpion tattoo on Liam's forearm during their NA meetings. The message was either a Bible quotation or some song lyric, but Frank tried hard not to notice, because he liked his sponsor and was afraid of what the message might reveal.

"You know, she's still rather striking," said Logan now.

"Who?"

"Your mother. Iris. She's very attractive for a woman her age. Maybe she could do some commercials for like, you know, older-type things."

"Older-type things?"

Like *Life Alert*. Frank tried to imagine Iris sprawled across a bathroom floor croaking *I've fallen and I can't get up* in her Marilyn Monroe whisper.

"I seem to recall she did a dog food commercial once," said Frank. "The dog lifted his leg on her in the middle of the take, but Iris was the one who got fired!"

Frank remembered that his mother had described this experience as the perfect metaphor for life in Hollywood.

"There's a lot of animal exploitation in our business," Logan said flatly.

Logan's natural empathy sometimes came out sideways.

"The point is," said Frank, "if Iris wanted to be making commercials, she'd be making commercials. She's the master of her own fate or destiny or universe . . . or whatever that phrase is. She prefers real estate, where she can convince people to commit to something they might not really want."

"Well . . ." said Logan.

"Look, all I'm saying is you don't need to be giving my mother any career advice at this late stage."

Iris was in her early seventies now. There was no bullshit about her, which was a mixed blessing, but she also had a brisk and calculated charm that she'd put to good use while selling real estate. She was still going to the office and showing houses, keeping her hand in, Iris liked to say, as if she were a hit man who wasn't yet ready to retire. Iris had given up acting when Frank was twelve, but the reminders of her career had continued to surface in reruns for a while to periodically embarrass him. One time when he was in high school, he remembered stumbling upon one of his mother's *performances* while flipping television channels. She was playing a loudmouth hooker in a tank top and hot pants on an old episode of *Police Woman*.

"Mother," he'd asked her afterward, oozing teenage scorn, "didn't you ever play a part where you were allowed to be, like, fully dressed . . . or function as, I don't know, just a normal, clothes-wearing person?"

"Yeah, wiseass," Iris had snapped. She'd been out that afternoon at an open house. "I played Mother Teresa in a TV movie once."

"I must have missed that one."

"Ha! I guess you did."

Logan crossed the room now and sat near the windows on a sleek Eames-style chair that didn't look at all comfortable and could barely accommodate his muscular frame. Frank blushed watching him. To still be blushing at forty-two felt embarrassing and unseemly, but nothing had prepared him for Logan.

They'd met six months earlier, watching the sunset from the beach at Paradise Cove. It was a very gusty day and so the wind kept blowing sand into Frank's eyes. Frank had gone to the beach because it was the fourth anniversary of Keith's death and staring out at the stormy Pacific, alone with his thoughts, had seemed appropriate for his mood. He was feeling unhappy that day, and not only because of Keith. He'd just come from his Tuesday NA meeting, where the moderator had told a long, harrowing story about the ways he'd financed his fentanyl habit—pawning his son's razor scooter and his dying aunt's wedding ring were two of the less appalling examples.

Sometimes, in the rooms, as the recovering addicts took turns with their shares, it felt to Frank like they were all in some grisly competition of *Can You Top This?* He didn't begrudge them that, not at his own meetings nor at the rehab facility where he now worked, handling the intake paperwork for its fraught clientele. It wasn't unusual at his job to encounter movie producers with six-figure monthly cocaine habits or Encino housewives who shot heroin between their toes to hide the track marks. Frank usually felt a gulping sadness when confronted with all this misfortune, but he also felt grateful for that feeling. The idea of growing accustomed to the grief and sadness of others, of getting desensitized, like a cop too long on the beat, worried him beyond all measure.

Not wanting to feel anything had been at the root of his own problems—when Keith had died in the bike crash and for that year afterward when he'd become addicted to painkillers. However, the pills, Oxys in his case (first discovered in the medicine chest, leftovers from Keith's shoulder surgery), never truly *killed* the pain. They only beat it back temporarily, to barely tolerable levels. *Pain-tolerators* is how Frank sometimes referred to these drugs during his own shares, a term that triggered some weary smiles around the room.

That day on the beach, Logan had sauntered up to Frank and started talking, as if they already knew each other.

"I grew up in the desert and never even saw the ocean until I moved here," he began, motioning toward the breaking waves. "It's still a shock every time I come to the beach, or not a shock exactly but more like a very pleasant surprise. I wonder if I'll ever get used to it. Know what I mean?"

Not really, Frank thought, but he didn't respond right away because this guy was so startlingly handsome that there had been a momentary disruption to his senses. Frank was nice looking, too, with a sweet and interesting face and a decent body, but being over forty, his appearance never provoked temporary amnesia in anyone.

"Well, people get used to things," Frank finally said, not really believing it.

The guy nodded and then asked, "You think that's an oil tanker out there?"

They stared into the distance.

"I guess," said Frank. "Or another barge of some kind. It's hard to tell from here."

"I've never even been out on the water."

"My dad had a job renting speed boats on Catalina when I was a kid," said Frank. "So I got a lot of free rides."

"Lucky! That must have been fun!"

The guy was so impressed by this ordinary childhood occurrence that Frank thought it might be time for him to reevaluate the memory himself.

"You know, I was obsessed with clipper ships when I was growing up," the guy suddenly said in a wistful tone, still looking out toward the water.

"Like the old tall ships?"

"Yep."

"That's a weird interest, isn't it? I mean, for a kid."

"Is it? I don't know. It was mine. There was this picture of the *Sovereign of the Seas*, this famous clipper, in my middle school library, and I used to stare at it sometimes, imagining long voyages and the rough lives of the sailors. There's lot of material on YouTube about these things if you care enough to look."

"So you weren't just collecting baseball cards back then?"

"Do kids even do that anymore?"

"Good point. They probably just download them from Pinterest."

They stopped talking then and looked into each other's eyes.

Frank looked away first. His face felt hot.

"Donald McKay was probably the best-known designer of the clippers."

"Yeah?"

"Yeah. But when they gave way to steamships, he lost his shipyard and his commissions and almost everything. He was like penniless."

"That's awful," said Frank.

"Not really."

"It isn't?"

"No. Because nobody could take away his accomplishments. He picked himself up and sort of pivoted.

He started designing the first kerosene locomotives, of all things. So it's not a bad story at all. It's actually a story of reinvention."

"Ah," laughed Frank. "I can see that."

A warm silence washed over them.

"I'm Logan, by the way," the guy then said, smiling and extending his hand.

He moved in with Frank three days later, because apparently, he had no place else to go. His apartment had been sublet right out from underneath him or the locks had been changed or his roommate practiced the dark arts. The details were rather vague, but at that time Logan was living in a cheap motel. Frank had dealt with enough of his own housing calamities back in New York, so it felt only natural to offer some assistance to a stranger. He did not like to linger over the idea that he might not have been quite so generous if the stranger hadn't been as genetically gifted as Logan. This was an innocent offer, Frank kept telling himself, mostly believing it. In fact, for a week Logan had slept on Frank's sofa in the little house in the hills, during which time they'd gotten along quite companionably, fixing their meals together in Frank's tiny kitchen and binge-watching *The Gilmore Girls* on Netflix, with Bertram stretched out on the back of the sofa, observing them both scornfully. Logan told some stories about the TV show he was on, which had begun to stream on an obscure network—the long waits to set up a shot, the mannequin-like skills required to satisfy someone called a continuity supervisor, all the dull monotony of being a featured extra. It must have been excruciating, thought Frank. He admired Logan's tolerance for this kind of bullshit. Then one night, after they'd tidied up the kitchen, Logan had simply followed Frank into his bedroom and joined him in his bed, without any discussion or preliminaries. Frank had uttered the words *This isn't really necessary* in a regrettably prissy tone, something that Logan had summarily (and thankfully) ignored.

Afterward, sprawled out on the sheets, spent and catching his breath, Frank had begun to laugh, but the laughter had suddenly morphed into hot tears. Logan watched Frank caringly and stroked his head. Frank was overwhelmed. He hadn't been with anyone since Keith. People thought gay men slept around a lot. They thought if you toured with a band, you slept around a lot, too. But Frank had been a gay man who had toured with a band and he could count on one (or maybe two) hands the number of guys he had ever slept with. So much for stereotypes. Or perhaps the stereotypes were accurate and he didn't know enough gay dudes or traveling musicians to make a determination. He and Logan had continued to enjoy themselves after that night, making their meals together, streaming some nicely written television shows, and having an altogether first-class time in bed—minus any more tears.

"So what's going to happen next?" Logan said now, leaning forward in the Eames-style chair.

"Tonight?" Frank said glumly. "Sleep, I suppose, and then maybe some nightmares."

"I'm serious," said Logan. "I think it's important to have a plan, like going to FEMA is a good first step, as your mother mentioned tonight, so you won't, like . . . drift."

Drift.

"That's an unusual word coming from you," said Frank. "Did Iris tell you to say that?"

"No. But I think she's worried about you, too."

Christ, thought Frank, they must have been doing more than discussing SAG dues out in the kitchen

"Jesus. It's only been three days," he said. "What's my mother expecting? That I'm going to have everything figured out already? You can go to FEMA yourself if you want, you know. Or you can clear out entirely, if that's what this is about. I have no intention of holding you back, Logan. I've told you that from the beginning. You're as free as a bird. Free as a bird!"

Frank wished he hadn't chosen that overused phrase or just said it twice. He never thought of birds as free, so much as aimless and sort of filthy, the way they shit everywhere.

"I only said that about drifting," Logan replied, "because I'm concerned about what might happen to you if you do . . . *drift*. I know I wasn't around when you had *the troubles*, but . . ."

"*The troubles?*" said Frank. "You make me sound like Northern Ireland in the seventies. Is that what you think? That I'm Northern Ireland in the seventies?"

"Of course not," said Logan.

"Because I'm not!"

"I know."

"I mean . . ." Logan started to say.

"I think I know what you mean."

When they'd had sex for the first time, the night of the hot tears, Frank had told Logan all about Keith getting killed in the accident and about the painkillers and his recovery, too, and he also told him how he was way behind the curve when it came to falling into bed with people.

"I have to feel a real connection before I can commit to anyone . . . in that way," Frank had said bashfully.

He'd probably said too much to Logan about that part, but he had hoped it would explain his messy, fugitive emotions in bed that night.

"Do you think that I'm using again?" Frank asked now.

"Like at this very moment? If I'm acting strangely, do you think it might be because I've literally just lost everything?"

"You haven't lost *everything*," said Logan. "I mean you still have . . . yourself. You still have *you*."

"No argument there," said Frank, patting his chest theatrically.

"And you still have, ummh, *me*."

"Do I? Do I *have* you, Logan?"

Frank said this in a teasing, melodramatic tone, but his heart swelled when he said it and then he rushed on, not waiting for a response.

"Can't you and my mother just accept that it's a crappy time right now?" he said. "Or would you both prefer I pee in a cup!?"

It occurred to Frank that his defensiveness and angry posturing sounded like someone who had already relapsed.

"I don't think that will be necessary," said Logan.

He smiled reassuringly.

It was virtually impossible to stay irritated with the guy.

"Great!" said Frank as he swatted at his pillow. "Then for now I hope we can simply settle for a good night's sleep."

CHAPTER THREE

Logan was trying to meditate by the pool. He was in his swim trunks, sitting in a lounge chair on the patio. He'd downloaded an app for something called *The Loving Kindness Technique*, which was supposed to help you spread all sorts of benevolent energy around. You were to repeat some affirmative phrases like *May I be safe in the universe* or *Let me give and receive appreciation today*, while maintaining an attitude of composure and self-care. This technique wasn't really working. Logan shifted in the chair and watched the sparkling surface of the water. He thought some more about a fellow background extra from *Windsor Valley High*. The guy had 30,000 Insta followers, which wasn't even all that many, but he was making serious money on social media, peddling men's grooming products; one of which was called *Under Carriage*, a body wash designed exclusively for a guy's balls. This person spoke with a bubbly momentum. In his YouTube videos, he was bluntly persuasive, a style that redirected you away from the bullying nature of his personality and let you focus on the things he was trying to get you to pay attention to. Logan had mentioned this person to Frank, but Frank had told Logan that there were other people he might want to imitate rather than someone hawking coconut rinse for your balls.

"I'm not trying to imitate him!" Logan had protested. "I'm just curious about how he's making it happen. He spent a week in Tahiti last Christmas and it didn't cost him a cent because he made a couple of posts about the resort on Instagram."

"So *he* says anyway," said Frank.

"But he has no reason to lie."

"He's an influencer. He has every reason to lie. But if you want to know how he is making this happen—well, the short answer is that people are gullible and the longer one is that social media has redefined the moral and ethical code of our present times. Ask Iris; she'll give you some thoughts about it."

Logan had, in fact, brought it up to Iris, but she'd only ranted about Twitter for five or six minutes and made some snide remarks about Chrissy Teigen, who that day had been tweeting some praise about public libraries.

"As if libraries were some hidden, woke resource that she alone had discovered!" Iris had seethed.

For someone who complained so much about pop culture, Iris sure followed it a lot. This was impressive, Logan thought, a woman her age keeping up with contemporary trends and using the word "woke" even if not in the proper context. Iris was one of the oldest people Logan had ever known, which was something he had told her recently.

"Jesus, Logan," she had responded, "that falls into the category of information best kept to yourself."

Logan and Frank had been staying with her for two weeks now. Logan liked it there. Iris's home was in a quiet, pleasant neighborhood, a few miles from the Santa Monica pier. The house wasn't particularly large or luxurious. It was a Spanish-style bungalow with a crisp, streamlined appeal and a casual, low-key glamour that might as well have been a reflection of Iris herself. Logan had developed a routine since he'd been at the house, which included swimming every morning in the kidney-shaped pool before he went to the studio. He had estimated the pool's square footage and then took that information and plugged it into his phone. He determined that if he swam 284 semicircles, it would be the equivalent of a mile. He ran most mornings, too, in the pretty neighborhood or along the beach. At the studio he worked out with free weights in a makeshift exercise trailer on the lot. You had to sign up for these privileges. The stars, or *the talent*, as they were called, took precedence over the extras and could jump them on the exercise list anytime they wanted.

Logan had lost his own free weights in the fire. Unless they had survived. He didn't know how hot a fire needed to be to melt cast iron or whatever they were made of. The neighborhood where Frank's house had stood, up in the hills, was still roped off. They weren't allowed to go back there yet and check for anything, though the landlord had told them that nothing was left. That would include the underwear he'd left on the bathroom floor that morning, and his toothbrush on the sink, and that day's script he'd forgotten on the bedside table. Personally, Logan hadn't lost much, but even the stupid things he remembered from that day made him feel sad. Logan would have preferred a membership to an actual gym, but he couldn't afford a decent one. His work on *Windsor Valley* didn't pay much. Frank might buy him some more weights if he asked, but it wasn't as if he had any real money either and Logan was reluctant to push the limits of Frank's generosity, especially since they were still grappling with what had happened and staying with Iris. He shouldn't even be thinking about weights with all those shattering stories on the news about people who had lost loved ones and who had nowhere else to go but the trailers set up by FEMA. Logan felt a slight chill as he glanced at Iris's pool. It was shameful to admit that his living situation had actually improved after the fire.

He was still terribly worried about Frank, who was in a predictable funk. His reflexive kindness, the quality that Logan had initially been attracted to, was now buried under a layer of uncertainty and gloom, reasonable responses in the aftermath of destruction, but this was something else casting doubt on their future. *Their future.* Logan had never thought of sharing a future with anyone, but Frank was completely different than any other guy Logan had ever been with. For one thing, he would listen. For another, he would smile at Logan's observations. They conversed, like people. Frank didn't just stare longingly at Logan's mouth as the sounds came out. Logan had been on the receiving end of greedy attention and grasping interest most of his adult life. He figured it was lucky that he could even recognize real hope and possibility when he saw it. He saw it in Frank. It didn't hurt that Logan found Frank's shuffling shyness impossibly sexy. After years of fending off advances and getting pounced on, it was fun for Logan, when it came to sex, to be the one making the first move. Frank's decency was perhaps the most endearing of his qualities and it was also the thing that concerned Logan the most when he gave thought to their future together—and to his own past. Until very recently he'd been able to avoid these thoughts, but now they were buzzing around him like flies.

It was a Saturday morning. Logan wasn't expected at the studio, which was why he was giving meditation a try. One of the other extras, not the influencer, someone else, a saucer-eyed young woman with a distracted smile and blasé manner, had mentioned the app to him. People were always peddling something on that set, but Logan tried to stay quiet there and out of the way, which he figured was not such a bad strategy for someone hired to be in the background. He would not be needed at the studio on Monday either. In fact, *Windsor Valley High* was on hiatus for the next thirteen weeks. One of the stars of the series, Tanner Van Dean, had a *Hulu* movie he would be filming during the break. Tanner had mentioned this so many times, he might as well have had T-shirts printed up. The actor was usually frosty and aloof, even though Logan had spent countless hours on the set with him, sitting side by side in fake classrooms, as if they really were in school. Tanner had never tried to include Logan in any actual conversation—if you didn't count the time he had cursed at him between takes. The star had accused Logan of wearing toxic-smelling cologne that was so foul, it was causing him to forget his lines. The smell had not been coming from Logan as it turned out, but from another guy who was sitting behind them in the shot. A nervous AD had quickly determined this after he had arrived to placate Tanner and sniff around the extras. Tanner had shrugged and nodded wearily in Logan's direction, a grudging apology, that was all he could muster. One of the costume people said that Logan shouldn't sweat Tanner's indifference. She said Tanner was probably annoyed because Logan never missed his marks, was pleasant to be around, and the crew liked him because he remembered everyone's name.

It seemed the rest of the cast of *Windsor Valley* would all be involved with some other pursuit during the hiatus, if only lining up various auditions for jobs they would never get. Logan had discovered something about actors since being on the show—they liked to catalog and assess their imminent opportunities and overall potential any chance they got. It was like bragging about what they would do if they ever won the lottery. As someone who had grown up without the burning desire for stardom and had arrived at his current job only through random circumstance, he felt fortunate to be free of these expectations. It was difficult enough to navigate in the real world with its normal risk of defeat and rejection.

Logan wouldn't be trying to land any other parts during the hiatus. Luckily, his distracted agent (she'd been recommended by that casting guy who discovered him at the Starbucks) seemed to have no strategies for advancing his career and was leaving him alone. Raising his profile was too risky right now anyway. That ugly business with Oliver Lash had resurfaced and who knew how that might play out. Logan was ashamed of his association with this person and what had transpired between them. He had not heard from Oliver for nearly a year, but now the man had been texting him since a few days before the wildfire. He had somehow discovered Logan's new cell number. There was probably someone at Verizon who owed Oliver a favor. So many people owed him favors. The messages were nonthreatening at first, simply checking in on Logan's well-being. Perhaps Oliver had seen Logan on *Windsor Valley High*, where he'd been hiding out in plain sight. Logan ignored these communications, even as they had grown creepier and more urgent. The latest one (received the day before) simply read, I KNOW WHAT YOU DID! Logan wondered how much longer he could go without having to tell Frank, and then it would all have to be revealed. He worried about what Iris might think, too. She already watched him as if she was well aware of everything that had happened and it was playing on an endless loop somewhere in her head.

Iris came out of the house through the French doors just then and stood on the patio, a short distance from Logan's lounge chair. She was wearing a white silk caftan and her hair was tied up in a bun on top of her head. She looked severe and unwavering, like a carved figurehead on the prow of one of the tall ships.

"Good morning, Logan. How was your swim?"

Wet, Logan wanted to say, but Iris did not appreciate sarcasm unless she was wielding it herself.

"Kind of abbreviated," said Logan. "I've been meditating."

"We used to call that being *lost in thought* when I was your age," said Iris.

She looked past the pool to the rest of her backyard, which was not large, but quite lush, with a sloping, healthy-looking lawn and some honeysuckle plants lined up along the perimeter. Two citrus trees stood like sentries at the far edge of the property.

"I think the point is to *empty* your mind of thought while meditating," said Logan, holding up his phone, "or at least that's what this app says."

"I was kidding," she replied. "Frank's father was an aficionado. Secret mantras. The whole bit. He was involved with TM for a time."

"Transcendental Meditation?"

"It was big out here in the seventies, started by some guru or yogi. Erik used to attend yoga conferences. He tried to get me to go with him once."

Logan barked out a small laugh.

"What?" asked Iris.

"*That* doesn't seem like your thing exactly."

Logan couldn't imagine Iris emptying her mind of thoughts even for a second. He imagined Iris's thoughts as lively and plentiful, like dogs scurrying to get off a leash.

She hesitated, as though she might counter his remark. "Fair enough," she said at last.

Logan reached for his T-shirt on the back of the lounge chair and put it on.

"I certainly hope I didn't interrupt your process?" said Iris. She waved her fingers in the air.

"Nope, I'm done," said Logan. "All meditated."

Iris reached down and yanked a weed that was sprouting near the edge of the patio. She didn't employ a gardener, something she considered to be a pointless expense. Iris had an old-fashioned push mower and mowed the lawn herself. *I grew up on a farm in Maine*, she had said (as if this explained anything) when Logan had seen her doing this not long after he and Frank had arrived. Frank said Iris sometimes liked to flaunt her eccentricities, as if she were playing a part in a TV movie, but she had seemed sincere enough about the mowing, shooing Logan away when he had offered to help.

"I went down to the farmer's market first thing and bought some organic eggs," she was saying now.

"Cool," said Logan. "I'm hungry. I was just giving some thought to breakfast."

"During your meditation, no doubt," said Iris.

Logan assumed she meant this to be amusing, so he smiled vaguely in her direction.

"Thanks for shopping for us," he said.

"The pool needs to be skimmed," Iris replied.

Iris often deflected simple expressions of gratitude. Logan assumed she thought that these communications were a waste of time, not that she didn't feel she deserved them. Logan was somewhat mesmerized by Iris, her weathered beauty, and sharp observations, but she intimidated him in equal measure. She was brusque, but oddly magnetic. Frank said her blunt charm was likely an advantage when she sold houses—her cool, surgical approach in the face of a buyer's emotion and worry. Logan wasn't so sure about that. He found her bluntness a little scary. Iris had warmed up to him slightly since he'd arrived here with Frank, but she still sighed wearily or gave him side glances if he said something that annoyed her. *My mother does not suffer fools well*, Frank had said on more than one occasion, but this was so obvious, there didn't seem to be any need for him to be pointing it out.

There was a bird making a fuss from somewhere near the hedges. It called out with a sweet, trilling urgency. Logan didn't know what kind of bird it was. There were people who had specific knowledge of birds. There was a term for these people, who had this type of expertise, but he didn't know what they were called either. He turned to Iris to tell her he would happily skim the pool and to ask if she knew anything about birds, but he saw that she wasn't there anymore. She had left him and gone inside.

In the kitchen, Logan watched Iris from the cooking island, where he sat on one of the acrylic and chrome stools, which were more comfortable than they looked. They spent most of their time in the kitchen, it seemed to Logan. Perhaps most families did. Had they already become a sort of family? The thought pleased him. Iris was adding various ingredients to an omelet. The omelet was not for Logan and would not be shared. Iris had stopped preparing meals for her guests. Nothing had been announced. She had simply stopped doing it a few days after he and Frank had arrived. It was as if Iris had taken a vow or been advised by someone to set down precise boundaries, but Logan felt it unlikely that Iris needed third party consultation to form any opinions of her own. She still put out coffee and cereal boxes in the morning and did the grocery shopping, too. It was like staying at a nice B&B with kitchen privileges. Logan had stayed in such a place once, with a burly guy who said he wrote spec scripts for *Netflix* and mostly just wanted to wrestle once they reached their plush, overdecorated room. Logan remembered spending most of that weekend in a poorly executed half nelson.

"Has Frank told you that he submitted all his FEMA paperwork?" he asked Iris.

Logan liked the idea of sharing something positive with Frank's mother as he sat in the sunny kitchen.

"No, he has not," said Iris, "though this is not a surprise."

"It's not a surprise that he's completed the paperwork or that he didn't tell you about it?" asked Logan.

"Both, I imagine," said Iris.

"I guess there are low-interest loans available for people who have survived the wildfires, funds for people to get back on their feet."

"Getting back on one's feet is an admirable goal," said Iris as she folded her omelet in the pan.

Logan got up from the stool and crossed the kitchen. He began to empty the dishwasher. He liked to make himself useful here, though the chores went as unacknowledged as his expressions of gratitude.

"What about *your* feet, Logan?" Iris asked now as she stood at the stove.

Logan looked down at his shoes. He was wearing a kind of slipper/sandal that the influencer had handed out to the other extras at the end of the previous day, a parting gift in honor of the hiatus.

"I'm sorry?" said Logan.

"Will you and my son be landing on your feet *together*, for lack of a better term?"

Logan paused, while sorting the clean silverware.

"I don't know if that has been . . . determined exactly," he said.

This was true and it wasn't just because of the chaos after the fire. Their relationship had never been discussed, not once since that first meeting on the beach, when Logan had approached Frank because he seemed so lonely that day, staring gloomily out to sea. His presence had lifted Frank's mood immediately, something that still gratified Logan when he remembered it. But in all the time since, no parameters had been set. It was one thing to make the first move in bed, but Logan had zero experience navigating the complexities of real-life commitments.

"Then have you submitted your own paperwork?" asked Iris. "Did you put in a claim for your own losses?"

"No, I didn't," said Logan.

"No?" said Iris.

She glanced at him over the frying pan.

"You don't think I would take any of Frank's funds, do you?"

There was a note of alarm in his voice.

"No. That is not what I think," said Iris. "You misunderstand me."

"That's good," sighed Logan. "I'm glad to hear it."

"I can't imagine that you have any designs on my son for long-term financial benefit," said Iris. "If that was your motivation, you could have done much better elsewhere."

There seemed to be no appropriate response to this, so Logan said nothing.

"I am speaking out of concern for you," Iris went on. "Frank has always been such a loner and he tends to change his mind very quickly—about people and places and things. My son is quite *mercurial*, if you haven't noticed."

Logan stared at her blankly.

"Moody," she translated.

"He's been happy since I've known him," said Logan. "Except since the wildfire."

"Yes, well, wildfires will do that to people. I'm just trying to tell you that Frank has his whims. Like that move to the East Coast and playing music on the streets, living the life of a panhandler. He was hurt by that ugly business with his band, and so he fled."

"Are you worried that I am another whim or that I will do something to make him, like, flee?" asked Logan.

"Neither of these things, or perhaps both," said Iris.

She had finished making her omelet and slid it from the frying pan onto a plate. She walked past Logan then, to the sink, where she washed up the pan, dried it, and left it on the counter.

"Now," she said, pointing to it, "you can scramble your eggs."

She took a carton of orange juice from the refrigerator and brought her omelet to the cooking island, where she sat on one of the stools and began to eat. The kitchen was modern and gleaming, but Logan felt it was ill-equipped, with a strange shortage of useful items. There weren't many plates, for instance, and only this one small frying pan. He'd already finished unloading the dishwasher because it was never more than half full.

"You know, I don't think that's true what you said about Frank being a loner," said Logan. "There was Keith, you know."

Frank was still asleep, but Logan glanced at the entrance to the kitchen and lowered his voice when he mentioned Keith's name.

"Of course," said Iris. "Keith."

"Yes," said Logan.

"Keith—the reason my son became addicted to drugs."

"What?" said Logan. "No. That's not right. Keith was not *the reason*. Frank never even took a painkiller until after Keith died. Maybe his death was more like a trigger."

"Is that what you think?"

"Yes."

"Well, you are entitled to your opinion."

"You can't really blame Keith for dying," said Logan.

"I can't?" said Iris. "And why not? Are we not allowed to blame people anymore? Has there been some new anti-blaming initiative passed? Is there a personal essay in the *Huffington Post* I should be reading?"

"Blaming people won't change anything," said Logan, "especially blaming dead people."

"I would have to agree with you there," said Iris. "And yet it is so strangely satisfying."

She glared at Logan as if daring him to challenge her flawed logic and then continued to eat small bites of her omelet. Iris swallowed and said, "They were only together a matter of months."

"Who?"

"My son . . . and this Keith."

"Around six months, I believe," said Logan.

"Three. Six. Nine. Whatever. It's not as if they were committed to each other for twenty or thirty years, weathering the ups and downs of a long-term relationship. Who knows how long they would have lasted if Keith had not died when he did? The relationship might have flamed out all on its own."

Logan stiffened at this unpleasant opinion. "That's not something anyone could have predicted," he said. "Predictions are kind of pointless, I think."

"Are they?" said Iris. "Many things can be predicted. Weather. Traffic. Football games."

"I'm not following you."

"I'm saying Erik and I knew nothing about Keith until after Keith's death. What does that tell you?"

"What does it tell *you*?"

"I think that should be obvious," said Iris. "Frank didn't consider the relationship important enough to share with us."

Maybe it's you he didn't consider important enough, thought Logan.

But he didn't say this. He simply picked up the frying pan, walked back to the stove, and began preparing his eggs.

"I have offended you," said Iris. "That was not my intention."

"It's not that," said Logan diplomatically, "but it seems you believe that Frank will either dump me or that I will hurt him in some way and then he will be sent spiraling again."

"These are two possible scenarios, are they not?"

"I'm not sure what you gain by discussing every possibility available to, like, your imagination."

"I can tell you what can be gained. Clarity."

"What kind of clarity?"

"There is only one kind of clarity, Logan. Truth. I do not doubt that you have feelings for my son, but I think there is something else, too. You give the impression of someone hiding something behind their back. I felt this when you first arrived and I'm thinking it now as I watch you scrambling your eggs."

Logan scraped his eggs on to a plate and took a deep breath. He had the eerie sense that Oliver Lash had entered the room and was looming above, watching from the ceiling. He turned to look at Iris and smiled broadly. He wished he could remember something from the meditation app to help him maintain that attitude of composure and self-care.

"I'm not sure what you mean," he said. "I'm really not that complicated, Iris."

"On the contrary," she replied. "We are all that complicated."

"By the way," said Logan, "may I ask you something? Would you have taken kindly to people quizzing you about your relationship with Erik when you first got together?"

Iris laughed and sipped some orange juice.

"I might have welcomed it," she said. "There were many issues people could have pointed out about Frank's father and me that I was likely not seeing for myself. I just didn't have many people in my life at that time offering commentary."

"Do you think it's fair of you to compare your own situation with Erik to what Frank had with Keith?" said Logan. *Or to what he might have with me?* he wanted to say.

"Is that what you think I'm doing? Comparing?" Iris laughed again, but not unkindly. "My marriage to Frank's father defies comparison to anything. And that statement can be taken any number of ways, both good and bad—and they'd all be correct. And let me also point out that my relationship to Erik was not *a situation*. It was a life."

They sat silently for a moment and then Iris said, "I only want my son to be happy and to remain sober, if that's not too much to ask."

"It's not too much to ask," said Logan as he sat down across from her and began to eat his eggs. "I just don't think you can control the answer."

Iris sighed, which might have been her only suitable response.

"Maybe after breakfast we can watch another movie," she said.

"I'd like that," said Logan. He smiled at her.

Iris pointed to a dollop of scrambled eggs at the corner of his mouth.

"You have egg on your face," she said dryly. He reached for a napkin.

Logan had grown up in Las Vegas and come to California at twenty-three, when he had finally decided to move out of his mother's apartment. It was an embarrassing age not to be on his own, but it was also because Samantha was getting married again. A new husband was to move in. This guy seemed pleasant enough, but earlier stepfathers (this would be number four) had made decent first impressions, too—before smashing everything in their lives to smithereens, with their drunken rants, financial chaos, and crazy-ass behavior. You couldn't say his mother didn't have a type. Logan also had no desire to be anywhere near another one of Samantha's honeymoon periods, where he'd have to sleep with a pillow clutched around his ears for a month or two. It was clearly time to go. He'd stuck around much longer than he should have. Samantha never exactly objected to her son being there, other than an occasional snide remark, and she never gouged him on the rent. She'd been sixteen when she'd gotten pregnant with Logan. The bio dad was a high school hookup, who had abandoned her and moved to Canada, as if it were still the Vietnam era and he was dodging the draft. Samantha's parenting style had been loose and distracted. While Logan was growing up, she treated him like a kid brother more than anything else—or maybe like somebody else's kid brother.

Logan's mother liked to tell people she'd been a showgirl and a blackjack dealer (this was Vegas, after all) but she hadn't been either of those things. She wasn't leggy enough for the floorshows and she had washed out in blackjack training because she lacked the instinct to spot card counters. She worked as a secretary in the office of a bail bondsman, a busy business near The Strip, where she'd met three of the four stepfathers. Samantha had friends who worked in the hotels and casinos. She was always coming home with gossip about big star performers whose egos had run amok, and Logan had seen plenty of examples of failed stardom in the city, a place where nighttime glitz and glamour was often revealed as harsh and ugly in the light of day.

He'd been working in a tourist trap restaurant since high school. His grades were okay, but college was not an option. The restaurant was not far from The Bellagio. It was called The Atrium. Logan was a dishwasher and parked cars there, until he started to wait tables and work behind the bar when he was old enough to serve alcohol. The place was designed to look like an Italian villa. The main dining room at The Atrium had a bunch of naked statues that leered at you while you ate, and there were some Roman columns made of pressed wood that jiggled and swayed if you bumped into them. Papier-mâché volcanoes sat in the middle of the tables, reminding people of the destruction of Pompeii, or at least reminding the people who knew anything about ancient history. The staff wore togas or gladiator outfits. There was an enormous stuffed lion near the entrance wearing a laurel wreath on its head for some reason.

Logan's tips were much better when he wore the gladiator outfit. It wasn't unusual for drunken patrons (men and women alike) to press cash into Logan's hands as he cleared the tables. They would smirk and ogle him optimistically. Logan never encouraged this kind of attention. He usually wore an expression of obliviousness, so nobody ever got too aggressive there, except for Larry, one of the night managers, who was always pestering him about messing around. He soon realized that the way he looked could intimidate some people. They would stammer and blush in his presence. Ironically, he had remained a virgin longer than anyone could have imagined. He'd known he was gay by the time he was twelve and felt no ambivalence about that fact, but he kept the news from Samantha, whose provincial sensibilities (she'd been raised in a tiny town on the Arizona border, in a family of noisy preachers) occasionally surfaced and manifested themselves in unpleasant ways. She referred to one of her coworkers as *a mean little pansy*, for instance, and rolled her eyes whenever they encountered a friendly, flamboyant neighbor who worked in *The Miss Behave* drag show at Caesars and rented the apartment across the hall.

Logan knew there was a kind of power attached to his looks, but he had no idea what to do about it. Even after he'd relented to Larry's advances (letting the guy go down on him inside the meat locker) after closing time one night, it hadn't gotten him anywhere. His schedule hadn't improved, and Larry wasn't any more likely to approve his days off or let him come in late either. If anything, he was less accommodating to Logan than he'd ever been, calling him *a big oaf* when he dropped a plate or broke a glass. Something had shifted between them. Logan filed this experience away in his head, but he didn't really know what to make of it, as he continued to chalk up disappointing hookups in a time-wasting way.

Hugo, another waiter from the restaurant, had moved to California. The summer after he left, he contacted Logan and told him he desperately needed a roommate. Logan didn't wait to be asked twice. The invitation had coincided with Samantha's newest engagement and her giddy, all-too-familiar reaction to it, as if navigating luckless relationships was her own version of *Groundhog Day*. Logan packed up his ancient Ford Focus and, in a cheerful, life-changing fashion, drove to California and an area on the outskirts of Venice. It was not a particularly pleasant neighborhood. Logan noticed there was something that looked like a junkyard at one end of the dead-end street and some stray dogs roaming around in a menacing manner. He'd been led to believe the house was near the beach, but this was not true. There certainly weren't any sweeping ocean views. It was a long drive to the water, as it turned out. The house itself was a rambling and ordinary ranch-style from the seventies. There was something dull and colorless about the structure, like a faded photograph.

Hugo was sitting alone on the front steps waiting for Logan, who parked on the street and exited the car.

"It's California, baby!" Hugo bellowed, before pulling Logan into a hug and bringing him inside the house for a tour.

Hugo didn't need one roommate; he usually needed several. There was a lot of turnover in the house, which was carved up into seven small spaces, not including the cluttered living area, outdated kitchen, and purple-tiled bathroom. The tiny *bedrooms* were separated by dividers that looked as thin as poster board. Each space resembled a walk-in closet, containing a twin bed and small dresser. No one who lived in the house was over twenty-five. Hugo rattled off a list of roommate names as he showed Logan around that first day and introduced him to a couple of nice-looking girls and a lanky guy sitting in the living area watching an episode of *Dragon Ball Z* in an absorbed fashion as they ate cereal from disposable bowls. They perked up when they saw him, but then turned quickly back to the TV screen. Logan figured the place, with its subdivisions and many residents, must be violating building codes, but when he mentioned this to Hugo, he just laughed and said, "Oliver's got all that covered. He knows everybody in town and people owe him favors—and so forth."

"Who's Oliver?"

"Oliver Lash. Our landlord. We should go see him," said Hugo. "I've told him you were coming."

They traveled in Hugo's Jeep. It was a twenty-minute drive through progressively better neighborhoods until they arrived at an upscale gated community called Beach Haven in Marina Del Rey. They were announced at the gate and waved through by a flexing security guard who seemed to be exploiting his resemblance to John Cena. Oliver's condo was nestled in a cluster of palm trees on a quiet, pristine cul-de-sac. When they got out of the car and strolled up the flagstone walkway, Logan was aware of a cool breeze that rattled the palms and felt totally lovely on his face. It was as if John Cena were controlling the atmosphere from a thermostat in the gatehouse.

Hugo knocked twice on a thick red door and then a voice from inside told them to enter. Oliver was sitting in a big peacock chair in the middle of a spacious, sunny room, filled with high-end Scandinavian furniture and floor-to-ceiling bookcases, which held no books, but contained numerous small sculptures and *objets d'art*. There were some Buddha-like statues in the corner of this large room and beside them a small trickling fountain on a tabletop.

Oliver, who was short and plump and wearing a kimono-type robe, looked something like a Buddha himself, except he was a standard-issue white guy sitting on an oversized pillow. He did not get up as they were introduced, but smiled eagerly at Logan, his eyes almost disappearing into his large fleshy face. His age was impossible to determine, Logan thought. He could have been thirty-five or sixty.

"Well," Oliver said. "You weren't exaggerating!"

This comment was directed to Hugo, but then to Logan he had said, "Your friend told me you were disturbingly handsome. I would say that is a fair assessment. Would you agree?"

Logan was used to having his looks discussed in this sort of detached and clinical way, right in front of him or behind his back or shouted out from across a room. He shrugged at Oliver in response.

"Ahhh, I like that," said Oliver, "no false modesty. And what do you think of your new accommodations?"

"I'm afraid Logan was expecting something a bit grander," said Hugo.

When Logan began to protest, Oliver put his hand up to silence them both.

"You do realize," Oliver said pleasantly, "that the only way to eventually afford a lovely neighborhood like this one or be anywhere near the water is to share the rent with a bunch of other financially challenged young people for a while until you can save, save, save, and move on up, as they say."

"I'm happy for the opportunity," said Logan, somewhat nervously, as if he had just been hired for a new job.

It *would* turn out to be something like work to live in the ranch house, with its cramped conditions, lack of privacy, and the ever-changing cast of characters. Logan stopped trying to remember the names of his roommates, unless it was someone he encountered often, in the long waits for the kitchen or bathroom. Oliver had installed a port-a-potty in the grassless, rocky backyard. It was put there, Logan assumed, so the residents weren't forced to piss out the windows. But these experiences were still ahead of him that first day.

After Oliver had spouted a few more stock phrases of welcome, he abruptly dismissed his visitors. As they were driving back to the ranch house, Logan turned to Hugo and teased, "So I'm disturbingly handsome, huh?"

"Fuck you, bro!" said Hugo.

He and Hugo had hooked up a few times in Vegas after their shifts at the restaurant, nothing too major, but it wasn't the kind of thing either one of them wanted to pursue in their makeshift environment. Plus, Hugo had already mentioned a boyfriend during the grand tour, some hunky carpenter in Fresno.

"Thanks for throwing me under the bus by telling Oliver I didn't like the place," said Logan. "I never told you that."

"You didn't have to. I saw your expression, man."

"But why tell him?" asked Logan.

"I find it's best to keep things aboveboard with Oliver," said Hugo.

"Okay, so what's his deal anyway?" Logan asked.

"What do you mean?" said Hugo.

"You know what I mean. Does he unexpectedly show up in our little dorm rooms in the middle of the night or something?"

Logan mimed jerking off.

Logan wasn't certain if this would be a total deal breaker for him. He had plenty of experience managing the lustful expectations of others. He just thought it better to get all the facts up front.

"Nah," said Hugo as he watched the road. "I don't think he's even queer. He doesn't hassle the women either. I don't think he's a sex guy."

"Well then, what *is* his story?"

"Oliver?" said Hugo. "Oh—Oliver's an entrepreneur."

This was true, in as much as Oliver was a part owner of various local businesses and seemed to know a lot of people. He acted as a sort of employment agency for the tenants in the house, staffing the restaurants and tourist shops along the beach, where he enjoyed some foggy connections. Later, after everything, Logan would come to believe that it wasn't financial ambition or the seduction angle that fueled Oliver; it was the simple desire for control. Oliver wanted to be the guy pulling the strings. He liked to strategize and anticipate next moves. The guy saw the world as his own personal chessboard. Oliver kept track of everyone's schedules and knew where Logan and his roommates were supposed to be at any given moment. No one would ever discuss Oliver in any detail, not even Hugo, after that first day. It was like some unwritten rule of the house. No speculation about their landlord and benefactor, as if they were bound by nondisclosure agreements. There were other rules, however. No drugs (not even weed) or overnight guests. These were written out on signs pasted to the refrigerator and a wall near the front door. Young people came and went, as if it were a youth hostel or a drug-free commune. Soon after Logan had arrived, Oliver arranged for him to wait tables at a mid-priced restaurant in Oxnard. The Sea Glass sat on a small bluff overlooking the Pacific. The place was listed in several guidebooks. Tourists flocked there, though they were not always the best tippers, so the money wasn't great. Logan had done better in Vegas actually, another town with tourists, but where recklessness and a gambler's optimism sometimes translated into generosity to the waitstaff.

Logan remained polite and appreciative in his dealings with Oliver, which were handled mostly by text, but he knew enough to realize it was an odd arrangement. It occurred to him that all he had done was trade one imperfect living situation for another. Then one morning, about a month after moving into the house, he was summoned to Oliver's condo for what Hugo said was probably some kind of status report. Oliver liked to check in on his tenants periodically. This was different from the first visit. For one thing, he arrived alone this time, and when he knocked on the door, there was no voice from within directing him to *Enter*. Oliver answered the door himself. He was dressed more formally, in a collared shirt, black slacks, and a thin tie, giving him an air of professionalism. When Logan entered the apartment, Oliver extended his hand in greeting, something he hadn't bothered to do when they first met.

He ushered Logan into the condo and brought him to a small table at the far end of the room. The table was covered in a cloth that depicted a scene of angry peasants meandering around the countryside. It looked familiar. Logan felt this must be a duplication of a famous painting, but he was afraid to ask Oliver about it as his question might reveal his ignorance of art, something the landlord, given the art on the walls and all the little sculptures on the bookcases, would no doubt frown upon. There was a copper teapot on the table, sitting on a trivet that was shaped like a large frog, and beside that two earthenware cups, a small pitcher of cream, and a sugar bowl. The tea was another new development.

Because of this formality, it went through Logan's mind that he was perhaps being fired from the restaurant, where he sometimes mixed up the California cuisine. This might be his exit interview. Or perhaps he was being kicked out of the house because Oliver had found someone more appropriate, someone who could identify the scene on the tablecloth. Maybe both things were true simultaneously and he'd be returning to Las Vegas that afternoon, where Samantha in a two-minute phone call the previous week had suggested that things had already taken a bad turn with husband number four. Logan was pondering these possibilities, staring into the teacup that Oliver had begun to fill.

"I wanted to check in with you and see how you are settling in. I'm glad I did," said Oliver. "You don't seem particularly happy to me."

"I don't?" said Logan, snapping to attention. He wondered if his overall happiness would be a determining factor when it came to eviction from the house. He smiled brightly then and practically batted his eyes. Sometimes his smile was enough to get people to forget their line of questioning, sometimes even their own names. This time Oliver simply chuckled. It was an odd, gruff sound, like gears grinding.

"You don't need to demonstrate for me," said Oliver. "I only wonder if you are being challenged enough at the restaurant. It seems like you are perhaps suited for other opportunities."

"It does?" said Logan.

"Well, it must be said, you're a very handsome young man."

Logan added some sugar to his tea. He did not believe the statement required a response, as Oliver had said this before, on the day he arrived.

"Perhaps there are benefits to this genetic advantage you might want to explore," continued Oliver. "You can't tell me that you haven't wondered about how your appearance might open some doors, how your looks might be a calling card."

Oh boy, thought Logan, here we go.

He pushed his teacup slightly forward on the table, folded his arms across his chest, and scooted back in his chair.

"Look," said Logan. "Practically everybody who lives around here is good-looking. There must be like an ordinance about it or something. I'm sure the market, or whatever you are referring to, is already saturated."

Oliver's gear-grinding laugh again.

"Then aren't you lucky that you have someone like me in your corner?" he said. "I hear about opportunities all the time for good-looking young men like you."

"Yeah, well, I'm not doing any porn," said Logan.

"My goodness," gasped Oliver. "Why would you think this is an offer of pornography?"

Oh, I don't know, thought Logan. My experience of the world.

There had been no shortage of sketchy opportunities

for him in Las Vegas, where he'd had offers to take part in everything from Boylesque Dance Revues to naked rodeos, some of which he had even half explored. He couldn't count the number of times that some seedy character had approached him on The Strip, passionately urging him to call a number or go to some website because it would change his life!

Logan remained silent and adjusted the wattage of his smile.

"Rest assured," said Oliver, "I do not, as a rule, associate with pornographers."

"Not as a rule, huh?" said Logan.

Oliver sighed wearily. He was either offended while pretending not to be or perhaps it was the other way around. He was employing a complicated facial maneuver which was hard to read.

"Look, I am only trying to be a friend here and make you aware of certain prospects," Oliver said now, "but if you prefer I reroute my generosity . . ."

He did not finish this sentence; he reached for his cup instead and sipped his tea rather furiously.

Logan thought of the long, traffic-choked drive to the Sea Glass that he had ahead of him that day, where he had pulled a double—and he also thought of the consequences of pissing off his new landlord.

"I guess hearing what you have to say can't hurt," he said.

"That's right," said Oliver, toasting him happily with his teacup. "I guess it can't."

CHAPTER FOUR

On her DVR, Iris had recorded dozens of films from *Turner Classic Movies*. Her love of movies had inspired her to be an actress and come to Hollywood in the first place. The fake lives she saw depicted as a child and teenager, on *The Late Show* or at that remote movie theater in Maine, were far more authentic and relevant to her than the one she was leading on the farm. They had been essential to her escape and she still believed in their power. So she was shocked to discover, one night over dinner about a week after Frank and Logan had landed on her doorstep, that her son's boyfriend had some serious holes in his movie knowledge. This was an unacceptable deficiency, Iris thought, especially for someone making his living in show business. It was like practicing psychiatry without ever having heard of Freud. She was unable to mask her annoyance when Logan had confused Jimmy Stewart with Gregory Peck, or when he'd told her he'd never seen a Bette Davis movie. Iris had thrown her napkin on the table and glared at Frank after that one.

"Why are you looking at me?" laughed Frank. "Do you think I should have enrolled him in some Queer Icon seminar at UCLA or something? Don't blame me, Mother. He's not exactly a boomer."

Logan had just sat there shrugging as they discussed this personal defect in front of him.

Almost every evening since then, she had led Logan to the living room after dinner, though she'd begun to refer to it as

The Screening Room. She had Logan sit on the long, narrow sofa that faced the television. The television was enormous. It took up half the opposite wall. This was where Iris began her lessons. Frank begged off from these cinematic tutorials, usually citing exhaustion from work and explaining that his education was already complete.

"I'm all done graduating from the Iris Flynn Film Society and Lecture Series," he'd say, and pad off to the guest room.

Erik, when he was alive, had loved old films, too. When Frank was a kid, they'd all go to an old revival house in Northridge, with its cracked mirrors in the lobby, torn seats, and faded glamour. Sometimes they would go there after Erik had returned from one of his trips away, from his periodic wanderings. It was a place where they would all reconnect as a family—there at the movies, those classic films flickering all over them in the dark. Or perhaps Iris was just remembering it that way? The reconnecting part. Perhaps Frank had entirely different memories and associated those trips to Northridge with his father's frequent absences instead. Iris sometimes wished she had the kind of rapport with her son that would allow her to ask him this type of thing, but there were other times when she had no desire to unearth any of Frank's resentments. They came up enough on their own. There was another realtor in Iris's office who had one of those "close" relationships with her grown daughter, where everything from the kid's past was up for grabs and open to interpretation. Tessa, who in business was confident and assertive, spent most of her time with her child apologizing for some slight or offense from the past she didn't remember committing. *Who the hell needs that?* Iris thought. She didn't intend to spend the rest of her life walking around with a target on her back, though she also had to acknowledge there wasn't exactly an abundance of time and opportunity left to get to know her son.

The first night of Logan's movie education Iris screened *Now, Voyager* to get the Bette Davis issue out of the way. She followed a pattern when they watched the movies, giving a brief overview of the film before it started, explaining the stars and the director, and then she'd fast-forward through the TCM hosts, who often irritated her with their *gee whiz* sincerity. Once the film began, if something else occurred to her, Iris would pause the movie and point that out, too. Logan didn't seem to mind these interruptions. Whenever she stopped a film, he would nod compliantly while she said whatever she needed to say. This was an attractive quality, even if Iris had a vague notion that this might have been how Logan had been directed to act during those fake classroom scenes on *Windsor Valley High*. However, the kid didn't always stay quiet. During the scene in *Now, Voyager*, where Paul Henreid lights two cigarettes in his mouth and hands one to Bette Davis, Logan had muttered, "Yuck. Smoking."

"Jesus, Logan!" Iris had snapped. "It was 1942. Everybody smoked then. Children were going through a pack a day. It was a different time. Get over yourself!"

The next movie they saw was *Harvey*. It was about Jimmy Stewart's friendship with a giant, invisible rabbit. There was a great character actress in this film who played Jimmy's sister. Her name was Josephine Hull. She had a scene at the end of the film that was almost impossible to play. She needed to stop Jimmy from getting an injection that would end all his delusions of Harvey forever. The scene required the actress to be hilarious and heartbreaking at the same time. Iris always watched this scene with admiration, but she knew if she asked the next hundred people she encountered, not one of them would have heard of Josephine Hull, maybe even a thousand people—and the woman had won an Oscar! This thought troubled her and she had wondered briefly if it might have something to do with her own lost career, but that was another subject, like Frank's resentments, better left unexamined.

"I thought we'd have a Hitchcock film today," said Iris, after they had rinsed their breakfast dishes and retired to The Screening Room. "You've heard of Hitchcock, I assume. Or maybe it's best if I make no assumptions."

"Yeah, of course," said Logan. "Like *Psycho*."

"That's right, like *Psycho*," said Iris. "But this morning I am introducing you to one of his more sophisticated thrillers."

Iris had a lot to say in advance of *To Catch a Thief*. Logan didn't know anything about Hitchcock and his creepy obsession with blondes or Cary Grant and how he got his start in show business as an acrobat or Grace Kelly, who had married Prince Rainier and become Princess Grace of Monaco a year after this movie was released. Midway through the film, after a few of her trademark disruptions, where Iris pointed out Edith Head's costumes and tried to explain the history of the French Resistance, Logan had turned to her and said, "You know, you sort of look like her."

Grace Kelly was driving rather wildly at the moment along the cliffs in the South of France, a scene that disturbed Iris to watch because of how the real-life princess would die thirty years later, careening off a similar road after suffering a stroke.

"I beg your pardon?" said Iris.

"You look like her or she looks like you. Well, not now, of course, but you from that photo," said Logan, pointing in the direction of the dining room, where her old headshot sat on the sideboard.

"Oh, don't be ridiculous," said Iris. "I didn't look

anything like Grace Kelly. If I'd looked like Grace Kelly, I would have won an Oscar and married a prince!"

"What's the trouble?"

Frank had come into the room, having just woken up. He was stifling a yawn and smoothing down his hair.

"Your chum Logan says I resemble Her Serene Highness Princess Grace of Monaco."

"Her," Logan said, pointing at the screen.

"No comment," said Frank as he settled between them on the sofa. "I plead the Fifth."

"You're not going to offend me by speaking the truth," said Iris.

"And yet I'd rather not take any chances," said Frank. "By the way, isn't it a little decadent to be inside watching movies on such a beautiful morning?"

"So says the person who's been sleeping through it," said Iris. "Now shut up and let's get back to the film."

They watched in silence for a little longer, until the scene where Cary and Grace go to bed together in her hotel room, except this was only implied, since it was 1955 and Hitchcock had to pan away during the big moment to some fake-looking fireworks.

"So were they actually doing it in real life?" asked Frank.

"Who?" said Iris.

"Those two," he said, gesturing toward the TV.

"I should think not," said Iris. "They were lifelong friends. Cary attended her funeral."

"She slept with a lot of her costars, though," said Frank. "Like Gable and Sinatra and Ray Milland, I think. I read that somewhere."

"People write things," said Iris testily, "as they tend to do. What possible difference does it make?"

"It's just that her image was so ladylike," said Frank, "the white gloves and everything—and yet apparently she really liked to hook up with her costars."

"Your mother is right," Logan piped up now. "What difference does it make?"

"I'm simply pointing something out about the hypocrisy of the 1950s," said Frank.

"No," said Iris. "You are not talking about the 1950s. You are talking specifically about this particular woman."

"But I'm still pointing out the hypocrisy," said Frank.

"Why are you slut-shaming Princess Grace?" said Logan.

He picked up the remote from the coffee table in front of them and paused the film.

"What's the matter with you?" said Frank.

"She's not around to defend herself, for one thing," said Iris.

"That's true," said Logan. "But that's not the worst of it. I mean what exactly would she be defending? That she enjoyed having sex with her handsome and famous costars? Where is the news flash in that?"

"Come on," said Frank.

"No! Look at her," Logan barked, pointing at the screen where Grace Kelly's face was frozen mid-frame. "She was so beautiful. I don't think you can understand the pressure on her or the expectations. Good looks aren't always the gift people think they are!"

"I suppose I *can't* understand," said Frank dryly. "I'll need to defer to you on the subject—and to my mother, of course, the princess's doppelgänger."

Iris mimed a royal wave as Logan continued to fume. *The kid's on to something*, she thought. Her own looks had provoked plenty of expectations in people, not to mention a few very unpleasant assumptions.

"I'm just saying," said Logan, "you shouldn't ever judge

the choices people make! People make questionable choices all the time! People do stupid, regrettable shit every day, in fact. But it shouldn't define them!"

"Holy crap, Logan," said Frank. "Look, I'm not trying to pass an ordinance against the woman. I was just offering some historic information. Lighten up."

"You're not even hearing what I'm saying! I'm saying somebody's missteps shouldn't seep into their legacy, or whatever you call it, like a stain, so that sixty or seventy years later, that's the information that gets passed around until it's the only thing we end up talking about!"

"But I thought you said her sleeping around wasn't even a misstep?" said Frank.

"Well . . . it's not," said Logan. "I'm talking generally now!"

"Generally?"

"Yeah," said Logan, "as in generally it's just a shitty thing to guess people's motivations or worthiness based on a collection of haphazard moments from their past."

"Jesus Christ," said Frank. "What's gotten into you?"

Iris had leaned forward on the sofa and was staring hard at them both. Logan noticed her watching and forced a laugh. He took a deep breath.

"I'm sorry," he said, his facial expression in disarray. "We just shot an episode about slut-shaming on *Windsor Valley* last week. I guess the lesson made more of an impact on me than I realized."

"I guess so," laughed Frank. "I've never seen you get angry like that before."

He reached over and mussed Logan's hair.

"What can I say?" said Logan, smoothing his hair back into place. "The power of television. Strange how that happens."

"Yes," said Iris, still watching him intensely. "Very strange indeed."

Logan returned her gaze for a moment and then quickly picked up the remote and pressed *Play*.

The movie continued without further interruption. Afterward, they all returned to the kitchen, where Logan volunteered to make Frank's breakfast and the frying pan was once again called into service. Iris took her place at the cooking island and opened her laptop to check her emails. She was mentoring, for lack of a better term, one of the kids in the real estate office, though this "kid" was a mother of three and must have been nearly thirty-five. Iris had offered to help with an open house later that day in Manhattan Beach and was waiting for a confirmation. There were no messages from the young woman. The only new message had a subject line that read:

Iris Flynn: Is that you?

Iris opened the email and began to read.

A few minutes later she pushed the laptop away and exhaled noisily.

"What's the matter now?" said Frank. "Did the Kardashians do something else to annoy you?"

He was sitting directly across from her. Iris glanced at her son and slid the laptop in front of him.

"You might as well read it," she said.

Logan was just then sliding Frank's omelet from the frying pan onto the plate in front of him.

"And you can read it, too, Logan," said Iris. "We should have no secrets from each other when we're all living under the same roof."

She said this quite pointedly, but Logan refused to look

her way. He stood behind Frank and read the email over his shoulder.

I am trying to locate my sister. Iris Flynn. I couldn't find any contact info for anyone living in Southern California with that name, only a list of television credits attributed to her (you?) on some Hollywood database. Then I looked under your married name and found this email on a real estate website. Are you a realtor now? You weren't using Erik's last name when you were acting. You never answered my letters after that last visit and you eventually stopped popping up on television. I guess that's when you moved on to real estate, assuming I've reached the right party. But how many women named Iris Gessemoni could there possibly be in Southern California? Gessemoni is uncommon enough, but you don't hear the name Iris much anymore either. Some of these old-fashioned names have been making a comeback. My twelve-year-old granddaughter, for instance, is named Opal, which is another name that doesn't exactly sound fresh as a daisy. I actually suggested "Daisy" to my daughter when she was considering options for the baby, but she doesn't like flower names as a rule (no offense) and so Opal it was. Cheryl, my daughter, wasn't even born the last time we saw each other. And Frank must be over forty by now. I remember him as a sad-eyed toddler. You probably have grandchildren, too, but how would I know? Oh, well. I've already taken too long to get to the point. Here's the thing, Iris. Mother has passed away. Died last night in her sleep, in her own bed, here at the farm. This is how she preferred it, of course. We had been discussing putting her into Assisted Living, but Mother always called this Assisted Dying and shut down the idea quickly enough. She'd been shaky on her feet for a while. I bought her one of those orthopedic canes at the CVS, which she sometimes picked up and heaved at us when she was angry. This will not come as a surprise, if you still have even the vaguest memories of Mother. Anyway, I felt you should be informed, not that I see you crying into the Pacific over the news, but she was our mother, after all. The funeral will be next Friday. Thibedeaux's is handling it. I'll let you know how it goes. I'm also reaching out because I will need your mailing address. There will be some papers that will require your signature, releases and such, since Mother stubbornly refused to set up a will. She won't be leaving much, rest assured, as you should be aware more than anyone. I can't imagine you'd have any interest in any items from here anyway, considering everything. So that's that. It suddenly seems strange to be writing my big sister after all this time. We probably wouldn't recognize each other if we passed on the street. I hope this note finds you and your family well. I always did wish you well, Iris—whether you believe that or not.

Yours truly,
Celeste

"I had a freakin' grandmother!" Frank shouted when he was finished reading. He was glaring at Iris across the cooking island. His eyes were livid.

"Of course you did," said Iris. "People have grandmothers. It's a thing."

"I mean I had a grandmother who was alive and kicking until about ten minutes ago?"

"Yes."

"You told me your parents were dead."

"That's true. I did."

"I even remember when you told me. We were doing family trees in the fifth grade. I asked you about your family. You didn't even look up from whatever you were doing. *All dead*, you told me."

"It felt that way to me."

"Is my grandfather still alive?"

"No. He's long gone," said Iris.

"Like really dead or will there be a follow-up email—FROM THE AUNT WHO I NEVER KNEW EXISTED!!!?"

"Oh, Frank, I was estranged from them, okay? We'd never been close. Your dad and I thought it was simply easier to tell you they had passed on, as his folks had."

"Easier for who exactly? I was living on the East Coast for years. I could have traveled up to the farm to see my grandmother some weekend."

"I don't think that would have gone over too well."

"How do you know?"

"I was acquainted with the woman," said Iris.

"Well, we'll never know now. You took that chance away from me!"

"It's not like you ever exhibited much curiosity about your family history," said Iris.

"Because when I was ten years old, you told me they were all dead!"

Iris shrugged.

"And why are you sharing your secret now anyway?" Frank asked.

"For one thing, you're sitting here right in front of me." said Iris. "I wasn't going to be able to avoid it. Or maybe I felt it was finally time to share."

"Geez, how old was your mom anyway?" asked Logan incredulously.

He was still standing there behind Frank with the frying pan in his hand.

"Older than dirt," replied Iris.

"He's only asking a question," said Frank.

"Okay then," said Iris. "Sorry. Ninety-six."

"Wow," said Logan.

"Yes, wow," said Iris.

"What caused this falling-out exactly?" said Frank, gesturing toward the laptop.

Iris sighed deeply again.

"It's complicated," said Iris.

"Auntie Celeste sounds a wee bit passive-aggressive in that message," said Frank.

"Then you should have met my mother. She was in her own category—aggressive-aggressive."

"There was some unnecessary info in that email, too," said Frank. "I mean, who describes a toddler as sad-eyed?"

"Well, there *is* some photographic evidence," Logan murmured.

The three of them remained silent until Frank looked at his mother and said, "I'd offer condolences to you, but that doesn't seem necessary under the circumstances."

Iris shrugged again.

"So now what?" asked Frank.

Iris got up and crossed to the French doors, where she stood for a long time thinking through the situation. She stared out at the backyard, which was now awash in blazing sunshine. There was more debris in the pool. She could see it from here, more leaves and blossoms, and something that looked like a small, drowned lizard, bobbing around.

"Hello! Hello!"

Frank had stood up and was waving his hands like a castaway trying to get her attention.

Iris turned back toward him. She could see he was observing her with almost zoological interest.

"So now what?" he repeated.

"I guess I need to make some arrangements," she said flatly.

"What kind of arrangements?" said Frank.

"So I can be in Maine by next Friday," said Iris.

"What are you talking about? You're not planning to go, are you?" said Frank, pointing at the computer screen. "That wasn't an invitation, more like a notification with some baggage attached."

"Who needs an invite to attend their mother's funeral?" said Iris.

"You mean the mother you haven't seen since . . . I was a sad-eyed toddler?" said Frank.

Iris went to the sink, picked up a wet sponge, and began to wipe down the countertops.

"If there was no love lost between you," said Frank, "why exactly do you feel the need to attend?"

Iris paused, weighing her answer.

"The woman gave me life," she finally said.

"How very New Testament of you," said Frank. "You don't think a nice floral arrangement might suffice?"

"I do not," said Iris.

"Again, let me repeat. I don't think your presence is expected," said Frank.

"Why should my sister assume that I won't attend?"

"In fairness, your absence for several decades might have led her to that conclusion," said Frank.

"Then Celeste is being a presumptuous twit," remarked Iris.

"Since I have no real-world knowledge of the woman, I wouldn't know," said Frank.

Iris threw the sponge in the sink.

"Anyway, you need to give this some more thought," said Frank. "You've just gotten the news. I imagine it must at least be somewhat of . . . an adjustment."

"That's a good point," said Logan. "What exactly are your *feelings*, Iris?"

She turned to look at him. Logan's eyes were wide with

concern, his even features now flushed with compassion. She was almost moved.

"I'm feeling that we need to arrange our flights," said Iris.

"What do you mean *our flights*?" said Frank.

"I will need you to come with me, of course."

"How do you figure that?"

"I might need your assistance," said Iris.

"I beg your pardon?" said Frank.

"I'm an old lady. I might fall. I might break a hip."

"Only if someone tackled you," said Frank.

"Well, she is older," whispered Logan.

"I can hear you," said Iris.

Logan mouthed an apology.

"I don't see how I can go," said Frank.

"This is a family emergency," said Iris.

"Yes," said Frank, "but it might make more sense if the family in question wasn't making a surprise guest appearance."

"Glib doesn't really suit you, Frank," said Iris.

"Look who's talking. And it's not as if I can just take time off work," he said.

"And why the hell not?" said Iris. "You've just lost all your possessions in a fire and now you've lost your grandmother, too. They don't need to know you never knew the woman. Are you telling me they're not going to give you some bereavement leave? At a rehab, a business founded on the guiding principles of sensitivity and compassion?"

Iris knew it might be awkward having Frank along, but she wasn't willing to leave him in California. Notions of her son's potential relapse were still swirling in her head, put there by Logan himself, and she did not think the kid was up to navigating a worst-case scenario on his own. Frank's presence, she imagined, might also prove beneficial from a practical standpoint.

"Hold up," said Frank. "I didn't know these people even existed until five minutes ago and now you want me drop everything and fly across the country. First the fire and now this. It's all too much."

"I'm sorry my mother didn't do a better job of coordinating schedules before she died."

"Oh, that's real nice," said Frank. "Anyway, what about Logan? What's he supposed to do?"

There was a note of concern in her son's voice that sounded slightly desperate. It answered any lingering doubts Iris had about Frank's feelings for his young boyfriend.

She thought for a second.

"He can come, too," she said. "My treat."

She imagined Logan would be a welcome distraction for Frank, something that might also be helpful in the long run. Plus she was growing fond of the kid.

"Really?" said Logan.

"Why not?" said Iris. "You're not playing high school for the next little while, are you?"

"Nope. I told you. We're on hiatus. And I've never been, like, anywhere," said Logan.

"Of course you haven't," said Iris. "See, Frank, there's another reason. Logan's never been, like, anywhere."

"I don't know," said Frank. "I mean, who are these people anyway?"

"Weren't you just saying that I've kept you from your family all these years? Now here's your chance to get a glimpse of them."

When Frank began to protest some more, Iris pointed a finger at him and shouted, "Enough! I need you to come with me . . . period!"

"Jesus. Whatever. Okay," said Frank, raising his hands in surrender, "I suppose I could maybe ask for some time off."

"There you go," said Iris. "Simple solutions to complex problems."

CHAPTER FIVE

"Jesus H. Christ! She's coming here!"

Celeste was staring at her phone in disbelief. She and Joe were sitting in the living room of the farmhouse. There was a mound of laundry next to her on the sofa, which she was supposed to be folding, and Joe was in his easy chair watching the game. The Pats were slaughtering the Jets.

"Who?" asked Joe, without taking his eyes off the screen.

"Iris. She's coming here for the funeral. She sent an email."

"Didn't I tell you that was a possibility?" said Joe.

He turned away from the game then and looked at his wife. The expression on his face was haughty and disapproving. He didn't look like himself at all.

"You did not tell me that," said Celeste.

This was not true. He had told her at least twice.

"I definitely said when you were writing that note, '*And what are you going to do if she shows up?*'"

"You don't need to sound so . . . victorious," said Celeste.

"I don't know why you felt the need to give her the news before Deb's funeral," said Joe.

"Because we don't need any trouble from her about the will and I figured she might get her nose out of joint if we didn't let her know right away. I certainly didn't expect her to jump on a plane!"

"Well, considering the tone of your message, it might have been like waving a red flag in her face. She's probably calling your bluff and won't even show up."

"She's not bluffing," said Celeste. "They've booked their flights. They're landing at the Jetport on Thursday and renting a car. Frank is coming with her. She didn't mention Erik."

"Divorced by this point most likely," said Joe, somewhat cheerfully. "It *is* Hollywood after all."

Then after a moment, he added, "She's really coming here, huh?"

Celeste ignored the eager tone in her husband's voice.

"And Frank will be bringing . . . his boyfriend," she said.

"Ah," said Joe. "Of course. The land of fruits and nuts."

"Now that's exactly what I'm worried about," said Celeste, throwing her hands up in the air. "Iris is going to be looking down on us as it is—the yokels. We don't need to give her any more ammunition."

"We are yokels, Cee, and I don't give a shit what your movie star sister thinks."

"Charming," said Celeste. "Please keep sharing that kind of stuff when they get here. And she's not even in show business anymore. She sells houses now."

"That figures," said Joe. "Real estate folks are kind of like actors, making shit up as they go along. And I'm not sure what you're so worried about. I can't imagine Iris has any interest in the farm, or what's left of it anyway. It's not exactly Malibu beachfront property."

"How do we know what she wants?" said Celeste. "We haven't seen the woman in forty years. We don't know anything about her."

"Look, she'll sign what she needs to sign when the time comes. I'm sure of it."

"From your lips," said Celeste.

Celeste knew her husband to be a sensible, levelheaded man, but then there was that soft spot he'd always had for

Iris, something he'd been trying to hide with wisecracks and half insults since the three of them were teenagers.

"If you were all that worried," Joe said now, "you might have taken more care with the message you sent."

"There was nothing wrong with my message!" said Celeste.

"It was snotty here and there."

"It was not!" Celeste replied. "And why shouldn't it be!? Or do I need to remind you that Iris not helping us out when we needed it was a major setback in our lives?"

"No need to remind me," said Joe. "I'm only pointing out that you can't, on the one hand, worry about how I might offend the woman, while not realizing that you probably already did."

"Says you," said Celeste.

Joe groaned and turned back to the game.

They weren't used to bickering like this. Celeste didn't think they did it particularly well. Lord knows there had been enough sadness and stress in their lives, but they rarely took it out on each other. Celeste was grateful for that, but she knew there were couples who enjoyed quarreling, even bragged about it. It was said that antagonism sometimes added a layer of excitement to a marriage. But her relationship with Joe had always fallen into a neutral zone. Chores on the farm, the challenges of parenthood, and simply making ends meet had been enough work for one lifetime. She didn't need another full-time job keeping a marriage together.

On the television, during a break from the action, photos were being shown of Tom Brady throughout his twenty-year football career.

"He looks younger than he did as a rookie," said Celeste, motioning to the screen. "How does he do that?"

Joe shrugged. "He don't eat tomatoes."

"Huh?"

"Too acidic."

"Oh please," said Celeste.

"And I've read that everything in his diet has to be organic and locally grown and it all has to be pH balanced, too," said Joe.

"What? Like a swimming pool?" said Celeste.

"I guess so," Joe replied.

"That's a bit woo-woo. Don't you think?"

"I don't care, not as long as the Pats keep winning."

"Aren't they saying he might not even finish his playing days in New England?"

"Hell no. That will never happen. Trust me. He'll never leave the Pats. Playing here is keeping him young."

"Well, he's also married to that Brazilian supermodel," said Celeste, "so that can't hurt either."

"Nope, you're right," Joe nodded, "it can't."

He winked at his wife.

"Take a deep breath about your sister, will ya," said Joe. "It's all going to work out."

Then Joe turned back to the television. His facial expression was nice and normal again. It was the contented look that crossed his face whenever he watched the Patriots play. Sports, Celeste realized, were a simple, uncomplicated pleasure for her husband in a life that hadn't always provided him that luxury, especially these days. He'd had his third heart attack the previous summer while he was on the roof of the farmhouse with Moody Prescott replacing shingles. That one had scared the crap out of her—and of Joe, too. Celeste could tell. Moody, not the brightest light in the harbor, had nevertheless prevented Joe from rolling right off the roof. It was the most serious heart attack of the three. The attacks, Joe said, felt as if they were building in strength, like thunderstorms forming in the sky, waiting to burst. He'd become more cautious after this last one. Joe took his pills now without complaint and had stopped making snide remarks about his Portland cardiologist, with his bad breath and terrible comb-over. And this time, after getting his latest stent, he had *not* joked with the nurses in the recovery room about bringing him a pot of black coffee and a pack of cigarettes. He was resigned and compliant now. This embarrassed Celeste a little (she was ashamed to admit), observing how her wise-ass husband, who had been unflustered and solid for decades, was suddenly aware of his own mortality. It seemed beneath him somehow. There was no more roof work in the sun and now he ordered egg white omelets for breakfast when they went to the Town Line Diner. And he somehow knew about Tom Brady's diet and how the guy didn't eat friggin' tomatoes. These were all new developments—and to Celeste, they were not entirely welcome.

They'd met fifty-five years earlier when Joe had come to the Flynns' farm during the three-week potato harvest. They were both seventeen then. Joe was from the next town over. Schools closed in that region of Maine in the early fall so the local farmers could hire teenagers to help out with various farm jobs. Celeste's father, who made no secret of wishing he'd been given sons instead of two daughters (one of whom was too pretty for her own good) always hired big, strapping boys during the harvest. At over six-foot-two, Joe was no exception. He wore a big shit-eating grin on his face the day he had come to the front door of the farmhouse looking for work. This grin did not please Jasper Flynn much. He distrusted smug happiness in general, and especially if it was being spread around by a complete stranger.

"What the hell are you smiling at?" the man had snapped at the boy as he opened the door.

"I don't know," answered Joe. "Maybe this will be my golden opportunity."

Jasper liked that response even less than the boy's grin. "There are no *opportunities* here, kid—just a chance to make a buck from some hard work."

Celeste and Iris were standing behind their father in the doorway as he conducted this little *interview*. They were peeking over his shoulder. He hadn't even invited the boy inside. Joe had leaned a little to the left and peeked back at the girls for a moment. He'd focused on Iris first, of course, as everybody did. At eighteen and very beautiful, she commanded all varieties of attention, but as soon as it was received, she would immediately dismiss it, as if it was nothing she cared about at all. This was how she acted that day with Joe. Her eyes slid away from him, like the sun slipping behind a cloud. She glanced past him into the front yard and then out over the fields and then beyond that, all the way to the horizon. Iris was known in the family and elsewhere, for these cold, thousand-mile stares. Joe, in this instant, seemed more amused than anything else, by the frosty, glaring snub. He shifted his gaze toward Celeste then and she had offered him a weary smile and a resigned shrug, her standard response after witnessing this type of snotty performance from her sister. Meanwhile, Jasper, with great reluctance, as if he was doing Joe the most enormous favor imaginable, hired the boy and began going over the particulars of the work expected of him, telling him that he should return to the farm the next morning at dawn.

Later, after dinner and its cleanup, after they had helped their mother can some green tomatoes (a messy job Iris particularly despised) and as they were climbing the stairs to their rooms, Celeste had said, "So what do you think of him?"

"Who?" asked Iris.

"That boy today."

"Mr. Golden Opportunity?" said Iris. "Another bullshit artist, no doubt."

Celeste remembered how Joe had won Father over eventually, with his strong work ethic and easygoing attitude, and Mother, too, whose expectations were even harder to satisfy. He'd charmed everyone, in fact, except Iris, who overlooked him, like an unwatered plant. She ignored him during the three-week potato harvest and then afterward, when Jasper hired the boy for weekend chores. Iris's reaction had less to do with Joe than with Iris herself. That's what Celeste always figured. Iris was singularly focused on her own plan to get the hell out of town. She might as well have had blinders on. She had no time for boys—or her own family, for that matter. As sisters, Celeste and Iris had never been close. It was as if they had been cut and styled from different patterns.

Iris would get her chance to escape soon enough. The following summer there would be a beauty contest in Augusta, sponsored by a movie theater chain. The winner would get prize money, a trip to Hollywood, and the promise of a screen test. From the moment she had heard about it, Iris didn't even pretend to entertain the possibility that she wouldn't win. She had already been voted Best Looking in her senior class, as well the County Potato Queen and the Blueberry Princess at the Fryeburg fair. Iris had been gathering compliments about her appearance since birth, like interest in a savings account. Not that Celeste thought her sister was particularly vain. There was more to it than that. Iris simply possessed an unwavering certainty about her future—and her good looks were a commodity, a product, something she could use as safe passage to break from her life on the farm. Celeste had gone to watch that pageant, even though

Iris hadn't expected anyone from the family to show up and cheer her on. It took place in a cavernous civic center on State Street near the capital. Celeste stood by herself in the back row. Her parents said they couldn't be bothered with such foolishness. Iris looked very beautiful in the spotlight. When she crossed the stage, Celeste heard a collective sigh from the crowd. She felt as conflicted as she usually did when her sister triggered some seismic reaction. So when Iris actually lost, when she was named second runner-up, Celeste would have expected to feel something like relief or even satisfaction, considering Iris's stack of royal titles and all that admiration that trailed her everywhere she went like wisps from a jet. But Celeste hadn't felt relief. She had stood in the back of that auditorium and found herself weeping, imagining her sister's bitter disappointment, the scuttling of her plans. It suddenly occurred to Celeste that she had probably trusted in Iris's determination and dreams as much as Iris did herself. Now it seemed like there had been a ripple in the universe. Up on the stage, as another, less beautiful, girl was crowned; Iris wore her usual indomitable expression. She retained the same resolute set to her shoulders, as if she'd been cast in bronze. She stared straight ahead. It would take more than a lost contest to stop Iris. It wasn't until a few days later, after she had packed up and left for California on a bus with her savings, that Celeste overheard her parents talking. Father, it seemed, had paid one of the local judges, a man he knew from the Rotary Club, a man with a gambling problem who was chronically short on cash, to vote against their daughter, because a blow to her confidence was what Jasper and Deb thought she needed and would finally bring her back down to earth. They had been wrong about that part, of course. They really didn't know Iris. They didn't know her at all.

CHAPTER SIX

The Jets really sucked. The Pats were up 28–0 and it wasn't even the half. *It must be terrible to be a Jets fan*, Joe thought. They were always waiting around for the second coming of Joe Namath. Then again, the Pats had sucked, too, before the Belichick-Brady era, and he'd lived through the Red Sox curse as well, for most of his life, before they'd finally turned it around. Miracle of miracles. He knew what it was like to be a foiled sports fan. He'd cried when the Mets beat the Sox in the '86 Series. He'd actually wept. That was over thirty years ago now, which seemed insane to him, that passage of time. Time sped away faster the older you got. Everyone knew that. But this wasn't just some theory people liked to spout. There was an actual reason for it. It had something to do with physics or maybe just simple math. When you were ten years old, one year was one tenth of your whole life. But at the age of seventy-two, as Joe was now, a year was a much smaller fraction than that, so twelve months seemed to pass by while you glanced out a window. He thought back over his life more often these days, probably because of his advancing age and his shitty heart. He could imagine his life piling up behind him, broken up into sections, like blocks of ice.

There was his childhood, of course, in Houlton, where he had lived with his widowed father and two older brothers. Joe's mother had died of a rare blood disease not long after he was born. He had been shuffled around to assorted relatives until it was time for him to start school and that's when he'd gone back to live with his father full time. His old man was a preoccupied and ornery piece of work, a carpenter with a mean and flashing temper. He'd never forgiven his wife for dying on him and leaving him three sons to raise. Joe learned early on to stay out of the man's way. He got pretty good at flying under the radar. His older brothers made that a little easier for him because they were always the ones getting into trouble, picking fights in school, brawling on people's front lawns. As a result, Joe's father watched his youngest boy, waiting for him to turn wild, too. But the boy didn't turn wild. He'd grown up without incident, not that he got any credit from his father for not going off the rails.

Joe considered his arrival at the Flynn farm as the real start to his life. For a long time, he thought this had something to do with Iris and his reaction to her. Seeing her was like being jolted awake after a very long sleep, though he'd noticed her a few months before that first day at the farm. She was coming out of a movie theater in Caribou. She looked so out of place there, standing alone on the sidewalk in that town of ordinary shops and boarded-up storefronts. It was if she had simply appeared, like a lovely sunrise, willed from people's imaginations. It wasn't only her beauty that set her apart, though that, of course, was an undeniable factor. There was also a restlessness to her, an energy, something he could see from across the street, something that might have been spotted from distant rooftops. Three months later, when he saw her at the farm, during Jasper's interview, when they locked eyes for a moment before she looked away, Joe knew he was lost. He told himself he could maybe win her over by ignoring her, by faking nonchalance in her presence. His indifference would take her by surprise. He would be like an unexpected bump in the road forcing her to slow down and take notice. He had nothing but time, he reasoned, and simply seeing Iris during the harvest or later when he worked at the farm on the weekends, as he was loading the truck or parceling out the fertilizer or dealing with the irrigation system, the wait seemed like the most worthwhile thing he had ever done in his life. He worked hard for Jasper, earning the man's respect. And he won Deb over, too, a tougher nut to crack. She watched him frostily as she fed him his lunch in the kitchen. He was quiet and polite with her, but he didn't overdo it. Like her husband, Deb distrusted casual friendliness. Joe stopped flaunting his natural sunniness in front of them to earn their trust. One thing he still regretted was that he had begun to flirt with Celeste as part of his quest for her sister. He thought it might get a rise out of Iris, who had exclusive rights and privileges to all avenues of attention. It wasn't as if Celeste wasn't pretty in her own right, but in the constant unavoidable comparison with her beautiful sister (people were quite blunt in their assessment of the girls), she would always be found on the losing end of a daily competition. Joe knew this could not have been an easy path for her to tread.

Celeste, no fool, had even pointedly questioned him about his sudden interest in her when he'd begun to loiter around. One time, early on, she was out on the porch shelling peas for supper as Joe was making small talk and getting ready to leave for the day.

"So why aren't you sniffing around after Iris?" asked Celeste. "She's probably around here somewhere."

"Your sister seems to prefer her own company," said Joe, smiling remotely.

"No argument there. But isn't that what you boys refer to as *a challenge*?"

"Not this boy," said Joe.

"Ah. The exception to the rule. Nice to meet you."

"Maybe I don't like fighting uphill battles."

"Ha!" laughed Celeste. "That's my sister, all right, a very uphill battle."

"I don't mean anything by it," said Joe.

"No. That's a good description of her. I suppose this means you're more interested in pushovers and such. Is that correct?"

"Something tells me you're no pushover," said Joe.

"You got that part right."

Celeste amused him. He had to give her that.

Joe eventually grew tired of waiting. Iris loved the movies and would visit that theater in Caribou one Saturday afternoon a month when she could arrange a ride with a family she regularly babysat for. This transportation deal was part of her babysitting wages. Joe had called the theater and got the times of when the movie would be let out. Then he paid one of his brothers ten bucks to let him borrow his pickup truck. He drove to Caribou, parked near the theater, and then paced up and down in front of the place a few hundred times, waiting for the patrons to spill out onto the street. It was the end of March, snow still piled high everywhere. But there was a hint of warmth to the day, the first real sign of the impending spring, and this seemed to reflect the optimism Joe felt about his plan. He was carrying a bag of school supplies from the stationery store next door, which was the alibi he had worked out in advance for when Iris registered her surprise at seeing him.

"Hey, Iris!" he shouted as she filed out with the small crowd, but she did not express any surprise at his presence. The look on her face was fixed and neutral.

"It's you," she said flatly.

"Yes," said Joe. "So it is."

He was breathing hard. His face was burning.

"I needed notebooks," he said, holding up his bag and motioning next door. "Had to hit Gelson's."

Iris gazed disinterestedly in the direction of the stationery store and then turned back to him.

"Did you now?" she said.

A stony silence settled over them.

"So how was the movie?" Joe said finally, pointing to the big poster they were standing in front of.

The movie was called *The Pumpkin Eater* and it was 118 minutes long, but that was all Joe knew about it. He kicked himself now for not doing more research. He might have even tried to see the film beforehand, so they might have discussed it. These regretful thoughts buzzed in his head as Iris began to speak.

"I liked it," she said. "Anne Bancroft was wonderful."

"Anne Bancroft. She was in the Helen Keller movie, right?"

"*The Miracle Worker*," said Iris. "Yes. She won the Oscar for it."

"I saw that one," said Joe.

"A lot of people did."

"It was a comedy, right?"

"*The Miracle Worker*?"

"No. This one," said Joe, motioning to the poster again.

"Not even accidentally," Iris answered coolly. "It's British. Harold Pinter wrote the screenplay."

Who the hell is Harold Pinter? thought Joe.

"Oh," he said. "I just assumed the movie was on the lighter side. You know, with a title like that?"

Iris looked at him blankly.

Come on, he wanted to say. *The Pumpkin Eater*!

But he didn't say this.

"So what was it about?" he asked.

Iris sighed heavily, as if she'd been interrupted while performing surgery.

"It was about a very depressed woman with nine children and a philandering husband."

"And it wasn't a comedy?" Joe joked.

Iris didn't exactly smile at this, but at least there was an adjustment to her facial expression, an expression he was still having trouble deciphering.

"It was a film about diminished expectations," Iris continued, "and about dashed hopes and ultimately, I suppose, about betrayal."

Jesus, I'm glad I didn't see it, thought Joe.

"It sounds interesting," he said.

"Does it?" asked Iris, staring hard at him. It was the first time she had ever done this without then glancing quickly away.

He blushed some more.

"Yes, it does," Joe stuttered awkwardly. "Or at least it sounds unusual."

He stared at the poster of Anne Bancroft in a negligee peering off into space looking somewhat beleaguered.

"She looks very young to have nine children," he said.

"I'm not sure if there were nine exactly," said Iris. "But there were a lot. That wasn't really the point."

She watched him. Then she did look away, scanning the sidewalks of downtown Caribou.

"I'm waiting for Mrs. Standish," Iris said. "She's giving me a ride back to the farm. She's running some errands now, so . . ."

This was the opening Joe had been waiting for.

"Yes, well," he grinned, "maybe I could give you a ride back instead."

"What do you mean, Joseph?"

Iris was the only one who called him that. His heart fluttered when she said his formal name.

"I have my brother's truck," he said. "I could drive you."

"And why would you do that?"

"Well, I was thinking, if you're hungry, we could go grab a bite at the Town Line Diner and then after that I know there's a new movie theater over in Allagash, so we could check if there was something on over there that you might want to see, I mean, if you were up for two movies in a day. Or we could just go out for ice cream after the diner or even a drive to the ocean. I don't have to have the truck back until late. We could make a night of it."

These words spilled out of Joe in a rapid, involuntary way. Like a burst pipe. Iris had continued to stare down the street as he spoke, but now she turned back and gazed at him in an unwavering way.

"These plans just occurred to you, huh?" said Iris.

Joe didn't know the best way to respond to that.

"I was thinking maybe it would be . . . fun," he finally stammered.

"What would make you think that?" replied Iris. "We haven't said two words to each other before this. I guess I'm supposed to be charmed that you are lurking outside a movie theater with my whole evening planned."

Joe shrugged helplessly.

"Do you think I have a secret desire to be swept off my feet? Is this the Caribou version of showing up on a white horse? I might like movies, but I certainly don't think I'm living in one."

Joe had expected a lot of reactions, but not this one. Her facial expression had now become obvious. Iris was livid. A feeling of humiliation rose in him like fever, but there was some anger mixed in there, too.

"I don't know shit about white horses," he said. "And I was hardly *lurking*. This is only me offering you a ride and asking you out to the Town Line. You don't have to be so nasty about it. I just thought—"

"Exactly. *You* just thought. You guys are always just thinking. Taking everything for granted."

Joe made an exaggerated turn to his right and then to his left.

"What guys?" he said. "I'm the only one standing here."

"And yet you might as well be a crowd scene. It's so . . . predictable."

Iris laughed unpleasantly and then scanned the street some more.

"Okay. Okay," said Joe. "Don't make a federal case out of it. Can't you just say *no* like a normal person?"

"Fine then," said Iris. "No."

"I really can't see why you're so bent out of shape about an offer of a movie and a damn ice cream," said Joe.

"So many offers."

"I think maybe you just don't want to admit we might have a nice time."

"Ahhh, now we've arrived at the *I know you better than you know yourself* portion of the program."

Joe stood there staring at her. Unfortunately, she was as stunning as he'd ever seen her. It was late afternoon and the fading amber light was making lovely shadows on her beautiful upturned face. And yet here he was, furious and grief-stricken at the same time. This was a new and complicated emotion for him. He had trouble even identifying it.

"What the hell's wrong with you anyway?" he said, waving his hands in the air.

"And now you're implying that something must be wrong with *me* because I don't want to spend the evening with *you*?" said Iris.

"You know, I knew you were snooty about your looks, but

I never realized you were as mean as a snake. But you want to know the weird thing? You wouldn't be able to talk like this if you didn't look like that. It's like you get a free pass from the universe for being . . . pretty. I'm sorry a lot of guys have gotten fresh with you or whatever this is about, but it doesn't give you the right—"

"How do you know what it gives me?" said Iris. "You don't know me or anything about my experiences, which of course is my point. And by the way, you wouldn't even be here if it wasn't for my looks, the ones that you say I'm so snooty about. So I don't really care if you think I'm as mean as a snake. Maybe I am. I didn't come with any guarantees. Why don't you give that a little thought?"

Joe scuffed his boots on the sidewalk.

"And just to be clear," said Iris, softening her tone ever so slightly. "Even if I had any interest in you, which I don't, there is no chance that Mrs. Standish would just leave me here with you or that my parents, when I called to tell them that my plans had changed and I was suddenly going out for the evening, would not demand that I return home immediately. So this plan of yours was seriously flawed from the start. And I can tell you something else of which I'm certain. If we did go out, we would run out of things to say to each other in about five minutes. No offense."

"Now she says, *No offense*," said Joe.

"And there's one more thing you should know," said Iris.

"And what would that be?"

"I don't think my sister would like it."

Joe walked away from this exchange embarrassed and smarting. The window of opportunity had been slammed on his fingers. In his brother's truck on the way home, he cursed Iris out, slamming the steering wheel and driving too fast, while cringing at his own stupidity.

The next weekend (he remembered it was April Fool's Day) the whole state got hit with a spring blizzard. He was back at the Flynn farm plowing out their long wraparound driveway—snow plowing being another one of his duties there. After the scene in Caribou, he'd been nervous about seeing Iris again. He couldn't let her believe that he was still pining away. He decided when he saw her next he'd plaster a middle-of-the-road smile on his face and act a little bored. If their eyes happened to meet, he'd be the one to glance away first. He certainly wasn't going to sulk in front of her. But Iris didn't make an appearance that day. It was Celeste who was outside, shoveling the porch steps and the path that led to the mailbox by the road. After Joe was finished with the driveway, she invited him inside for hot chocolate, but even as a kid, he preferred coffee, the stronger the better. He sat at the kitchen table as Celeste brewed the coffee, as she stood at the ancient, converted woodstove making her hot chocolate. There was no sign of Jasper or Deb, but it was a large property and there was no shortage of chores. Or perhaps they had dug themselves out earlier and gone to town to run errands. For all Joe knew, Iris could be at another movie somewhere, soaking up more annoying opinions. The storm had ended and the sky had been rinsed clean. Late morning sunshine was spilling into the room, making spidery shadows on the pale yellow walls and cabinets. Joe liked this old kitchen. He liked the table he was sitting at, with its wax tablecloth. He liked the curtains with their jaunty hummingbird pattern. He liked how the space was functional, but neat as a pin. Deb insisted on that. It couldn't have been any more different from his own crowded and filthy kitchen eight miles away, with its mismatched chairs and every surface covered with his dad's fishing and wildlife magazines, the sink perpetually stacked with dirty dishes. Joe's brothers would rinse a plate only if they were forced to, if they needed one for a meal. He honestly couldn't remember ever seeing the sink empty, a depressing and perfect example of his chaotic childhood.

Celeste placed Joe's coffee on the table in front of him and then she brought her own mug over and sat down.

"I thought we were done with winter," Joe said wistfully, motioning outside.

"Did you? And why would you think that?" Celeste replied. "Where have you been living your whole life?"

"It was sixty degrees last week."

"So?"

"So nothing. I just expected spring from here on out."

"Ha," scoffed Celeste. "I read something once. Expectations are just disappointments waiting to happen."

"Now that's a grim attitude," said Joe.

"You think so?" Celeste asked.

"You don't have any expectations, I suppose," said Joe.

"I didn't say that. I expected this hot chocolate to taste pretty good."

"Mmmh. I see," said Joe.

"What? What do you see?"

"Expectations are okay when you think you can control the outcome yourself. Is that it?"

There was a brief pause before Celeste answered.

"Now that you mention it."

She smiled at him over her mug. Joe could see that it was true. Celeste was someone without any illusions—about herself and probably anything around her. He wondered what that must feel like. Lonely, he imagined. It must feel lonely to have no illusion of hope, because isn't that what expectations were, a sort of symptom of hope? He thought of his own expectations, the way he always imagined his father and brothers would suddenly stop being such assholes and pull it together at home, though he wasn't even sure what that would look like, other than a clean sink. And then he thought about what happened with Iris the previous Saturday, and his foolish romantic notions leading up to all of it. He wasn't sorry he had these notions, only that they had been misdirected. He smiled back at Celeste. He wondered if her resigned attitude had something to do with growing up around a sister who had cornered the market on hope and anticipation, the way a fire can suck all the oxygen out of a room. To someone like Iris, with her shining appearance and confidence, expectation must seem like nothing more than a self-fulfilling prophesy or simple routine, a milk bottle delivered to her front door. It occurred to Joe just then that Iris and her blazing impact had somehow led him and Celeste to this very moment, as they sat there eyeing each other across a table.

"The coffee's good," said Joe.

"Of course it is," said Celeste. "Did you expect anything less?"

The Jets rookie quarterback threw a Pick 6. Pandemonium ensued in Foxboro. The cameras spent some time focusing on the mayhem in the stands and then there was a close-up of the baby-faced quarterback as he walked to the sidelines. His chin was quivering.

"Poor kid," said Celeste, motioning to the screen.

"Why should we feel bad for him?"

"He's got a mother somewhere," said Celeste, "who's probably watching this. She might even be at the game."

"Well, I'm sure his thirty-million-dollar contract will console her," said Joe.

Celeste chuckled and went back to folding the laundry.

Joe continued to stare at the television screen, but he was still distracted. It must be this news about Iris returning. He was thinking some more about the shape of his life and how the Flynns were his only *real* family. One of his brawling brothers had been dead for fifty years. He'd been killed in a motorcycle accident the day of the moon landing. He'd struck a moose on a desolate stretch of road. Joe's other brother had enlisted right afterward, maybe out of grief. Lonnie and Cal had always been inseparable. Cal came back from the service strung out and nuts, though he'd never even made it to Vietnam. He'd been stationed in Texas the whole time, inspecting parachutes. He'd moved to Florida eventually. Last Joe heard, he lived near the Everglades and worked trapping snakes and gators for carnival sideshows, which seemed about right. He might even be dead by now. They hadn't heard from him in decades. Joe's father had continued to flail around in the little house in Houlton, grousing about the neighbors and the changing world. He died after falling off a ladder when he was eighty. They'd never been close. The old bastard hadn't even come to their wedding, and he'd only seen Cheryl, his own granddaughter, a few times—when Celeste had dragged the kid over to his place on holidays, thinking that being in the presence of the adorable little girl might provide a shock to his system, a lightning bolt that would turn the guy into some other person entirely. But that hadn't happened.

Joe had enjoyed the hard work of the farm. He liked tilling the clay soil and the careful digging at harvest time. He even got superstitious about using a favorite garden fork that he felt did less damage to the tubers. After Iris had departed for California, it seemed that Joe had been tapped to fill the void. Not just in terms of her chores, such as they were, but even by taking her place at the dinner table. He was immediately absorbed into the family. If Jasper and Deb considered their older daughter's sudden departure an unforgivable betrayal, to acknowledge the loss would have felt like a colossal waste of time to them. They simply wrote Iris off, banished her from their conversations unless it was to criticize some news they received of her new life in California. Memories of Iris and her rejection of him drifted through Joe's mind for years and years. It went without saying that he and Celeste would get together; proximity and fate seemed to take care of that. Not that there wasn't a genuine attraction between them, but even at the beginning it felt less like a spark than the memory of one.

"I suppose I'll need to write back and tell them that they can stay with us," Celeste was saying now, pulling Joe back into the present.

"Huh?" said Joe, glancing away from the television. "What do you mean *with us*?"

"You know—*with us*. As in, *here*. I'm not sure that we have much choice anyway."

"Of course we do. Everything is a choice. Like sending that email in the first place was a choice."

"Enough about that," said Celeste.

"And now you want to have these people move in? What the hell are you thinking, Cee?"

"I'm thinking that we need Iris to sign those papers."

"And?"

"And so we need to at least appear welcoming."

"How long do you think that will last once she shows up?" said Joe.

"I think we can all get through the funeral and a brief visit."

"You think so, huh? Any recollections of the last time? Besides, where do you think we're going to put them?"

"There's plenty of space. Frank and his friend can have the daybed in the sunroom."

"There's a bunch of junk in there," said Joe.

"Just some boxes for the flea market. Opal can help me move them to the barn."

"And where are you going to park your sister?"

"I suppose we can put her in Mother's room."

"You think she's going to take kindly to that?"

"Why not?"

"Oh, I don't know. Coming back here after forty years to curl up in the bed where the mother she couldn't stand just died?"

"Well, I was going to change the sheets first," said Celeste.

"Come on. Is that really the kind of welcome you're talking about?"

"Perhaps you're right."

"Yeah, perhaps I'm right."

"Maybe we could move into Mother's room and she can take ours," said Celeste.

"Like hell!"

"All right, all right. Maybe Mother's room isn't a great choice for anyone right now."

"Agreed."

"Iris could take Opal's room and Opal could move in with us while they're here. We'll get the foldaway from up in the attic."

"Why should the kid have to get displaced?" said Joe.

"She'll look at it as an adventure."

"Sharing a room with her grandparents? Opal is almost thirteen, not six. She's more likely to put pillows over our heads and smother us in our sleep."

Celeste sighed deeply. She looked hard at Joe.

"I'm not sure how we're going to explain why Opal is living with us," she said.

"Why do we owe them any explanations? They've come here to kick us out of our beds."

"No. I mean it," said Celeste. "I mentioned Cheryl in the email and Opal, too, in passing, but nothing about . . . about the situation."

"We're certainly not the only grandparents to step in to raise a grandchild," said Joe. "Besides, everybody's got a situation."

He imagined Iris and Erik probably thought they had a situation when Frank told them he liked boys, but he didn't mention this example to Celeste because he didn't want her to scold him again. For the record, he didn't give a crap about what people got up to together and he'd been around long enough not to be surprised by anything either. Opal had tried explaining the meaning of *gender fluidity* to him recently. She had watched him slyly, expecting him to freak out.

"Oh, we had all that," Joe told her. "But back then it was just called swinging both ways."

"No. That's not it. Gender fluidity is something different, Grandpa," she told him.

"Don't worry. By the time you're my age, there will be some other words for it."

"By the time I'm your age, maybe there won't have to be a word for it at all and people can just . . . be, like, themselves . . . without any labels at all."

That Opal was a funny one.

"Opal is a child," Celeste said now, still debating the sleeping arrangements, "and moving her in with us is a reasonable solution."

"No, the reasonable solution is to have your TV star sister and her traveling California circus stay at a hotel, which is something they can obviously afford."

"Well, maybe that's exactly what they will do and all this concern of yours will be for nothing."

"Yeah. We'll see," said Joe.

He'd meant what he'd said to Celeste. Joe didn't give a goddamn what people thought, but he didn't like the idea of having to explain the Opal situation either. When he watched his granddaughter these days, curious and smart as a whip, she reminded him so much of Cheryl as a youngster that he was gripped by a fierce sadness, consumed in a fog of déjà vu. He had been quite close to his daughter as she was growing up—or that's how his memory had it. He admired her keen and slippery intelligence, got a kick out of her dry sense of humor. These were unusual traits in a kid. And for a while she even liked to memorize Red Sox statistics and debate lineups with him over breakfast—until she outgrew all of that. He chose to focus on those happier memories. There had always been something strangely fearless about Cheryl, even when she was small. She was that rare child who didn't worry about creatures lurking in the dark, who never asked to sleep with the lights on. If Cheryl heard a noise in the middle of the night, she'd be the first one up to investigate—and no matter how often she was forbidden, she'd fly off the roof of the barn every fall into leaf piles.

Being a daredevil wasn't so unusual, but Joe worried this fearlessness would lead her into the unruly behavior that he had witnessed in his older brothers. Once the girl hit her teens, he and Celeste worried about drugs, too. Drugs were every parent's knee-jerk worst nightmare. But whenever they tried to raise the subject with their daughter, it was embarrassing and awkward and felt like they were delivering public service announcements. They might have lacked credibility on that front. Their own youth had been basically drug free. Up on the farm, consumed with the day-to-day, the sixties counterculture had simply passed Joe and Celeste by.

Cheryl had responded to their drug concerns with weary amusement.

"Don't you realize that your little girl enjoys control too much to give it away voluntarily?" she had told them. "And I'm not exactly the kind of person who responds to peer pressure."

This was true. She must have been about fifteen at the time and her tone that day had been slightly mocking. She had hugged each of them extravagantly afterward, as if performing a skit about silly, moronic parents. Joe had since concluded that he probably never really knew his daughter. Then again, the older Joe got, the less he felt he knew anything. This was another crap symptom of age, the recognition of your own ignorance.

As it turned out, Cheryl's fearlessness and sharp adolescent curiosity had not led her into drug experimentation, but instead had directed her into *causes*, from where she charged forth with a raging energy. Even as a little girl, she had been opinionated, whether it was about the stupidity of her classmates or some injustice at school. By the time she reached adolescence, she would bring a wide range of subjects to the dinner table every night—everything from endangered wolves in Montana to floating islands of plastic in the Indian Ocean.

"Okay, okay," Joe would tell his daughter as she ranted. "We'll buy your war bonds. Now eat your damn supper."

Cheryl's determination reminded Joe of Iris. Celeste must have felt the same way, though that was one subject they chose not to discuss. But whereas Iris's resolve was rooted in the personal, in escaping the town and making a name for herself, Cheryl was more interested in actions that could impact global change. This first became apparent when she was given a two-week suspension in high school for dousing herself in red acrylic paint during a school assembly and rolling around on the stage of the auditorium. She was protesting the clubbing of baby seals. She shrieked *Assassins!* into a hand-held microphone until the assistant principal had to drag her away kicking and screaming. A fussy guidance counselor had told Joe and Celeste after this that in his opinion they should get their daughter into therapy—pronto. *Her intensity is alarming*, the man had said in an urgent, conspiratorial whisper, a style that made Joe want to bounce him off the walls of his office. Joe's view (long formed) was that you did not seek *outside* help for *inside* problems. The guidance counselor might as well have advised that Cheryl be treated with potions or leeches. Their daughter, after all, was not some sad sack, curled up in a blanket or lost behind a vacant stare. She was engaged and spirited—not to mention a top student. If she had been a boy, Joe wondered, would the school authorities have chalked up her protest to a harmless prank? Not long before Cheryl's incident, the football team had left a couple of freshman recruits in the woods in their underwear on a freezing cold night as part of a hazing ritual. There was barely any grumbling in town about that, and nobody got suspended for it either, even though one of the freshmen had lost a toe to frostbite.

Joe wanted to believe that all this concern about his daughter was an overreaction. He had an unlikely ally in this—his mother-in-law. Cheryl was born years after Jasper's death. Maybe widowhood had softened some of Deb's rough edges, but there was no denying she'd been charmed by her granddaughter from the first. She admired her *pluck*. That was the word Deb used for it. When Celeste would scold Cheryl at the dinner table for gabbing too much, it was Deb who would always defend her.

"Let the kid talk," she'd say. "She's more entertaining than you or even the television."

After the trouble at school, Celeste sided with that smarmy administrator. She wouldn't listen to Joe, who was in denial, or to Deb, who thought the girl could do no wrong.

"I think we *do* need to get her some help," Celeste told Joe as they were lying in bed a few days after the incident, going over it again.

"For what? It's not like she's on drugs. She's just . . . passionate," Joe had replied.

"Don't you see?" said Celeste. "What just happened was its own version of an overdose. The girl DOUSED HERSELF IN BLOOD in front of her entire school!"

"Fake blood," said Joe.

"You know what I mean. There is something terribly extreme about our girl these days. She's changed. It's not just that she has opinions. She's in a fever about them. We should have seen this coming. Look how many friends she's lost this past year!"

"We didn't like most of them anyway," Joe joked, but his voice sounded hollow even to himself.

"We've got a problem on our hands, whether you want to believe it or not. We should bring her to Augusta so she can talk to somebody. We're in over our heads here, Joe."

"How can someone who has never met us before," he replied, "someone who doesn't know us from nothin', possibly tell us anything about our girl we don't already know?"

"You sound like a jackass," said Celeste.

In the end, Cheryl was the one who shut down the idea. She was cold, but lucid in her response. It was simply a protest, she told them, a peaceful protest, over a disgusting and indefensible practice of animal cruelty. They could stuff her in the car and drag her to Augusta if they felt like it, but no one could get her to utter a word once she got there. She had no intention of defending herself to some pompous shrink.

"But hey, it's your money," she said.

Being privy to her parents' financial worries, this was a pointed and rather unpleasant remark. As a compromise,

Cheryl did agree to refrain from further melodramatic scenes and promised not to cover herself in any more paint.

"I'll stop trying to educate my peers, if that's what you're asking me to do," she told them.

"Come on," said Joe. "You think any of those kids are actually traveling up to Canada to club baby seals?"

"I don't know how those dipshits spend their weekends," Cheryl had said and then she had smiled at them, sort of, as she deployed two more mocking hugs.

She'd still get fiery around the dinner table, but there were no more guerrilla tactics in her high school. She joined an environmental group in Bangor, where she told Joe and Celeste she answered phones on the weekends and approached people on the sidewalk with petitions to sign. Joe chose to believe that her work was really this benign, but Celeste had her doubts. Two years later Cheryl was accepted to the University of New Hampshire to study environmental science, but before the end of her freshman year, she had dropped out to travel west with a ragtag group of activists who patterned themselves after Greenpeace, but without the pledge of non-violence. They planned to sabotage some Japanese whaling ship that they heard was traveling to the Bering Sea, though they had been misinformed about that part. It was somewhere off Antarctica. Not that it mattered, because Cheryl was arrested before they reached their destination, with enough powerful explosives in her backpack to blow up a fleet. The first Joe and Celeste knew anything about this, the first time they realized that their daughter wasn't in her dorm room studying for some organic chemistry exam, was when she'd called while in custody from Seattle. Celeste, on hearing the news, had thrown up in the kitchen sink.

Their world became a blur after that. They quickly went through their paltry savings and whatever they still had in the girl's college fund to pay for her legal defense. She was held without bail. Deb agreed to remortgage the farm to help with the expenses, but as a result, her granddaughter would forever lose her *favorite* status. Cheryl's lawyer was optimistic at first, given the girl's age and clean record, but then it was discovered that she'd been sending terrorist threats to tuna companies and some government officials who her environmental group had identified as war criminals. In the end, she was given a five-year sentence. It could have been worse, the lawyer had told them. Though someone else had made the explosives, Cheryl was the one carrying them. This had been deliberate, as she was the youngest and most innocent looking of the bunch. The federal prosecutor had referred to their daughter as a mass murderer in the making, who had been hindered only by a few random circumstances.

It was before the trial, on their first visit to the prison facility in Seattle, that Cheryl revealed to Joe and Celeste that she was going to have a baby. The father was a Japanese man, an expert on the whaling industry. Cheryl had met him in Durham, where he had come to lecture. He had inspired her recent activism, but it had only been a fling. The man had returned to Japan before she realized she was pregnant. Later she learned that he had been killed in a car wreck in Osaka. Joe and Celeste had sat there in that prison meeting room, with its stark furnishings, the bolted-down tables and benches, the dusty light spilling across Cheryl's face as she spoke to them in a low, reserved tone, as if she were delivering a monologue on a stage. Cheryl was four months along, not even showing. It sounded like one of those melodramatic plots in those old movies of the week, where Iris might show up as the husband's flashy mistress or some random friend with no backstory of her own. At first, Joe tried to believe that his daughter was discussing someone else, some other unfortunate girl who had been arrested with her, and that he had lost the thread of the story—though the denial evaporated quickly as Celeste gripped his hand so fiercely, it would remain sore for days. Celeste stayed silent the whole time and shed no tears. She looked like one of Cheryl's seals, like she had been clubbed over the head. Joe watched the other tables with their grim, hunched visitors and wondered what had led them all here. He thought of Celeste's three miscarriages. The doctors had thought she would never be able to carry a child to term, but then it had finally happened, when they were forty. Now the miracle baby was sitting in front of them in prison garb telling some impossible story as if it were the most natural thing in the world. Joe had to remind himself to breathe. All of it had finally caught up with him. Cheryl had stopped talking and was watching her parents with what appeared to be a combination of remorse and expectation. He hoped she was remorseful. The attorney would later tell them it remained unclear how far her regret extended. Joe knew in that moment, sitting across from his daughter, that whatever he said next would be remembered forever. So he reached across the table and took Cheryl's hand.

"Well, my girl," he'd said, his voice suddenly breaking, "we're here for you. Just tell us what you need."

CHAPTER SEVEN

When they boarded the flight to Boston, Logan had clambered to sit by the window like an excited five-year-old. They were seated three across, with Iris on the aisle and Frank between them. It had been years since Iris had flown anywhere. The last time was when she and Erik had visited Frank in New York, soon after he'd been bounced from the band and relocated. That must have been twelve years ago. She considered asking Frank to confirm this, but he seemed happily occupied watching Logan gaze at the clouds. Leave well enough alone, she thought. Besides, any mention of that earlier trip would likely remind Frank of how poorly it had all gone. He wouldn't be shy about sharing the particulars either, trotting out all the details like a forensic accountant. Her own memories of that time were slightly less distinct. She and Frank had not gotten on well. She remembered that. He was annoyed with her for not loving his adopted city as much as he did. It was true. She didn't love New York, but she had thought Frank might be overdoing it. The tours he gave them of his noisy Brooklyn neighborhood and a few famous attractions were a bit too smug and eager, like he was rushing a frat. Iris could appreciate New York's gritty beauty, its bustling possibilities, but the place mostly reminded her of some rude drunk at a party who didn't know when to shut the hell up, someone who would eventually stumble into a corner and throw up on themselves.

One night while they were there, Frank had a gig at a

shadowy and smoke-filled club in the East Village. The space was long and narrow, like an old-fashioned diner. The rude and burly bartenders seemed half drunk themselves. It was the first time Iris and Erik had seen their son perform since he had left the band, the first time they'd seen him perform solo since he was a teenager at school talent shows. He didn't go on until after midnight, a lousy slot, and once he did, the crowd was so buzzed and noisy, nobody was listening. This was a shame, thought Iris, because though Frank's solid guitar skills were no surprise to her, she had forgotten what a sweet and lovely voice he possessed. She grew livid that the rowdy patrons wouldn't stay quiet, as he worked his way through a set of mellow troubadour covers, which were probably a bad choice for the clientele. She wanted to tell them all to shut up but realized how stupid she'd look if she began screaming at strangers in the dark, defending her little boy up on the stage who was a grown man in his thirties. Erik, sensing all this, held her hand the whole time, crinkling his eyes at her, willing her to lighten up. Afterward, when Frank joined them at their table, instead of praising his performance, as Erik had done, Iris had complained bitterly about the crowd and the venue and told her boy he was wasting his time in a place like that. Frank had sneered at her and said, *Tell me what you really think, Mother*. It was not her finest moment, but sometimes the need to share her opinions felt unstoppable, like a seizure. She had never considered it necessary to apologize for speaking the truth. Iris admired outspokenness. She had a thick skin after her years in show business. There was a ton of bullshit in Hollywood, schmoozers and duplicitous sharks, but there was also brutal honesty and cruel assessments put forth with surgical precision and she'd almost gotten used to that part.

Now on the plane, she thought back to that night in the bar and wondered why she hadn't offered Frank a little motherly kindness. Well, she hadn't exactly been *that type of mother* was the simplest answer. When Frank was growing up, she often felt that she had to offset Erik's grinning indulgence, his lax parenting style. Somebody had to keep their hand on the tiller. Even on that trip, with Frank a grown man, Erik had been relegated to his role of cheerleader, which he'd played in his usual winning fashion. At that point in their lives, her husband wasn't away from home so often. His dalliances and gallivanting had ceased by then and he was working steadily, steadily for him anyway, renting out jet skis again in Catalina. Iris and Erik's relationship had softened, become more conventional, now that they were older. These conventions, Iris realized, might have benefitted her son if he had been around them earlier. Who knows what opinions Frank had formed, what road map he followed in his own relationships, after observing their unusual marriage? At least she and Erik had loved each other and stayed together. That had to count for something.

Iris sighed and leaned back against the headrest. She noticed one of the flight attendants looked like her old friend Ginny. She hadn't seen Ginny for years and for a moment Iris wondered if this might even be her, in her own post-Hollywood second act. But of course, that was a ridiculous notion, since the flight attendant was maybe thirty and Ginny was older than Iris. Iris shook her head at this odd senior moment. But then she thought of Ginny some more. It was Ginny who had dragged her to the acting classes. They'd met during a three-episode arc on *Here Come the Brides*, playing scheming dance hall girls. Later in their friendship, when Iris was complaining about the stupid, unplayable roles she was being offered, Ginny had hollered, "Then do something about it! Hone your fucking craft!"

Soon after that, Iris had accompanied her to Actors Studio West.

The Studio was situated in a one-story stucco building in an ordinary Hollywood neighborhood a few blocks from the Sunset Strip. It was basically one large room with lots of folding chairs, a small, curtainless stage, and some semi-familiar faces milling about at any given time. The rotating moderators were *legit famous*, however—which was a term Iris had recently heard Logan use. Actors like Bruce Dern or Ellen Burstyn would show up to walk them through scenes and offer critiques. Iris worked hard at the Studio. Some of the exercises felt like party games, but she loved every minute of them. Up on the stage, the moderator might whisper some given circumstances in the ears of the actors—*You're terrified of water, but you need to cross a bridge*; *You're madly in love with the actor standing to your right, but he doesn't know; You are looking through a bakery window and haven't eaten for three days*—and then they'd go to work without being able to utter a word. Iris watched as these directions would change the physicality of everyone's behavior. Surrounded by such talented, dedicated actors, Iris was inspired for the first time in her career. After a few months of classes, she signed up to perform her first real monologue, something from *The Country Girl*, not realizing that Lee Strasberg himself, the guiding force behind The Actors Studio, would be moderating that night. When Strasberg was the moderator, scene night was jam-packed. He was sometimes merciless, cutting a scene short to deliver a sharp or dismissive critique before sending a trembling actor back to their seat. On that evening, Strasberg let Iris get about ten lines in before he shouted, "Stop!" Then he got up and stepped onto the stage. He crossed to where Iris stood and whispered in her ear, "Georgie doesn't just want Frank to stand on his own two feet, she *needs* him to." Iris thought for a moment. She nodded at Strasberg. He left the stage and motioned for her to start again. When she did, it was with a new layer of urgency and desperation. After she'd finished the monologue, Iris gathered her props and sat back down in her chair. Lee Strasberg stood. He turned to address her directly.

"What's your reason for being here?" he asked. "And I don't mean the character, I mean you."

Iris considered the possibility that he was about to kick her out of the class, but she did not panic.

After a moment she said, "I want to get better."

"You work, don't you?" said Strasberg.

"Not the kind of jobs I want," Iris said flatly. She held his gaze.

"I see," said Strasberg. "You know, I gave you that adjustment because I had a hunch about you. Not much throws you, does it?"

"No," said Iris, "not much."

There wasn't a sound in the room. Everyone's eyes were on her.

"Well," said Strasberg. "It was extraordinary. You were quite extraordinary. No notes."

There was a pause after he said this, while Iris held her breath and chewed the inside of her cheek. His tone had been unemotional and matter-of-fact. He pivoted away from her then and motioned for the next scene to begin.

A few weeks after this, Iris discovered that she was pregnant with Frank. She and Erik needed to move because the lease on their apartment was up and now they needed a larger space. They found a small house on the other side of the Valley, a lengthy drive from Hollywood. Classes were no longer convenient and, with another mouth to feed, harder to justify. In some hopeful corner of her brain, Iris did imagine going back, but when this did not happen, she filed it away as one of life's ordinary compromises. Iris was hardly one of those unfortunate people to wallow in regret and it wasn't as if she and Erik hadn't wanted to be parents. Though she would never land any major films, be a regular on a series, or segue to Broadway, Iris did relive that Strasberg moment a thousand times, while taking pratfalls on failed pilots or reciting terrible, mind-numbing dialogue or fending off the advances of asshole casting directors. That one moment of real praise, she would come to realize, was the highlight of her life as an actor. Now on the plane to Boston, remembering all this, with Frank and Logan beside her, she let herself ponder the lost opportunities and near misses that had made up the steeple chase of her career. She remembered her talent, too, as one might remember a friend from one's youth who had inexplicably packed up and moved away, leaving no forwarding address.

CHAPTER EIGHT

Frank was watching his mother with real interest, but she didn't appear to notice. She was sighing irritably, as if someone had just stolen her parking space.

"What are you sighing about?" he asked.

"Nothing," said Iris. "Nothing at all."

"Are you sure about that?" said Frank.

Iris straightened up in her seat.

"I was just wondering," she said, motioning down the narrow aisle, "why do all these flight attendants look like professional assassins? They look as if they could eat their young."

Frank stared in the direction she was pointing. He did not believe his mother was sighing about the flight attendants.

"They just look exhausted to me," said Frank, "if anything."

"More like fed up. That one there just threw nuts at an old man!"

"Maybe he deserved it," said Frank.

Iris said nothing.

"You know it's hard to wait on people," said Frank.

Iris shrugged.

"But I guess you never had to do much of that, did you?" Frank asked.

"What do you mean?"

"Wait on people."

"You mean if we're not counting you?"

"No. I mean, like, restaurant work. The service industry. I did a lot of serving and grunt work in restaurants, especially my last year in New York. And these folks up here have to do it accompanied by turbulence while reciting safety procedures."

"I *played* a lot of waitresses," Iris said flatly. "And some flight attendants, too."

"Did you really just say that?"

"What's the matter now?"

"If I have to tell you," said Frank, "there's no point in explaining it."

There was a long pause after that as they sat amid the muffled hissing sound of the pressurized cabin. Logan had drifted off and was dozing now, his face pressed against the tiny window, a trickle of drool trailing from the corner of his mouth.

Frank turned back toward his mother.

"Okay," he said. "We have about another five hours on this plane. You're a captive audience . . . or I guess I am, so would you be willing to share a bit more about what has brought us here?"

"To this flight?"

"I'm referring to what brought on this long estrangement from your family. There's obviously a story there."

"There are stories everywhere," said Iris.

"Okay. Your reluctance is duly noted, but don't you think you need to give me some context before we arrive on the East Coast, if only to prevent me from saying something . . . insensitive?"

"It has been my experience," said Iris, "that having adequate context does not always inoculate one from being insensitive and I do not believe that I am *required* to tell you anything."

"Oh, come on, Mother. This is so stupid. Can't you just talk to me?"

Iris sighed some more and glared at the passing flight attendant, the one who had hurled the nuts.

"Let's see. What can I tell you that might satisfy your curiosity? That my parents were ice cold and wildly unsupportive people who wanted me to toe the line, keep my mouth shut, and remain on the farm for my entire life to further their own goals and aspirations?"

"Is that true? Is that what they wanted? Indentured servitude?"

"Yes. Essentially."

"I guess that's a start. I mean, in terms of explanation," said Frank. "I take it that your sister agreed to their terms and remained on the farm?"

"That was Celeste's choice, yes, and she was welcome to it, but it was not mine."

Frank paused before his next question. He leaned in and whispered it.

"Were they abusive?"

"Who?"

"Your parents, of course."

"Not in the way that you are implying," said Iris.

"I'm not implying anything. I am asking a question."

"Then they were not abusive in the way that you are asking the question."

"In what way am I asking?"

"In the daytime talk show sort of way."

"And what way is that?"

"You are asking if I was beaten to a pulp or fiddled with or otherwise molested."

Frank stammered a protest, but he wasn't sure how to respond, as this was exactly what he had meant.

"Anyway, the answer to that question is no," said Iris.

"Well, I'm glad to hear it," said Frank.

"I'm glad that you're glad," she said.

A brief awkwardness settled over them.

"The word *abuse* conjures certain images, though, doesn't it?" said Iris. "But there are many ways that family members can fail each other."

"True enough," said Frank. He shifted in his seat. "And one of these ways, if I understand you correctly, is that your parents did not approve of the life that you wanted to live, and this prompted your escape from Potatoville."

"Do you even need me for this conversation?"

"I'm just trying to get a picture in my head," said Frank.

The picture in Frank's head was of the battle between his mother's burgeoning iron will, her teenage drive to make something of herself, and his grandparents' need to meet all the challenges pertaining to life on the farm. His imagination didn't extend to the specific details of potato farming, but he assumed these duties were varied and endless. Frank could see how his grandparents (whom he visualized as Auntie Em and Uncle Henry in *The Wizard of Oz*) might object to their little girl chasing flimsy Hollywood dreams. This even seemed to make sense, and in his mind he was even beginning to side with them. In a parallel train of thought, as the plane flew over the Midwest, he was reminded of his own youthful ambitions and how they hadn't exactly been cultivated as he was pursuing them. Frank was contemplating the best way to advance this thought when Iris said, "I know what you're thinking. You think you have this all figured out."

"No, not necessarily," said Frank, "but I don't believe it is unprecedented for parents and children to, how shall we say, not see eye to eye on career options."

Iris leaned in closer to him.

"I assume by that *gotcha* expression on your face," she said, "that you are referring to our own relationship."

Frank remained silent.

"Well, all I can say in response," Iris continued, "is that I do not remember disowning you because you were panhandling on the street—and unlike my parents, I am certain I did not send you any hate mail either."

"I was not panhandling! And what do you mean by hate mail?"

"I don't know what else you could call it when you are chastised in various letters about the disgrace you have brought on the family name because you have been *behaving like a common slut with your titties hanging out for all the world to see.*"

"Titties hanging out? You weren't doing pornography, were you?"

"No, you dimwit. You know what I was doing. I was on sitcoms, running around in bikinis and miniskirts, but shaming me was the common theme of their communications."

"Really?"

"To Father and Mother, there was no real difference. I might as well have been starring in *Deep Throat*."

"You could have spared me that image," said Frank.

"You asked," said Iris.

"Your father really called you a slut? Or was that your mother?"

"Both, actually. Sometimes they would take turns in the same letter. Different pens, different handwriting. Same general idea."

"How long did this go on?"

"Oh, years."

"Did you ever respond to them?"

"I was too shocked at first. I mean Father and Mother

were not religious fanatics or anything. Just your standard Methodists. They went to church once or twice a year, but there was such fervor attached to those letters. I would read them and almost expect the paper in my hands to burst into flames. I did eventually write them, to try and reason with them, calm them down. There must have been some faulty unknown gene in me still trying to seek their approval. I tried to explain myself and my career. I was trying to justify the entire acting profession, I suppose. I was on shaky ground with this, considering the roles I was landing at the time. I mean, I wasn't doing Shakespeare on PBS."

"Well, did it calm them down?"

"Hardly, but the letters would stop for a while. Then they'd see me in something else and let loose again."

"Jesus."

"Once I had a bit part in a terrible biker movie. Joe Namath was the star, if you can believe it."

"I think we saw that one on TV. Dad made us watch it."

"Entirely possible," said Iris. "The point is I only walked across the screen for like ten seconds, but the next thing I know, I get a two-page letter from your grandparents about the costume I was wearing, some hot pants and a ripped halter top. I had LEERED INTO THE CAMERA, they wrote, all in caps. Oh, the humiliation! They couldn't show their faces in town! When would I stop with my Hollywood decadence? But here's the thing. They must have lined up and paid their money to see that movie, like everyone else. Why did they even subject themselves?"

"Maybe they had their own faulty genes and couldn't stop seeking you out," said Frank.

"I don't know how they knew I was even in that film. I was hardly giving them career updates at the time, though I did write them once about an episode of *The Flying Nun* I was in where I wasn't doing anything sexy at all and wore a habit the whole time."

"Did that help?"

"Nothing helped. And eventually, at some point, I came to my senses and stopped trying to rationalize my existence to them. I wrote a note telling them that their *slut of a daughter* would not be reading any more of their unsolicited opinions, so they should stop writing them, and while they were at it, I suggested they could both do me a big favor and drop dead."

"Yikes," said Frank.

"Your father did not approve of that, but I certainly did not need his approval to cut them off. He was a cockeyed optimist as you know. He hated their letters, but he thought they would come around eventually. He wanted to write to Father and Mother himself. They didn't even know him. I had sent them a telegram when we married, which was never even acknowledged. I told Erik that he was overestimating his charms if he thought he could sway them."

"Who knows?" said Frank. "He might have."

"Now you're the one doing the overestimating. At any rate, after I sent them that note, there was no more hate mail, no communication whatsoever."

"Did it bother you?"

"No. I felt lighter or liberated, something like that, as if I'd shed a skin."

"And where was your sister in all this?"

"Celeste? Oh—in some land of the willfully ignorant. She'd send these yearly Christmas letters about the happenings on the farm, as if everything was normal, as if I cared anything about it, as if I hadn't tunneled my way out of there with a spoon. She'd share bits of gossip about people in town I either didn't remember or wished I'd never met. And then she'd praise her husband Joseph to the heavens, his work ethic, and salt-of-the-earth qualities, as if I hadn't been acquainted with the guy when he was just another teenage doofus."

"Isn't it possible that she didn't know about the hate mail?"

"No. That is not possible. Some years later, after I sent the note telling my parents to drop dead, my father did, in fact, die. Celeste contacted me. He had died, without warning, of some type of lung embolism. Celeste told me that just before Father lost consciousness in the emergency room, he told her that he regretted our estrangement more than anything in his life. She then told me that Mother was bereft and unable to speak on the phone, but that she, too, lamented the behavior that had caused all these hard feelings—and that she, Mother, that is, was requesting my presence at the funeral."

"And so you went?"

"Yes, we all did. You were two years old."

"I was there? *That's* the visit Celeste was referring to in her email?

"Yes."

There was a loud snort from Logan just then, who was twitching in his sleep, like a dog dreaming of chasing rabbits. They turned to watch him for a moment and then Frank looked back at his mother.

"I take it that visit did not repair the familial bond."

"You could say that, because, you see, my sister had lied about the whole thing. Father had died, all right, but instantly. He never even made it to the emergency room, so there were no deathbed musings. And Mother was not so bereft she could not speak, because, well, she just wasn't made that way—and she had not changed her mind about her harlot daughter either."

"When did you find all this out?"

"After the funeral. Celeste approached me about giving

them a loan for the farm. Your father was out walking with you in the fields. I remember she brought it up while we sat in the sunroom. She had Joseph try to explain what they needed the loan for—some pointless expansion. Mother was there, too, sitting on a wicker chair, with her perfect posture and pursed lips. She had been distant and cool since our arrival, all through the visiting hours at the funeral home and the funeral itself. I had attributed this to her grief. I hadn't expected the woman, no matter what Celeste had told me over the phone, to throw her arms around me and beg forgiveness. I was willing to wait for that. But it wasn't until they asked me about the investment, that it became clear to me that Celeste had tricked me into coming there simply for this conversation. I suppose she thought that she could convince me to hand over my cash if she saw me in person. I declined, of course. It was Mother who confirmed the charade as she rose from her chair. '*Just so you know*,' she said, '*this was all your sister's doing. I wanted none of it. I hated the idea of coming to you with our hands out. I told them they should be ashamed to ask you and that you were too selfish to even consider helping the family. You have always only helped yourself, Iris. It's oddly pleasurable to know that I was right about you all along and so was your father.*' The fury from those letters was still blazing in her eyes."

"Shit," said Frank. "That sucks. And then what happened?"

"I told Mother that it was nice that I could finally do something to please her at long last and then I went outside to find you and your father and we packed our bags and flew away home."

"And now that we're flying back," said Frank, "what do you hope to achieve?"

Iris paused then, leaned forward, and pretended to

refasten her tray table. Then she settled back against her seat again and folded her arms.

"Why don't we just say closure," she said, "and leave it at that."

Iris turned away then, folding her tent. Frank knew she was finished with her disclosures for the time being. He thought of what she'd told him. At Harmony West, the rehab where he'd gotten sober and now worked, there was a counselor who referred to the clients' lives as *crooked little paths.* What his mother had just described was her own path or at least some portion of it. Her revelation was ugly and unpleasant, but she had moved on with her life. Frank had heard far worse at the rehab and in his NA meetings, of course, where most of the hard luck stories focused on how people had been swallowed up by disaster and adversity before (or after) tumbling into their addictions. The triumph in those rehab stories was in the sobriety itself. That same counselor said you were not supposed to judge anyone else's journey, but Frank sometimes had trouble with that piece, though he appreciated the twelve-step aspect and the serenity prayer, too. He liked that you could study the steps, see them as your daily homework. You moved from one step to another, as if advancing your way through a foreign language, going from basic conversation to fluency. Though sometimes you had to reverse course and learn them all over again.

At first, when he'd arrived at the rehab, Frank had real trouble with the concept of a higher power and the idea of turning your life over to it. It was hard to put your trust in God, considering all the shitty things that happened in the world on a minute-by-minute basis under His or Her watch. It would be like handing your car keys over to a killer on the lam. But Frank was told that cynicism was normal for people in his position, meaning people who were dragging themselves back from the edge, and that he didn't need to think of the higher power in a set religious way. In fact, he could leave religion out of it entirely.

At the beginning of his stay at Harmony West, there was a client in his morning group, an affable crackhead, who said he liked to think of his higher power as the sun and the moon and the stars. Frank was impressed by that simple idea. It was helpful information. That's when Frank had begun conjuring other guitarists he admired as his higher power—guys like Ritchie Valens, Jim Croce or Ricky Nelson, who had all been taken away too soon. It amused him to think of these guys watching over him, a fraternal order of musicians escorting him to sobriety from the great beyond. All these dudes had been killed in plane crashes, weirdly enough. This was an odd thing to remember now, at 30,000 feet.

Just then, as if on cue, the plane banked sharply to the left and plummeted a couple hundred feet. The seat belt sign was instantly illuminated and there were some murmured expletives throughout the cabin. A toddler sitting in the row in front of them began to cry, while the nut-throwing flight attendant walked unsteadily down the aisle, smiling icily at everyone.

"I wonder how much time this pilot has had in the air," Iris muttered.

Frank's mother was someone often on the lookout for incompetence—especially in professional types, whom she distrusted on principle and thought were treated with way too much deference by society. Iris especially despised doctors ("*Fifty percent of them graduated in the bottom half of their class!*" she liked to say), though she'd been lucky enough to avoid the medical establishment for most of her life until the arthritis in her spine had gotten the better of her. Still, she rarely took anything for the pain. In fact, Frank knew that she had hidden her medication after he'd shown up after the fire. He had seen the pills in her kitchen cabinet, but then she'd quickly moved them, hidden them away somewhere. Frank wasn't sure whether to be insulted by her suspicion or touched by her concern. But recent events had not shaken his sobriety after all. Keith's death had perhaps redefined loss and his reaction to it forever.

Iris was not finished with the pilot, who had just announced over the intercom that the plane would be moving to a different altitude, in search of smoother air. He made a dumb joke about not charging them extra for the roller coaster ride.

"Did his voice sound slurry to you?" asked Iris when he signed off.

"That was a Southern accent, Mother," said Frank.

She ignored him.

"For all we know, he downed a few cocktails in the airport bar before takeoff," she said.

Frank said nothing, and soon enough Iris got quiet again and settled back into her seat, but he still had plane crashes on his mind. He had never been a nervous flyer and was usually more rational than to believe that his thoughts alone could bring on cataclysmic engine failure. However, the wildfire and its aftermath had perhaps confirmed a belief that every terrible thing was possible after all. The day of the fire, he hadn't been prepared. He'd had to evacuate two other times since coming back to California. Frank understood the idea of precaution, the necessity for the drill, a by-product of his location in the world, the way it was for Florida residents during hurricane season. But this hadn't translated into actual fear. He didn't think anything awful would happen that day. Those other evacuations were before Logan moved in, and back then he hadn't even bothered to contact Iris. He'd stayed in an unoccupied room at the rehab with a packed suitcase and a yowling Bertram in a cat crate, until the all-clear had come and then he'd gone home. This time was different. The fire spread so rapidly, exponentially, and then the winds had unexpectedly shifted. He'd gone to work early and hadn't even gotten word of the warnings and sudden evacuations until it was too late. Later, when his landlord called to say the neighborhood was consumed, that his house was no longer standing, the impossibility of the news had actually brought Keith to mind and the terrible image of his crushed body in the morgue. Frank had somehow let himself believe that he'd already paid his dues as far as tragedy was concerned. Clearly he hadn't. So why couldn't the plane crash right now? If it did, Frank thought, there would be no headlines about him, nothing about his great promise being extinguished from the universe. Not like after Ritchie Valens had gone down on that flight with Buddy Holly and the Big Bopper—the day the music died.

There wouldn't even be a real obituary for him since Iris would be gone, too, and so who would be around to write it? Not those phantom family members they were traveling to see in Maine. Maybe Liam, his NA sponsor, would draft something and post it on Facebook, or perhaps the executive director at the rehab might put something in the newsletter. Frank imagined the executive director's lifeless prose (one of Frank's jobs was to punch up her memos) as she described his cut-short, random existence in a conventional way. Whatever she wrote would probably focus on his work at the rehab and maybe even how he had been a client there. It's not like Frank didn't value sobriety as an accomplishment. He did. It was one of the most important things he had ever achieved, but he wished he could be remembered for something other than *not gulping down painkillers*. He turned to look at Logan then, who had slept through the turbulence and was still drooling beside him. Frank shook his head, as if to free himself of any more morose thoughts. Then he reached over and put his hand on Logan's knee, ever so gently, so as not to wake him.

CHAPTER NINE

As the plane was making its final descent into Portland, Logan looked out the window and saw the Old Port and the city's business district sprawled out before him like markers on a board game. And then, at the edge of his line of sight, he spotted a stately lighthouse perched above the craggy coastline. Logan experienced an involuntary jolt as he remembered a book he had loved as a child that was set in New England. It was a meticulously illustrated book about a boy who was sent to live with his grandmother for the summer on the coast of Maine. The boy was not happy to be sent away from his friends or his Midwestern habits, but his parents were going on a trip or one of them was ill or there was some other reason. Logan couldn't remember that part now. The grandmother lived in a big, shingle-style house that gave the impression of a colossal cruise ship.

The house sat on a bluff that overlooked a rocky beach and a small, enclosed harbor, where fishing boats bobbed on the waves. The grandmother took the boy on various adventures every day of his visit. One time they took a long, dangerous hike along a cliff to an old lighthouse and then climbed its spiral staircase to the very top. As they gazed out to sea, the grandmother entertained the boy with tales of hurricanes and shipwrecks and miraculous rescues.

Another time the grandmother took the boy clamming. She had him look for small holes in the mud at low tide, no bigger than the tip of your index finger. That's where the clams were hidden. She used an ordinary (new) bathroom plunger to fish them out, which passed for humor in the story, though it was not exactly a comic romp.

Then there was the day when the grandmother and the boy walked in the opposite direction, away from the sea, until they came to a long row of blueberry bushes which sat at the edge of some dark woods. Here they gathered big, fat blueberries in gallon jugs, which they took back to the grandmother's enormous country-style kitchen. They made pies and muffins from scratch to sell to the tourists, which they did from card tables that they set up along the main road out of town. With the blueberry proceeds, the boy bought some materials to make a bamboo raft, which he took to a narrow channel near the harbor. The boy used an old sheet that he tied to a makeshift mast and in this way he was able to sail along the channel, until the wind picked up and the boy and the raft were swept out to sea. This was when the boy had to rely on all his grandmother's lessons of the summer (which Logan remembered as amounting to patience, perseverance, and an upbeat attitude) as he navigated the raft to safety. The raft came to shore near the old lighthouse, where the grandmother was inexplicably waiting for the boy with open arms and a slice of leftover blueberry pie.

More of the book's episodic plot came rushing back to Logan in the rental car, as they drove north to meet Iris's family. The book had comforted him as a child. He'd read it in his bed at night in the small second bedroom of the Las Vegas apartment that he shared with his mother. It was a plain space that didn't even feel like his own room because it was also used as Samantha's walk-in closet. Overstuffed clothing racks and a tall shelf for her shoes lined the walls. He remembered that Samantha was between husbands when he first read this book (it had been left by somebody in the building's laundry room) but she had other distractions and had not wanted to hear anything about it. She'd put her hand up to silence him whenever Logan tried to discuss it with her.

He wanted to tell Frank how much he had loved this book, how the vivid descriptions had given him a sense of place and home, something he'd never experienced in real life, growing up the way he did in Vegas. It would also be nice to share something about his past that had not been embellished, abbreviated, or completely sanitized, especially since he couldn't talk about what was really on his mind. When they had been changing flights in Boston, when Logan had turned his phone back on, there was another voicemail from Oliver Lash—this one more threatening than the others. Something about how if Logan knew what was good for him, he had better make things right as soon as possible. It might not have been as hostile as that, but Logan couldn't know for sure. He had deleted the message immediately, but he knew Oliver had not raised his voice in the message because Oliver never raised his voice. He made you aware of his displeasure by enunciating his words very clearly and hitting his consonants hard.

They had been traveling for many hours since California and the stress over almost missing their connecting flight to Portland and a mix-up at the rental agency still permeated the car's atmosphere. Logan could tell that Frank wasn't in the mood for small talk or reminiscences about books from his childhood. Frank needed to focus on his driving. Logan sat in the back seat and watched the passing countryside, happy to see that it measured up well with those images from the children's book. As they drove, the rocky coastline gave way to salt marshes and pine forests and then they passed through charming chocolate-box villages. The rolling hills in the distance were ablaze with fall color, as if hidden under patchwork quilts. It was all quite beautiful. This must be why people who were born in the East always said they missed the seasons, thought Logan.

Iris was shouting directions at Frank that were diametrically opposed to the instructions the GPS was spouting out.

"You seem to forget I lived here," said Iris.

"A lifetime ago, Mother," said Frank. "When this was probably all cow paths."

This comment was conspicuously ignored.

"Well, I can tell you that *she* didn't live here," said Iris, gesturing toward the GPS on the dashboard, where a caustic female voice with a quasi-English accent was telling Frank to take the inland route.

"I like her accent," said Logan. "It's Australian, right? Like that Gecko, only classier."

"That is not Australian," said Iris. "It is computer-generated British."

"You're both wrong," said Frank. "The accent is South African."

"What does it matter?" said Iris. "The stupid Brit is going to get us all lost anyway!"

The GPS did not get them lost. On the contrary, they arrived in Harborville slightly ahead of schedule, a fact that Iris declined to acknowledge.

CHAPTER TEN

Opal was watching her grandmother from the doorway of the bedroom. Celeste was standing in front of a full-length mirror, which hung rather unevenly on the back of her closet door.

"What are you doing?" the girl asked.

"What does it look like I'm doing?" Celeste responded, turning briefly to look at her.

"Why are you watching yourself like that?"

"That's the purpose of a mirror the last time I checked," said Celeste.

"I've never seen you look in a mirror before," said Opal.

There was a tone of amused wonder in the girl's voice, something that Celeste found vaguely irritating.

"I've looked in this mirror every day of my life," said Celeste.

"Not like that you haven't."

"How long have you been standing there anyway? It's not nice to spy. It's especially not nice to spy on your poor old grandmother."

Opal was endlessly observant, as Cheryl had been at that age, but at least there was a little less judgment attached to it.

"Who's spying?" said Opal, leaning against the doorjamb. "I'm just standing here. And isn't this my room, too?"

Her tone was less amused now than pointed. She motioned to the rollaway cot tucked between the oak bureaus.

"Okay, okay," said Celeste. "It's only temporary. We've told you."

Joe had been right. Opal was not at all pleased that she needed to give her room up to make space for the California contingent and was sufficiently mortified that she'd be bunking with her grandparents.

"Gross!" she'd shouted when they'd told her about the sleeping arrangements. "That's just plain wrong."

"You'll muddle through," Celeste had said.

And in the end, Opal didn't make much of a fuss. The girl was less resistant than she might have been because the move was compelled by her great-grandmother's death. Opal was a good kid at heart. Celeste liked that term—*at heart*. It was a nicer way of saying *underneath it all*. Their granddaughter was also precocious and articulate, but not in the ways that made you want to give her a swift kick in the ass.

"Well, since you're standing there," Celeste asked now. "Does this look all right?"

She pivoted away from the mirror and faced Opal, pointing exaggeratedly at herself. Celeste was wearing a dress that she had found in the back of her closet. It was a simple cotton dress with a full skirt and a wide belt made of a thin netted fabric. It was something she'd worn to a summer wedding. Dorothy Hill's daughter, as she remembered it. The girl's first marriage. She was divorcing husband number two, the last she heard, and had long ago moved to Boston. The dress certainly wasn't new or stylish. It wasn't the summer either. It was an unusually warm October for Maine, so Celeste thought she could get away with wearing it. The dress was a rather nice shade of blue. Periwinkle or cornflower. It might have been cobalt. Celeste didn't bother much with colors.

"I like . . . the color," Opal said hesitantly.

"But otherwise?"

"Is this because those people are coming?"

"Is what because those people are coming?"

"You wearing a new dress and asking me about it. Suddenly caring about how you look."

"This is not a *new* dress and you make it sound like I usually walk around here looking like Bigfoot."

Opal shrugged, as if that's exactly what she did mean.

"You always tell me not to be vain and that girls get too much pressure about their looks and how it's unfair and how I shouldn't play into it. Isn't that what you say?"

"Jesus, kiddo. Forget it. I'm only asking if I'm in danger of scaring small children."

Celeste turned back to the mirror.

"Grandpa said she was an actress on television," said Opal.

"Who?"

"Your sister."

"Well, she was on television. I'm not sure how much of an actress she was. She was no Katharine Hepburn."

"Who?" asked Opal.

"Scarlett Johansson," said Celeste.

"Oh."

"What else did your grandpa say?"

"He said she was full of herself, but I didn't know what that meant, so then he said conceited."

"Both true," said Celeste.

"I asked him if she had anything to be conceited about."

"And what did your grandpa say to that?"

"He said she was very beautiful, like a sunrise."

"Did he? Like a sunrise. Imagine."

"But he also said she acted as if her looks were her own doing, as if she'd earned them or something. when they were just a lucky break."

"I guess that was her own business, how she thought of them."

"And he said she was actually the Potato Princess at the fair, which seems totally embarrassing."

"Does it?"

"Yes."

"I wouldn't suggest you telling her that when you meet her."

"And you're not," said Opal.

"I'm not what?"

"Scary. You look nice."

"Oh. Thanks, kiddo."

At that moment there was the sound of a car turning into the driveway from the main road.

"I think they're here," said Opal, rushing across the room to the window.

"They made better time than I expected," said Celeste.

She moved away from the mirror then and stood next to her granddaughter, looking out the window and down on the circular drive as the visitors began to materialize from their rental car. A man got out of the driver's side. He was fortyish and nice looking. He wore tan slacks and a white dress shirt. He stood there gazing at his surroundings and tucking his shirt in. Celeste assumed this was Frank, the serious toddler all grown up. A younger man bounded out of the back seat next, like a golden retriever. He was saying something in a friendly tone, but the words were indecipherable and were being ignored by his companion. This must be the boyfriend, Lance or Leo. Celeste couldn't remember what Iris had written in her email. There *was* something a little golden about him. It was *The Sunrise* who emerged next from the passenger seat of the vehicle, except now she was an old lady. Celeste knew that this was her sister, but it took her a moment for her eyes to make the adjustment. The first thing she noticed was that Iris's hair was cut shorter and she wasn't dyeing it, unless the silver was a dye, which perhaps it was, because it shimmered attractively in the fading sunlight. Getting out of the car had taken her a while. Celeste noticed that, too. Perhaps Iris was regretting her decision to show up here after all this time. She stood now, rather stiffly in the driveway. Iris still had a way of holding herself, as if waiting to be photographed. This was a sort of muscle memory tied to youthful vanity, thought Celeste. Iris was wearing a complicated and expensive-looking cream-colored outfit with a cape draped perfectly about her shoulders. The overall effect was of elegance and understated glamour. How had she managed this after a cross-country trip and a five-hour drive? She was forty years older, but Iris had apparently retained some semblance of beauty after all. At least she wasn't in full-on movie star mode. At least she wasn't wearing mammoth sunglasses, Celeste thought, or any kind of turban. Celeste backed away from the window and wondered if she had time to change out of the periwinkle dress and back into her stretch pants and sweatshirt.

Opal, who had been silent while observing the scene outside, now crossed quickly to one of the bureaus and opened the top drawer.

"What are you doing?" asked Celeste.

The girl returned with the faux diamond necklace Joe had bought Celeste for her seventieth birthday.

"Wear this," said Opal. "I like the way it sparkles and it will go with the dress."

CHAPTER ELEVEN

When they got to the farmhouse, after the car had pulled into the driveway and rolled to a stop, Logan shouted, "We've arrived!" Frank smiled tightly at him in the rearview mirror, while Iris remained silent, staring out the passenger window. Logan assumed her silence, after forty years away, made some sense. Frank exited the car first and a moment later Logan climbed out of the back seat. He took a very deep breath. The scent of New England seemed to be a mix of pinecones, autumn leaves, and something else he couldn't identify—maybe a whiff of that Yankee determination Frank had mentioned when trying to explain his mother and her origins.

"It's really gorgeous here," said Logan.

He motioned to a cluster of maple trees in the yard that were blushing with color and to the potato fields beyond that went on as far as one could see.

Frank stood by the car, staring up at the house.

"It looks very lived in," said Logan, following his gaze.

In fact, the farmhouse was quite rundown and badly in need of a paint job. There were cracks in the foundation, clearly visible, and the front porch was sagging, as if it needed to be shored up with a hydraulic lift. Frank did not respond to Logan's observations. Like Iris, who remained in the car, he appeared lost in thought. Frank tapped lightly on the hood and Iris finally opened the door and took her time getting out. She stood very straight, watching the house. Logan was unable to categorize the expression on her face. Presently the front door opened and an older woman in a very blue dress followed by a pretty young girl with a ponytail and wearing a Billie Eilish T-shirt came out to greet them. The woman crossed to the edge of the porch and the girl stood behind her. Iris watched the woman, and the woman watched Iris. There were a few beats of uncomfortable silence as this scrutiny continued and then the woman stepped down off the porch and approached.

"So it's really you, then," said the woman.

"The last time I checked," said Iris.

"Forty years does something to a person, doesn't it?" the woman said, rather evenly, so that Logan couldn't tell if she was making the comment about Iris or herself or perhaps human beings at large.

He wondered if the two women might embrace. For a moment this seemed like a real possibility. They might have been weighing this idea themselves, but neither of them made the first move, so the opportunity was lost. Frank had come around from his side of the car just then with his hand extended, like an affable politician.

"I'm Frank," he said.

"Of course," said the woman. She took his hand and then leaned in and gave him a hug.

"I'm your Aunt Celeste. But you can call me Cee if you prefer."

"I might need to get used to *Aunt Celeste* first, if that's okay, but thanks for giving me the option," chuckled Frank.

Celeste smiled warmly at this and looked over at Iris.

"He favors Erik," said Celeste, and then to Frank she added, "You're tall like your father. You have his features."

"Erik is dead," Iris said flatly. "Three years now. Non-Hodgkin's lymphoma."

"Well, shit!" gasped Celeste.

"Yes," said Iris.

"I didn't know."

"Well, how could you?" said Iris, adjusting her silk cape.

"I'm surprised somehow," said Celeste. "I don't know why. He seemed so indestructible to me, such a lively, athletic guy. Of course, I only met him the once and we were all so young then."

Celeste said this to no one in particular. She might have been directing these comments at the universe. At first no one responded. Everyone stood still. The news of Erik's death swirled around them, like a cloud of dust, momentarily choking out the possibility of further conversation or movement. Then Frank nodded at his aunt and said, "Yes, you're right. Pop did give that impression—of invincibility."

Logan could see that Frank was doing his best to defuse the awkwardness, mitigate any of his aunt's embarrassment, and placate his mother, too. Trying to put other people at ease, thought Logan, was just one aspect of Frank's personality. It served him well in his work at the rehab and now in navigating reunions with long-lost relatives.

"At any rate, I'm terribly sorry," said Celeste, reaching out to touch Iris's arm.

The expression on Iris's face started to soften, thought Logan, but then she recovered her equilibrium and took a step away from her sister. She motioned disinterestedly to her right.

"That is Logan," said Iris, "my son's companion."

"Boyfriend," said Frank.

"I think I prefer *beau*," said Logan.

"You do?" said Frank.

Iris cleared her throat.

"I'm pleased to know you," said Celeste, nodding at Logan. "Call me Cee."

"I'll do that," said Logan.

Celeste turned back to the porch then.

"And this is Opal," she said. "My granddaughter. Cheryl's girl."

Opal bounced on the balls of her feet and waved somewhat nonchalantly at the little group, though Logan could see she was watching each one of them intently, memorizing their faces like a sketch artist.

"I like Billie, too," he called up to her, pointing to the shirt. "She's the best."

Opal smiled at this and nodded, as if the accuracy of this opinion required no further acknowledgment.

"Billie Eilish is a singer," explained Celeste, leaning in toward Iris. "With a twelve-year-old in the house, Joe and I have a daily education when it comes to music—among other things. We've heard Billie's song 'Sea Eyes' about five hundred times."

"'Ocean Eyes,'" Opal corrected her grandmother from the porch, though less snottily than she might have.

"'Ocean Eyes,'" laughed Celeste. "You'd think I'd remember."

"I know who she is," said Iris in a blank, unsmiling way. "She's the current *It* girl of pop."

Opal let this statement stand without comment.

"My mother doesn't have any twelve-year-olds at home," said Frank, "but she knows stuff like that, about pop culture and so forth. She likes to stay informed, you might say. She doesn't like to let the world pass her by."

"Ha," laughed Celeste. "This is not a surprise. She was always like that. You couldn't tell your mother much of anything that she hadn't already figured out for herself."

Celeste and Frank shared a knowing smile.

"I'm right here, you know," said Iris.

"Joe calls her *Billie Eye Lash*," Celeste said now.

"And it wasn't funny the first fifty times Grandpa said it," said Opal.

"And where *is* Joseph?" asked Iris, looking around somewhat exaggeratedly, as if he might suddenly appear from under the porch.

Logan, who was still unfamiliar with this cast of characters, had a panicky moment when he thought there might be another disclosure about a dead husband. He was relieved when Celeste gestured in the direction of the main road and told them that Joe was at the hardware store.

"Please come on in," she said now, ushering them up the slanting stairs of the porch. "You must all be exhausted. I hope your drive from Portland wasn't too much."

"I saw a lighthouse," said Logan.

"No foolin', sweetie," said Celeste. "We got a lot of 'em!"

Opal held the screen door open as the visitors followed Celeste into the small, dimly lit vestibule, where there was a line of coat hooks (fully engaged) along one wall and on the floor a collection of discarded shoes and other items not quite swept into a corner—which Iris regarded somewhat contemptuously.

"Hey! I know you. I've seen you on TV!"

Opal had shouted this happily.

Frank laughed out loud.

"Well, your great-aunt was a busy actress at one time," he said. "You probably caught her on one of those *TV Land* reruns."

"Not her," said Opal. "Him!"

She was pointing excitedly at Logan.

"You sit next to Tanner Van Dean on *Windsor Valley High*!"

"Oh, you're right!" Logan said happily. "That would be me!"

"Bless us and save us," mumbled Iris as she moved with great purpose into another part of the house.

CHAPTER TWELVE

Joe pulled his pickup truck behind the car in the driveway. Iris and company had arrived. The rental car was an Audi. He'd never owned a foreign car. Joe's father used to rail about German products and Japanese ones, too. Joe had spent most of his life ignoring stupid and offensive things his father had said, but perhaps the car thing had stuck. His father had been a machinist mate on an escort carrier in the North Atlantic in World War II, where his task group received a Presidential Citation for sinking ten German U-boats in one day. He was then transferred to a light cruiser bound for the Pacific, where his ship was involved in the Battle of Iwo Jima. He watched the surrender ceremonies in Tokyo Harbor from the deck of his ship in September 1945. It was often hard for Joe to reconcile his dad's heroic war record with the mean and petty man he turned out to be, but he still couldn't help imagining what the old man would say about an Audi parked in the driveway. Though having a half-Japanese great-granddaughter would have already caused the man's head to explode.

As Joe stepped onto the sagging porch, he thought of what the visitors' first impression must have been of the house. It was in terrible shape. The house felt like the physical manifestation of his body's betrayal and collapse. He'd had to slow down considerably after the heart attacks and he simply wasn't able to keep up with the small repairs around the place, which were accumulating at a disturbing rate. As for the bigger fixes, like raising the porch or replacing the roof, they simply didn't have the cash. When Celeste first heard that Iris would be coming to the funeral and would (as it turned out) be staying with them, she had some anxious moments. How were they ever going to make the farmhouse presentable before her arrival? Celeste had spun around, pointing out cracks in the plaster, the swollen doors that wouldn't shut, the worn floorboards, until she'd suddenly plopped down onto the couch.

"Screw it!" she'd said. "My sister should see how we live. We'll present her with the evidence. It will give her even more reason to do the right thing and sign the paperwork."

"Good plan," Joe had replied. "Besides, four days isn't enough time to transform this place into the Bush Compound anyway."

When Joe entered the house, he could hear the buzz and murmur of conversation coming from the kitchen. He walked down the poorly lit hallway to make his appearance, but when he got there, he stood in the door for a moment—just watching. They were all seated around the table, sort of squeezed in. Apparently, they were to be eating dinner in the cluttered kitchen, instead of the dining room. The table was already set, and Joe could smell some garlicky spaghetti sauce heating on the stove. Everyone was drinking lemonade from paper cups. After making the decision to forgo any last-minute renovations, his wife had really leaned into this idea of *not* trying to impress her sister. Celeste was in an animated discussion with a guy who Joe assumed to be the nephew. The other guy was too young. It pleased Joe to see Celeste smiling, considering how all week long she'd been flinging worst-case scenarios about. His granddaughter appeared happy, too, having her own little conversation with the young guy who must be the boyfriend. He really didn't look much older than a boy himself. Then again, almost everyone seemed impossibly young to Joe these days. Iris's son must have robbed the cradle, he thought, or was that even a phrase anyone used anymore? Did the gays have their own expression for it? The kid was fit and muscular, but it was the kind of body created in a gym and not obtained through actual *labor*. You could tell he didn't look like that by hauling construction panels for a living. He was in the middle of telling Opal a story. She was hanging on his every word with an airy, blissful expression on her face, as if it were Christmas morning. Joe found it oddly disorienting to see his granddaughter so mesmerized by a stranger.

These were only momentary observations, because now Joe was focused on Iris. Though she wasn't part of either conversation, Iris was seated at the head of the table in a queenly manner, observing. It was almost twilight. The overheard light had not yet been turned on in the kitchen. What was left of the day coursed through the window above the sink, bathing Iris in a soft, flattering light. It occurred to him that she might have chosen this chair for that particular reason. Later, when they were alone, Celeste would point out how old Iris had gotten and he would reluctantly agree. She was older, of course, but watching her from the doorway, unnoticed, it struck him that the years had been very kind to his sister-in-law. Joe had heard that phrase before, about the kindness of time, but now he felt he understood it. Wealth and privilege could have played a part in that kindness, softening the blows bestowed by an accumulation of years. For all he knew, Iris might have personal trainers or masseuses. She might have a cook who prepared the same kind of meals Tom Brady favored, the ones that kept him young. But Iris was not young; she had simply aged gracefully.

"Joe!" Celeste called out when she noticed him standing there.

She proceeded to introduce him to the boys, who each stood and shook his hand. Iris stood, too, with some effort, he thought.

"Hello, Joseph," she said.

Her tone was friendlier than he'd imagined, but he thought it would be awkward and unappreciated if he embraced her. Iris might stiff-arm him if he tried. He was slightly annoyed that Iris still had the ability to get in his head, to gob-smack him.

"The return of Iris Flynn," he finally said after a long pause, smiling ruefully in her direction.

Then he heard Celeste whisper, "Home again, home again, jiggity-jig," as she rose quickly from the table and crossed to the stove.

CHAPTER THIRTEEN

Iris was staying in her old bedroom. It was Opal's room these days, but the girl had been banished to sleep elsewhere. The room had thankfully not morphed into anything too pink or frilly. It had rust-colored walls and an oversized duvet on the bed depicting a lightning storm or perhaps something from a *Harry Potter* book. The room was artfully cluttered with the concerns of a preadolescent girl—or specifically this preadolescent girl. An effort had been made to neaten up the space or perhaps not. There were posters (more Billie Eilish!) and some wry, sarcastic sayings taped up here and there throughout the room like *I'll Clap When I'm Impressed* or *Don't Take Yourself So Seriously, No One Else Does*. An old mahogany bureau with missing nobs (was it possibly the same one that had belonged to her as a girl?), and a large overfull bookcase ran along one side of the room. School books and papers were piled to a teetering level on two chairs in the corner. An enormous fishing net containing some barely inflated balloons was draped from the ceiling, suggesting (ironically, Iris imagined) the aftermath of a party. The room did not resemble in the slightest the stark empty space Iris had inhabited when she had lived here. Father and Mother had not considered it to be her room at all. They owned the house and all its contents. They were quite adamant on this point and repeated it often. She might as well have been a boarder or a foreign exchange student. That was how Iris thought of it, even as she was living through the experience. Ever since the teddy bear stage, Father and Mother had dictated the room's color and what Iris could hang on the walls or even place on the bed. Decoration was a frivolous expense! Personal expression was an exercise in vanity! Iris remembered Celeste pleading with them about the issue and after much discussion they had allowed their younger daughter to put up some innocuous wildlife prints and to paint the moldings and trim in her room a muted yellow. Iris, however, did not appreciate her sister's strategy. She refused to beg when it came to matters of interior design. She preferred blank walls to the bitter pill of negotiation.

Iris turned over in the bed and smoothed down the duvet. Michelle Obama's memoir was on Opal's bedside table along with a couple of graphic novels set in distant locales, and a neon lamp shaped like a unicorn. Opal was an unusual twelve-year-old. Despite her fascination with all things *Windsor Valley High*, she was obviously a girl of many interests and was curiously self-possessed. It was unclear where her mother was and why the girl was living here with her grandparents. Iris had sought some discreet clarification from Celeste at one point during dinner, but that query was all but ignored. There had been lots of other information to absorb in the hours since she'd arrived. The deteriorated condition of the farmhouse had been the first thing she had noticed and then the state of Celeste and Joe themselves. Joe had grown barrel-chested and did not look at all well. His complexion was florid and his bushy eyebrows needed to be trimmed. Celeste mentioned that he had heart problems and then later Joe had told some confusing story about being saved from falling off the roof by Moody Prescott, a boy Iris remembered from school as nice enough, but hardly a Rhodes scholar. Celeste appeared healthy, though her face was careworn and she'd lost her trim figure. The dress she was wearing, an alarming shade of blue, only accentuated this fact, since it was tightly cinched at her waist.

Joe, it turned out, had not just been running errands at the hardware store, as Iris had assumed. He worked there as a clerk. The farm was no longer functioning, not as a potato farm at least. Celeste also had a job. She was a waitress two nights a week at a local café and she also sold random things at flea markets across the state. Opal helped with these junk sales.

When Iris had first arrived with Frank and Logan, they had all sat around the kitchen table in an aimless fashion, waiting for Joe to return. The kitchen, familiar and strange at the same time, was faded, just like her sister. Lemonade had been served and a plate of chessman cookies passed around with some conjured enthusiasm. Frank immediately fell into an easy conversation with his aunt, about life in Maine, the history of the area, the miserable winters, and many other subjects he had never broached with Iris herself. Opal's identification of Logan had already lent a surreal quality to the visit. The girl peppered him with so many affectionate questions about the plot twists and character motivations on his teen soap opera that it might as well have been a Barbara Walters interview. Logan accepted this adulation with such friendly indulgence, you would have thought he had been handed a lifetime achievement award. He answered the girl's questions with such care and discretion, it was as if a publicist were in the room giving him secret hand signals. This was a skill of sorts, this measured diplomacy, so Iris found herself watching Logan with curiosity. He had surprised her once again.

There were some memorable moments from the spaghetti dinner.

Joe spoke in the same insinuating, jokey tone of his youth. "So, Iris," he had said at one point, while twirling pasta on his fork. "Weinstein."

The name drifted there for a moment, like poison gas. Everybody stopped talking.

"I beg your pardon," said Iris.

"You know. Harvey Weinstein. Any creepy dealings with that guy?"

"Oh, really, Joe!" wailed Celeste.

It was unclear to Iris whether her sister was secretly amused by her husband's boorishness or was planning to dump a bowl of spaghetti over his head.

"No," said Iris, patting her mouth with a paper napkin. "I never met that pig. I was traveling in a different orbit. Not to mention, I was mostly out of the business when he was slithering his way up through the Hollywood ranks."

"Well, the man should be horsewhipped," replied Joe.

"No kidding," said Iris.

"Glad you were never interfered with," said Joe.

"I didn't say that," said Iris. "There were other lowlifes, just not that particular one. I'm afraid there will always be lowlifes, even if they have to run for cover temporarily."

"Maybe not always," said Logan. "We had to have sexual harassment training on our show recently and one of our episodes was all about implied consent. I learned a lot. Everybody did."

"See, Iris," said Joe. "The kid's solved it all for you."

"Grandpa!" said Opal.

"What?" asked Joe.

"I know your sarcastic voice."

"Don't be fresh to your grandpa," said Celeste.

"Tell *him* to not be fresh," said Opal. "I saw that episode. It was awesome."

"I have no doubt, darlin'," said Joe. "I was just having some fun. I apologize to our visiting celebrity."

Opal had excitedly told her grandfather about Logan's claim to fame almost as soon as Joe had settled himself at the table.

"No apology necessary," said Logan, flashing that grin of his, which Iris had come to believe he sometimes brandished like a weapon.

"When was the last time we had such a starry dinner?" Joe asked out loud, but to no one in particular, so there was no response.

"Two TV stars at our table," Joe continued. "Or is it three? You on a soap, too, or doing Viagra commercials or something?"

This was directed at Frank.

"Nope," Frank smiled tolerantly. "I am most definitely a nonprofessional."

"He's a musician, actually," said Logan. "He's a guitarist and a singer."

"Cool," said Opal, glancing down at her Billie Eilish T-shirt.

"Was," said Frank, frowning in Logan's direction.

"He works in one of those rehab places for people on drugs," explained Celeste.

"Oh," Joe sniffed. "Okay."

"He was talented," said Iris.

She was surprised that she had said this out loud, but then she said it again.

"Frank was talented."

"Really? *Was* I?" Frank asked.

His tone was flip and dismissive.

He looked into his mother's eyes across the table.

"You were," said Iris. Then she said, "You are."

"Yet sometimes talent isn't enough," said Frank.

"No," said Iris. "Sometimes it isn't."

Frank raised his cup of lemonade in the air, like he was making a toast.

Iris was aware everyone was watching this unhappy exchange.

"Well, what Cee and I lack in *talent*," said Joe, making air quotes, "we make up for with an ability to put one foot in front of the other. But sometimes that's not enough either."

He was trying to be cute again, thought Iris. He probably figured that his three houseguests were spoiled California layabouts. But what could he possibly know about the hustle and grind associated with being a working actor or of selling real estate in a depressed housing market? Joe was likely confusing her (and Logan, too) with vapid celebrities who thought real bravery was posing for a selfie without any makeup. And she could imagine what he and Celeste thought of Frank's work at the rehab—summer camp for pampered people who lacked willpower. She knew what they were thinking because sometimes she had this very thought herself. She was grateful they hadn't quizzed Frank about his work at Harmony West because any discussion would likely lead him to mentioning his own *journey of addiction* (as Frank sometimes referred to it) and then her sister and brother-in-law would no doubt be left pondering Iris's accountability in the matter, something she still had not worked out for herself.

"So do you all like it out there, in California?" asked Joe as they continued to eat. "I'm sure it must be nice and all, but you folks are always in the headlines, what with the wildfires and mudslides and the ongoing threat of the big quake. It must feel like you're living in the middle of an obstacle course or a video game."

Another uneasy silence descended.

"What's the matter now?" said Joe. "I'm sure it's a beautiful obstacle course."

"It's not that," said Frank.

"What do you mean?" asked Joe.

"What he means is," said Celeste, "before you got here, Frank was telling us how he lost his home to the wildfires not three weeks ago."

"You serious?" said Joe, somewhat horrified.

"It's not exactly something I'd joke about," said Frank sadly.

"Well, that's some hard cheese," said Joe.

"Yeah," said Frank with the gush of a sigh.

"Jesum. How much info did I miss before I got here?" asked Joe.

Everyone stared at him and no one replied. "I mean, were you able to save anything? From the fire?" Joe asked.

"No," said Frank, wincing. "There wasn't any time."

"Well, at least you lived to tell the tale," said Joe.

"Bertram didn't make it," said Logan.

"Who's Bertram?" asked Joe.

"Frank's cat," said Logan.

"Oh no," said Celeste sympathetically. "I didn't realize."

"I guess you didn't get all the dope after all," said Joe.

"Your cat!" said Opal. "I'm sorry. How old was he?"

"Twelve," said Frank.

"So sad," said Opal.

"It is," said Logan. "He was a real character, that one. Sometimes he'd just sit and stare at me like we'd known each other in a past life."

"Our physical science teacher asked a sort of philosophy question last week," said Opal. "If there was a fire in a museum and you could only save a cat or a painting, which one would you save?"

"That's an odd question for a science class, isn't it?" asked Iris.

"Ms. Fairchild wanted to be a concert pianist, but never finished at the Berklee College of Music," said Opal.

The girl said this as if it was an explanation. Perhaps it was. Iris knew firsthand that thwarted ambition led people on strange paths. Sometimes it made them more judgmental of whatever dream they had abandoned. Maybe thwarted ambition had brought Ms. Fairchild to Northern Maine so she could pose grim hypotheticals to a seventh grade class.

"What would a cat be doing in a museum?" asked Logan.

"I don't think that's the point, Logan," said Iris.

"Mice," said Joe.

"What?" said Celeste.

"They might have a mouse problem at the museum."

"Oh yeah," said Logan.

"I think the answer to Ms. Fairchild's question would depend on the painting," said Celeste. "Wouldn't it?"

"Or the cat," said Logan.

"Yeah, the class couldn't make up its mind either," said Opal.

Everyone was quiet then. They stared at their spaghetti dinners, which were in various stages of completion.

"Well, I would have saved Bertram," said Frank, with some gloomy intensity.

Iris was eager to steer the subject away from California calamities and dead pets, but it was hard to deflect Joe from barreling forth. He'd become like a human divining rod for awkward subjects.

"So where have you boys been living since the fire?" he asked.

"They're staying with Iris," said Celeste.

"Well, good on you, Iris," said Joe.

"They didn't have much choice," said Iris, "unless they wanted to live in the La Brea Tar Pits."

"What are the La Brea Tar Pits?" said Opal.

"It's an ice age excavation site in the middle of Los Angeles," Iris responded, "where a group of tar pits bubbled up and the bones of dead animals were preserved going back about thirty thousand years."

"Oh," said Opal, smiling and looking genuinely interested. "Good to know."

Iris regarded this likable child for a moment and found herself smiling back.

Dinner ended shortly after this and then they were shown to their rooms.

Iris was grateful to be alone. It had been an exhausting trip and a challenging evening. She shut off the neon light and pulled the duvet around her. The long plane trip had taken the stuffing out of her. Not to mention her son's needling questions on the flight and the drive up from Portland, punctuated by Logan's chirpy travelogue narration. Then being faced with Celeste and Joe over dinner after forty years! They were like the Ghosts of Christmas Past. She hadn't wanted to stay here. She would have preferred the Motel 6 in Bangor. It was Frank who had insisted they come to the farmhouse, after Celeste had made the offer. She assumed the least she could do was let him meet his aunt and uncle in their natural habitat—if that's what he really wanted. Frank had seemed happy at dinner, at least when they weren't discussing the fire or Bertram. That had pleased her. She sometimes regretted that Frank had been an only child and a lonely one, too, but she did not regret keeping him in the dark about his relatives on the East Coast. Landing in a family, like most things, was a stupid accident, and she had no desire to treat this trip home like its own ice age excavation or get into any more debates with Frank. She had more on her mind.

CHAPTER FOURTEEN

"I'm sorry about Grandpa tonight," said Opal.

She had walked Frank and Logan to the sunroom after dinner and was showing them the daybed where they were to sleep. They were following her with their luggage, retrieved from the car. She was carrying folded sheets in her outstretched hands and displaying a manner of sober efficiency. The room was neat and streamlined, unlike the other rooms of the house. Opal had told them it had been cleaned out in anticipation of their visit. Her tone suggested this was a bigger job than they might have imagined. Large windows ran along one side of the room. The daybed was tucked against the opposite wall, which was painted a steel gray. A couple of wicker chairs were strewn about and there was small side table next to the bed with a faux-Tiffany lamp bathing the room in a cozy radiance.

"What are you apologizing for?" asked Frank.

"His jokes, I guess," said Opal.

"I think that's a common affliction in grandads—corny jokes," said Frank.

"I think he's funny," said Logan.

That was a generous assessment, thought Frank, but it seemed to please Opal, whose eyes suddenly brightened. Logan stowed their bags near the bed and then he took the linens out of her hands.

"He doesn't mean to be, like, offensive," said Opal.

"Well, I wouldn't worry about it," said Frank pleasantly. "I've heard worse."

Frank was thinking about his general experience of the world and of his mother in particular. Maybe he should apologize for Iris, to make things even, he thought, though it wasn't so much for anything the woman had said, so much as the way she had sat there at the head of the table in a sort of regal funk, glancing somewhat disappointingly at the peeling wallpaper.

"Family," Opal sighed, as if she were a weary, middle-aged woman and not a spirited twelve-year-old.

"Yes. *Our* family," said Frank, offering her a smile.

Opal smiled back at him.

"It's nice you're here," she said. "It's good to have cousins."

But when she said this, her gaze fell only on Logan, who was not her actual relative. He was someone who pretended to read textbooks in the blurred background of *Windsor Valley High*. Logan's celebrity status here, in the wilds of Maine, was a development that no one could have foreseen. At one point during dinner, when he was still on the receiving end of Opal's eager interrogation, Iris had said, "*Can someone please ask George Clooney Jr. to pass the garlic bread*?"

"Grandma told me I should apologize for the narrow bed," said Opal, motioning in its direction.

It *was* quite narrow, observed Frank. It was barely the width of an army cot.

"We'll manage!" grinned Logan as he snapped one of the sheets in the air and spread it over the bed.

His tone was so drenched with happy anticipation that Frank found himself blushing, an embarrassing response in front of his young cousin, but she didn't seem to notice. She was still busy staring adoringly at Logan.

"Can I ask you just one more question about *Windsor Valley*?" said Opal.

How many more questions can there be? thought Frank.

"Go ahead," said Logan as he struggled to fit a pillowcase over one of the sunroom's throw cushions.

"Do you ever hang out with Tanner Van Dean, like, after hours?"

"No, unfortunately," said Logan. "I'd love to and he's such a chill guy, but he's so busy with the show, being the star and all. There's no time to socialize."

"That sucks," said Opal.

"Yes, it does," said Logan and then he glanced briefly at Frank, who raised his eyebrows. It was considerate, he thought, for Logan to preserve Opal's illusions about the show and its stars, as Tanner Van Dean was not a chill guy at all, but a raging narcissist. Frank knew that the extras referred to the guy as *Tanner Van Go-Fuck-Yourself*.

"Grandma says to let us know if you need anything," said Opal.

She started to back out of the room.

"We appreciate that," said Frank.

Logan waved theatrically at her, as if from the deck of a ship, which Opal of course found very amusing.

"Good night," she said happily, and then she departed, leaving them alone.

"Sweet kid," said Logan.

"Yes, in a *hopelessly devoted to you* sort of way," said Frank.

"Come on. You're not jealous, are you?"

"Don't be ridiculous," said Frank, but he assumed jealousy was probably mixed in there somewhere.

"Do you know what the story is with her mother?" asked Logan.

"Cousin Cheryl? I don't have a clue."

"Your aunt and uncle seem to make a pretty good team," said Logan. "I like them. Don't you?"

"Yeah, I guess so," said Frank, and this was true, but he had to remind himself that they had only been here a few hours and a week ago he hadn't known they existed.

"How do you think Iris is holding up?" Logan asked now.

"What do you mean?"

"Being back home."

"I'm not sure if my mother ever thought of this as her home."

"You know what I mean. How is she doing?"

"How would I know?" said Frank. "She was pretty remote tonight. That's for sure. She could have phoned in that performance."

"There must be a lot of history for her here."

"So there is," said Frank, remembering the conversation they'd had on the plane. "But she doesn't make it any easier for herself, does she?"

"I think your mother is doing the best she can," said Logan.

"I think my mother would agree with you," said Frank.

Logan was fluffing the pillows.

"The bed's all made," he said triumphantly.

Logan stood with his hands on his hips. There was a mischievous look in his eye.

"I'm going to hit the bathroom," he said.

He rummaged in his duffel for a toothbrush and toothpaste and squeezed Frank's shoulder before leaving the room. Frank blushed some more. They still hadn't had sex since before the wildfire. Frank didn't know why he was keeping Logan at arm's length, except perhaps a defense mechanism had finally clicked in after all this time. He couldn't keep falling for the guy, especially if it was now more hopeless than ever. An insolvent middle-aged, recovering addict might never be a likely match for a young and gorgeous television heartthrob, even one from the zip code of *Windsor Valley High*, but the wildfire had only served to put an exclamation point to that fact. It was still hard for Frank to accept the sheer fact of the fire. How many times was he expected to bounce back and start from scratch? Was this what life amounted to? A toddler's stacking game, where you build and build, only to see it all come crashing down. Frank imagined Keith telling him what a terrible metaphor that was. He still sometimes fancied Keith making witty remarks from the sidelines, a ghost-centric fantasy he liked to indulge. Keith would have grieved Bertram, of course, and cursed the fire, but he might also point out Frank's *uniquely Californian* lifestyle—what with the teenager-impersonating boyfriend and the fact that they were crashing with his aging, glamorous mother, a woman who used to make a living as a flashy blonde on sitcoms. Keith's understanding of California had leaned heavily on outdated hippie and surfer stereotypes, as well as a vague and naïve idea of showbiz gathered from screen parodies of Hollywood itself. Even this trip to Maine might amuse Keith. Frank meeting his long-lost relatives would surely appeal to his archivist sensibilities.

Frank crossed the room now. He undressed, folded his clothes, and placed them on one of the wicker chairs. There were no shades on the windows, but the holly bushes were quite overgrown. He could hear them scraping against the glass in the breeze and the nearest neighbors he'd been told were a half mile away, so he was unconcerned about modesty. He crawled into the daybed and waited. If Logan had any ideas about tonight, he would tell him that he was exhausted from the long trip and overwhelmed after meeting his new family. Logan was being very patient.

Frank settled into the bed. His pillow or the cushion that was taking the place of a pillow was too large for his head. He considered tossing it on the floor. Then it occurred to him that he could not remember a time in his entire life when he had slept without a pillow or some variation of one. This included the dives he had stayed in when touring with the band, and the sketchy sublets and couch surfing he had done in New York, even the camping trips with Erik when he was a child, where he always had a tiny foam camp pillow that rolled up in his sleeping bag. These thoughts reminded him of all the nights he had been on this planet and the strange circumstances that had brought him to this bed now, in the place where his mother had grown up. Frank liked the notion of doing something he'd never done before in his whole life, so he tossed the cushion on to the wicker chair on top of his clothes. The universe seemed very random at that moment. He thought some more of Keith and of Logan, too. He remembered seeing a movie once, a romantic little indie, where a young gay couple spent a good deal of the action discussing their relationship and how it stacked up against the soulmate theory. One of these guys resisted the soulmate idea because he said finding that certain someone was just an accident of location. Theoretically there were *soulmates* for you in every country, on all the different continents. There were probably thousands of such people for you, in fact, but you'd never have a chance to meet any of them. Frank felt the film was disingenuous in this regard, however, because as this cynical character kept denying the idea that he and the other guy were soulmates, you were obviously meant to believe the opposite was true—and then this was proven in the predictable last scene, set in a crowded train station, when the two men fell happily into each other's arms.

If Keith had been his soulmate, Frank thought, then how

could Logan be one, too? They were comically opposite—Keith with his keen, academic air and Logan with his artless, wide-eyed observations.

And yet.

He thought some more about his own parents and their curious conflicting natures, their complicated, undeniable love for each other. He figured he'd gotten all the wrong parts of them when the fixed aspects of his personality had pooled up in his DNA. He'd inherited some of Iris's artistic ambition, but none of her practical nature, something that might have been useful for him in navigating a career; and though he'd roamed around for years, somewhat aimlessly, without a clear-cut path, he'd inherited none of Erik's carefree disposition, which would have obviously lightened the journey. It saddened Frank now to think of what might have been if these traits had somehow been reversed or more evenly distributed. He'd be a different person entirely, maybe somebody who would know exactly what he should say to Logan, who at that moment had come back into the sunroom.

Logan crossed the room and stood over the bed. He noticed the discarded cushion.

"No pillow?" he said.

"I've decided to reinvent myself," said Frank

"By remaining pillowless?" said Logan. "I don't understand."

"I don't either. I'm just trying to figure things out."

"Like what exactly?" said Logan.

"I don't know," said Frank. "If I knew that . . ."

His voice trailed off. He felt ridiculous. It was pointless.

"I just don't know," Frank repeated.

"It's normal not to know things," said Logan. "That's the way of the world."

Frank smiled at this very Logan-like observation, but a moment later he felt the tears spilling down his cheeks.

"Jesus, Frank!" said Logan. "What's the matter?"

Frank's throat felt constricted, like he was having an allergic reaction. The sunroom walls were a gray blur. He took a very deep breath. Frank remained silent. But he wanted to tell Logan that he had been absolutely right with what he'd said back in California, following the fire, about how Frank hadn't lost everything after all. His wishful thinking, it seemed, had survived intact. He was feeling it now.

Logan began to undress quickly, tossing his clothes aside. He pulled his T-shirt over his head and stepped out of his shorts. He stood for a moment in front of Frank, who was once again astonished by his presence. Then Logan leaned over and switched off the lamp, before climbing into the bed and pulling Frank toward him in the dark.

CHAPTER FIFTEEN

Opal was sitting on the porch steps. It was early the next morning. Her grandparents were already up and out of the house, running errands at the Hannaford for the gathering that was to take place here after the funeral service. Her grandmother had asked her to sweep off the porch and to pile all the stuff in the vestibule into cardboard boxes and bring everything to the barn. This she would do after she sat here awhile. Her friends were all coming to the funeral parlor, not to pay their respects, but to get a peek at Logan. She had been texting about him almost as soon as she figured out who he was. Being related to a celebrity (she'd told everybody he was *married* to her gay cousin!) was irresistible news. Her best friend Amelia texted "*I...can't...even!*" about twenty times with an assortment of fireworks emojis. This Iris person, Opal's great-aunt, had been on television, too, but it was three hundred years ago, so no one cared. Opal thought she saw a resemblance between her grandmother and Iris, except Iris looked like she could be one of those senior citizens in an Old Navy commercial and she probably worked out at Curves every day. She looked too rested over dinner for someone who had been traveling cross-country, which probably meant she knew how to apply makeup so effectively that you couldn't tell she had any on. How could her grandmother compete with that? Her grandparents both seemed a little off during dinner. Opal couldn't put her finger on it, but it must have something to do with this woman. Iris's cool stares, perfect clothes, and too-straight posture had messed with the energy of the house. Opal hoped she wasn't touching anything in her room.

Just then the screen door swung open and banged shut behind her. It was Logan joining her on the porch. She smiled up at him. He was wearing maroon shorts and a Captain America T-shirt. It was still unseasonably warm. Logan's hair was wet from the shower. When he sat next to her on the steps, she could smell his almond extract shampoo.

"Sorry," said Logan. "Did I scare you?"

"It takes more than that," said Opal.

"I seem to make a lot of unnecessary noise. People tell me."

"That screen door is always banging. Grandpa was supposed to take the screens off by now, but he hasn't gotten around to it. He says the warm weather is a sign from the universe to be lazy this fall. But he's not lazy. He just gets tired because of his heart."

"He seemed energetic enough at dinner last night."

"Yeah," said Opal. "I was just thinking about that."

"There must be a lot of chores here," said Logan, scanning what he could see of the property.

"Not like a real working farm," said Opal. "But they keep me busy sometimes."

"The chores?"

"No. I mean my grandparents, but I guess it's the same thing."

"Joe and Celeste seem pretty cool. You must like it here. Do you?" asked Logan.

"What do you mean?"

"You don't understand the question?"

"Sure, I like it. It's my home," said Opal, shrugging vaguely.

"That's good. People don't always like their homes."

"Did you?"

"You mean growing up?" said Logan. "No actually. I did not."

"Where *did* you grow up?"

"Las Vegas," said Logan.

"Las Vegas! Like with the gambling and Circus Circus?"

"That's the place."

"Wow!" said Opal. This would be another fun fact for Amelia. "But you didn't like it out there?"

"Nope."

"Because of the gambling?"

"Maybe that was part of it."

"What was the other part?" asked Opal.

She flicked at a spider crawling in her direction. It tumbled down the steps.

"I don't know. I guess because it's such a temporary place in the world," said Logan.

"How do you mean?"

"I mean everyone is passing through. You feel like you are part of all that movement when you live out there, even if you're just standing still."

"Is that why you left?"

"In a way. I left because I felt sort of stuck. I figured if I didn't leave, I might never leave at all."

Opal wasn't sure how to respond to that, so she remained silent.

"Are your parents still there?" she asked after a long pause.

"My mother is."

"Do you miss her?" asked Opal.

"Not exactly," said Logan.

He stared out at the property again.

"Oh."

"Anyway, the point is nothing felt permanent out there. Not like this."

Logan gestured toward a row of mammoth oaks near the main road.

"See those trees. It probably took a hundred years for them to grow that tall. And that stone wall over there, bordering the field. It could have been here since the Revolutionary War."

"Not that one," said Opal. "That was a project of Grandma's when I was eight. I helped her find the rocks and then I hauled them for her."

"Well, you know what I mean."

"Where's Frank?" Opal said now.

"Still asleep. We kind of had a late night."

"Wasn't the bed comfortable?"

"The bed was fine. But what about your grandparents? Where are they?"

"Running errands for the reception or whatever you call it after the funeral service."

"I'm sorry about your great-grandmother, by the way," said Logan.

"It's okay, she was *really, really* old."

"I know. Right? Did you like her?"

People didn't usually ask such direct questions of Opal. She felt like she had stumbled into an episode of *Windsor Valley High*, where you couldn't even stand around your locker without having a meaningful conversation.

"I'll tell you what I did like," she said. "She used to talk to me about my mother. She told me stories about when my mom was a girl. My grandparents don't talk about her much. I think it makes them sad."

"Where is your mother, if you don't mind me asking?" asked Logan.

"Portland, Oregon. Sometimes I just say Portland so people will think I mean Maine, because that's not so far away. But it's Portland, Oregon."

"Have you ever lived with her?"

"No. She thinks it's best that I stay here. She doesn't have the most stable kind of life. She's visited me a few times when I was little and we FaceTime every couple of weeks. There's been some talk of me spending the summer with her and I wish she would come out here sometime, but so far it's just talk. I was supposed to go there last June, but she lost her job and was in the middle of switching apartments again and then Grandpa got sick and I didn't want to leave him."

"So you've lived here your whole life, then?"

"Yeah, except for when I was born. I was born outside of Seattle in a federal prison."

"You were what?" said Logan.

"I was born in prison. My mother was there for five years. She had me at the beginning of her sentence and then my grandparents took me back here."

"Is that right?"

Logan was watching her intently. Opal could tell he was trying to figure out if she was teasing or making up a story just to impress him.

"Yep. It's really true."

"I'm so sorry. I didn't mean to pry."

"You didn't. My grandparents don't exactly want me broadcasting the news, but they didn't swear me to secrecy or anything. I know it sucks for them—their only child went to jail. I mean, most everyone in town knows, but I think they're worried about what you all might think—or maybe just Iris."

"Why should that matter?" said Logan.

"I don't really know. But she seems to have a judgy way about her, don't you think?"

"I like to believe Iris is just misunderstood," said Logan.

"You really think that?"

"Sort of."

Opal noticed the spider she had flicked making its way up the steps again.

"So my mom tried to blow up this whaling ship when she was in college."

"You don't need to tell me," said Logan.

"That's okay," she said. "We're just talking. She was an environmental activist. She got caught holding the explosives and she had made a bunch of threats to some important people. She wasn't robbing banks or anything. That's exactly what she said the first time she came to visit, when I was six. She told me the whole story then. My grandparents were pissed at her for telling me like that, but it's not like someone in town wouldn't have eventually said something. The news of her arrest was a big deal around here, I guess. I think it was better for her to tell me right off. Don't you?"

"I suppose so," said Logan. "But I think it's more important how you feel about it. Is your dad in the picture?"

"No. He died in a car accident before I was born. He was Japanese, like a Japanese citizen. He was an activist, too, and a professor, my mom says. They had, like, a relationship when he was in America, but it didn't last long. He never even knew she was pregnant."

"That's a rough deal," said Logan.

"Is it? People think it's some kind of tragedy, but it's just my life. I feel worse for my friends whose parents get divorced all of a sudden and then they have to get used to new apartments and custody schedules or whatever, but my life has just been my life for as long as I can remember."

"I know what you mean," said Logan. "I didn't have a dad growing up either. When people would hear that, they'd look at me with sorrow or something. But how do you miss something you never even had?"

"Exactly," said Opal. "Did he die, too?"

"Nah, he moved to Canada when he heard my mother was going to have me."

"Have you ever wanted to meet him?" asked Opal.

"The guy who left the country to avoid having anything to do with me? Can't say as I have."

They were quiet for a while after this, staring out at the hundred-year-old oaks.

Then Opal said, "Grandma asked me to do some cleanup. I should get started before they get back here."

"I'm happy to help," said Logan. "I've been told I take direction well."

"Deal," laughed Opal, and then they both stood.

"You know, kid," said Logan, "that backstory of yours is powerful stuff. It will set you apart as you get older. It's bound to give you strength and maybe someday you can go to Japan and find some more of your family, like Frank just did when he came here."

"Yeah, I know," said Opal as she left the porch in search of a broom. "I had already figured that part out for myself."

CHAPTER SIXTEEN

Frank sat in the car waiting for Iris and Logan to come out of the farmhouse. The visiting hours at the funeral home would be starting soon. He wasn't sure what to expect in terms of attendance, especially since he'd never met his grandmother and couldn't gauge her local popularity. It was the middle of a Friday afternoon. A light rain was predicted. Frank wondered if this might impact the turnout, though there wouldn't be any kind of graveside service. Deb was being cremated, as his father had been. Erik didn't have an actual wake. There had been a brief, informal memorial service at Paradise Cove a month after his death, with Iris and a few of his father's ragtag friends, or as Iris referred to them—*that bunch of loud mouths and lost souls.* His mother had retained her famous composure throughout that service, which was a mostly silent affair, with everyone simply looking out to sea, alone with their various memories, except for an odd moment when Kipper, a hard-drinking old friend of Erik's, had spontaneously read a poem about heartbreak by Edna St. Vincent Millay (Kipper reading poetry!) and then began to sob like a child. Frank's idea of releasing balloons on the beach had been nixed due to environmental concerns, but also because Iris considered it a TV movie cliché.

"Well, you should know," Frank had said.

After the service, which had dispersed quickly after Kipper's weepy poem, they had all charted a boat from the marina where Erik sometimes worked. They scattered his ashes a few miles off Catalina. The ashes were oddly thick. They had the consistency of wet sand or maybe Play-Doh. "Goddamn it to hell!" Iris had fumed as she attempted to scoop them out of their container. His father, Frank had to imagine, would have been greatly amused by this. One more chance to make his presence felt. Frank was just out of rehab at the time, shaky and seasick, but grateful to be sober, which was the last and best gift he would ever give his father. Iris had gripped his hand at one point, after the ashes had been dispersed, as they were returning to land, but it was difficult to tell whether this action stemmed from rising emotion or because she was trying to steady herself on the boat. Her carefully made-up face gave nothing away.

When Keith had died, the year before Erik, Frank had initially handled everything—the identification of the body at the hospital, the notification of Keith's family and employers, packing his things—with almost Iris-like self-possession. Keith's parents arranged to have their only son transported to Delaware, where he was to be buried in the family cemetery. The Cabotsons were an old WASP family. Keith had told Frank that his relatives had come over on the *Mayflower*.

"That must have been an awfully big boat," Frank had teased at the time, considering the number of privileged white people who liked to make that specific ancestral claim.

Keith's parents knew that their son had begun a relationship with Frank, but they had never formally met. Even through the haze of their shock and grief, they had attempted to be cordial and even solicitous. Frank said he would contact them to get the details regarding the funeral as he fully intended on being there. But the next night, alone in the apartment, with death's administrative tasks behind him, Frank had begun to slip, to lose his mind. It was the night he had smashed another guitar. It was the night he had reached into the medicine chest and taken a handful of Keith's leftover OxyContin. Frank had not gone to Delaware for the funeral. He did not get around to asking Keith's parents for the details. And they, in turn, did not reach out to him. Frank was too consumed with sadness, too high at the time, to be insulted. They were strangers to each other, after all, and their only common ground was now lost to them forever. During his soberer moments over the next few weeks, he had packed up most of Keith's possessions and mailed the boxes to Keith's family home. He had saved a box for himself—one that contained Keith's spare glasses, his Orioles cap, the sweater he was wearing when they went out to the diner, a great photo of Keith in his early twenties sitting on a rock in Central Park, looking windblown and sexy, and the books from his nightstand, including a first edition of James Baldwin's *Go Tell It on the Mountain* he'd found at a flea market. Frank had inherited Bertram, too, who had wandered aimlessly around the apartment meowing pitifully in the first weeks after Keith's death, a miserable soundtrack. All now gone in the fire. Keith would not hesitate to point out that Frank was luckier than most because at least he and Logan had never been in harm's way and because his mother, whatever her issues, had offered them a soft landing.

Iris coming out of the farmhouse interrupted these specific thoughts. She looked quite striking as she stood on the porch pensively regarding the gray sky. She was wearing a sleek, fitted violet dress and an expensive-looking wrap. Not quite red carpet ready, but eye-popping for a small town in Maine. Did she feel some responsibility to look the part of the visiting Hollywood actress? Did she not want anyone to forget that fact? She walked across the porch and down the steps now with the purposeful stride of a star, if a bit gingerly, given her age and the challenges of her arthritis.

Iris opened the passenger door of the rental car and climbed in.

"Do you think it will rain?" she asked.

"Perhaps," said Frank. "We have umbrellas in the trunk if it does."

"Always prepared," said Iris, but not very pleasantly. She turned around to look in the back seat.

"Where is Logan?"

"He's coming. He's helping Opal pick out something to wear."

"How very *Queer Eye* of him," said Iris.

"I think she values his opinion because he's on television," said Frank.

"Clearly, but has she seen how he dresses?"

Frank laughed out loud.

Iris peered back toward the house.

"They've been running around cleaning up in there all morning," she said.

"I know," said Frank. "There are people coming over after the service."

"But for us, they couldn't even kick the shoes out of the way in the hall."

"So?"

"It's odd. That's all I have to say on the subject."

It probably wasn't all she had to say, thought Frank, but he was content to move on.

"So how are you doing?" he said, "You look very pretty, Mother."

"I relinquished *pretty* in my forties. I'll settle for *good for her age*."

"Well, then you have succeeded," said Frank, though he

didn't believe what she'd said about relinquishing anything. "But are you doing okay? I mean, being here after all these years. You seemed somewhat subdued last night and this morning at breakfast."

She watched Frank curiously.

"Is that a word you use with people at the rehab?" she asked.

"Which one?"

"*Subdued*. It's a therapeutic term."

"No, it isn't. It's simply a descriptive word I'm using right now in the driveway of my mother's childhood home to check in with her."

"Well then, to answer your question, no, I do not feel *subdued* or *suppressed* or *vanquished* or *subjugated*. I feel, to put it quite bluntly, just like myself."

"Silly me," said Frank. "I should have known."

"If I was quiet this morning, maybe it's because it was hard to get a word in edgewise with Logan pontificating to his number one fan. They need their own podcast, those two, and yet let's hope that no one gives them the idea."

"They are sort of cute together, aren't they?" said Frank. "An unexpected bond."

"Well, they are practically the same age," said Iris.

"Very funny," said Frank. "Opal's an interesting kid, though. Don't you think?"

"She is," said Iris.

"She has a tough story," said Frank. "Logan was telling me. Her mother was an eco-terrorist or something and did time for trying to blow up a ship. Opal was born in prison. And apparently Cheryl is still having some issues and that's why Joe and Celeste are raising her. It sounds complicated."

"Ahhh, I see," said Iris, "the reason for the secrecy."

"Please don't bring any of this up unless they do. You can't blame them for not detailing their little girl's indictments over bacon and eggs this morning."

"I had blueberry yogurt myself, which was two days past its expiration date."

"You know what I mean. Anyway, the kid's dad died before she was born, in Japan. He was Japanese."

"Ahhh, I see."

"Mother, please stop saying *Ahhh, I see*, as if you're collecting clues to a murder mystery."

Frank tapped on the horn to rush Logan along.

"You know," he said, "it must be hard being a kid of color in a town like this."

"I am not acquainted with Harborville's current racial demographics. However, you can see that the child is resilient."

"You always did value resiliency in children."

"I value resiliency in anyone."

Just then Logan came out of the house dressed in a blue blazer and pleated dress pants.

"Look at that," said Iris. "Who was the one giving the fashion advice in there? He looks quite nice, if a bit like an escapee from a yacht club."

"Don't tease him," said Frank as Logan scrambled off the porch and got into the back seat.

"You clean up nicely, Logan," said Iris, once he was settled in.

"Very handsome," said Frank, winking at him in the rearview mirror.

Images of the previous evening (the end of their drought) were flickering in Frank's mind. If his mother hadn't been sitting next to him, he'd be getting hard again.

"I wasn't sure what to wear," said Logan. "I've never been

to a wake before."

"Airlines, lighthouses, send-offs for the dead," said Iris. "We keep contributing to your education, don't we, dear?"

CHAPTER SEVENTEEN

"I'm not sure why she couldn't have waited for us," said Celeste, watching from the bedroom window as the rental car pulled out of the driveway.

"Didn't she say that Frank wanted to see the town?" replied Joe.

"I know that's what she said, but it didn't need to be now, did it?"

Celeste turned back toward her husband. He was wearing a chocolate brown suit that was a size too small, accentuating the paunch spilling over his belt. She imagined what her mother would say about his appearance.

You look like ten pounds of potatoes shoved into a five-pound sack.

"Why *not* now?" said Joe.

"We're on our way to Mother's wake. It might have been nice if we could have arrived together and entered the funeral home at the same time, as sisters."

"And what would that prove?"

"It wouldn't prove a damn thing, but it might have at least been cordial of her."

"Has *cordial* ever been a word that anyone has used to describe Iris?" said Joe, smiling wistfully.

Celeste squinted at him. She was suddenly annoyed, or perhaps it was not so sudden.

"Don't act so amused," she said. "Don't sound so admiring."

Joe loosened a lug on his belt.

"That's not how I sound. That's how you're hearing it."

"Is it now?" said Celeste.

"I'm only wondering why you would expect Iris to show up here as the kind of person she has never been in the first place."

"And I'm wondering why she should fly across the country, with Frank and Logan trailing after her, only to avoid us once she gets here."

"How is she avoiding us, Cee? She sat with us all through dinner last night and at breakfast this morning."

"She might as well be avoiding us. She sat there perched like a bird on a branch, tolerating us."

"Is that what birds do on their branches?"

"You know what I'm saying."

"I'm not really sure that I do."

"Fine, then. Pretend that you don't."

"Maybe you're misreading her. I think she's probably like the rest of us, just set in her ways."

"I don't have dyslexia when it comes to my sister. I'm reading her just fine. And the last thing she'd ever admit to, by the way, is that she's just like anybody else."

"I actually have no idea what she believes," said Joe. "But maybe she's come back to set things straight and reunite before it's too late."

"Are you going to keep doing that?"

"Doing what?"

"Defending her. Giving her the benefit of the doubt. Could you be a little less predictable?"

"I didn't realize I was defending her. I thought I was trying to make you feel better."

"You know how you can make me feel better?" asked Celeste.

"How?"

"By not defending her."

"How am I even doing that? I'm not sure what you think she has done."

Celeste didn't know how to answer that. She wasn't sure either. It was a feeling she had more than anything else. That Iris was up to something. But she knew better than to tell Joe that her side of the argument hinged on a vague notion she couldn't explain. She didn't say anything but moved across the room with a confidence that suggested she didn't need to dignify his question with a response. She picked up her black dress from the bed and stepped into it. It was a simple frock with a Queen Anne neckline that she'd worn to half a dozen funerals for friends and neighbors in the past two years. She thought of it as her death dress. She turned to the mirror and watched herself stoically.

"Did you see what she had on? She was wearing another cape, for crying out loud. Mother was always after her about putting on airs. I can imagine what she would have said."

"She won't be saying much today," Joe scoffed. He had sat down on the bed and was tying his shoes. "But maybe that's exactly why she decided to dress that way, as a statement to your dead mother."

"Well, she'll be disappointed that there's no red carpet at *Thibedeaux's*," said Celeste.

Then she remembered that the rug in the funeral home's entryway was a deep shade of burgundy.

"She's show folk," said Joe. "They all look sort of polished to me."

"More like laminated," said Celeste. "Her face is too smooth. Botox, no doubt, or a chemical peel."

"Chemical what?" said Joe. "Look, I can't imagine how she'd have to act for you to adjust your opinion of her."

Celeste turned slowly away from the mirror and faced her husband.

"I could say the same, " she said.

"And what's that supposed to mean?"

Are we really going to do this right now? Celeste thought. *Sure, why not?*

"Your opinion of my sister has been unchanged for over fifty years."

Joe looked up from his shoes. Celeste could see he was attempting to arrange his face to convey innocence or confusion. He looked like a teenager caught shoplifting in a convenience store. Celeste assumed he was weighing a response, probably wondering if one of his wisecracks might be enough to defuse whatever was happening.

"I watched you," said Celeste. "I watched you watching her from the doorway yesterday when you got back from the store. It was still there, all over you, like a rash. You were still the kid who came to our front door and was seeing her for the first time."

"Cee, that's the stupidest—"

Celeste put her hand up.

"I don't want to get into it. It doesn't matter at this late date. We're all as old as dirt. It's okay if once or twice every fifty years I get reminded that I was the consolation prize, but please don't insult me by denying it. Now let's grab Opal, jump in the car, and get this show on the road."

She patted her husband's shoulder and walked out of the bedroom. Opal was standing right there in the hallway with the same *guilty as charged* expression on her face that Celeste had just seen on Joe.

"Why didn't you come in and sit on the floor with a bowl

of popcorn if you wanted to hear what we had to say?" Celeste said to the girl.

Opal was not the kind of kid to make excuses for herself (it would have been beneath her) so she simply shrugged at her grandmother.

"And what in the world are you wearing?" asked Celeste, taking a step back to get a better look.

Opal had on a fringed skirt and a pullover that was a shade of shimmering yellow. There was a piece of feathered material tied loosely at her neck, and on top of her head, she wore a tiny pillbox hat, with red piping, something that she must have found deep in her great-grandmother's closet—half organ grinder's monkey, half high fashion.

Joe emerged just then from the bedroom. He looked from his granddaughter to Celeste and then back again.

"Hurray for Hollywood," he muttered, and then moved past them toward the stairs.

CHAPTER EIGHTEEN

Iris settled into the passenger seat as Frank drove away from the farmhouse. They were on their way to inspect downtown Harborville, this place from where she had fled *as if shot out of a cannon*. That was the way Celeste had described it over breakfast, when Frank had briefly attempted to quiz his aunt regarding his mother's fabled past. Iris had shifted in her chair while witnessing this and glanced at them both over the table in such a manner as to shut down any further discussion on the subject. Who knows what might have been said if Iris hadn't been within earshot? The notion that opinions and theories about her could be floated and discussed without the proper context was quite irritating. It was how she used to feel after leaving a casting call, that feeling of powerlessness that would sometimes creep over her.

As the car turned onto Main Street, the sudden appearance of the downtown area, with its cobblestone sidewalks and faux gas lamps, stunned Iris into an astonished silence. The village was unrecognizable to her, less restored than completely reinvented, as if from someone's Hallmark Channel imagination. There was a coffeehouse called *It's a Grind* and a place that sold ice cream cones called *Ye Olde Ice Cream Shoppe*. In fact, most of the *shoppes* in town displayed some cute type of spelling or cursive lettering on their signs. Clusters of poplar trees had been planted on every block, and there was something that looked like a bandstand in the town square. Peculiar little art galleries and gift shops dotted this new landscape, along with an entire store specializing, it seemed, in clothes for your pet—*Lovey's Animal Kingdom*, it was called.

"Well, this isn't exactly the county seat of desolation," said Frank.

"Don't be ridiculous," said Iris. "Obviously, it didn't look like this back when I was living here. There were no plant-based muffin shops or mason jar emporiums when I was a girl. There was none of this . . . *ornamentation*."

Her tone was accusatory, but it was unclear where she was casting the blame.

"It does look like it might have been designed by the hipster grandson of Norman Rockwell," said Frank. "But it *is* rather charming, you have to admit?"

"I'm not sure that I have to admit that."

"I love it," said Logan happily from the back seat. "It reminds me of *The Gilmore Girls*."

"Heaven help us," said Iris.

"Celeste said you wouldn't recognize it," said Frank. "It must be the influx of cash from that tech company on the outskirts of town they told us about."

Freaks and Geeks is what Joe had called the tech conglomerate that had moved here from Boston, taking advantage of tax breaks and buying up the land from a string of failing farms.

"Yes, now the farms are long gone, but you can buy a really nice decaf cappuccino," said Iris, frowning out the window.

"Where's the harbor anyway?" asked Logan.

"Excuse me?" said Iris.

"The town's called Harborville, isn't?"

"The closest harbor is thirty miles east," said Iris. "I always felt the founders exhausted their imagination on naming the town and gave up after that."

"I still love it," said Logan. "Even without an ocean."

Iris wasn't sure what she had expected, probably the same deterioration that she had observed back at the farmhouse, with its weather-beaten façade and elderly occupants. Harborville had been such a grim and lonesome spot when she was a child, a neglected old mill town, where the mill had been closed for so many years that even the old-timers couldn't agree on what it had once manufactured. When Iris had returned to the town for her father's funeral, in the late seventies, the place had been plunged even further into oblivion, as if it was sinking into quicksand. Most of the storefronts had been shuttered by then or had been torched for their insurance payouts. Iris remembered the smell of ash in the air and trash blowing along the empty streets, as if it were the establishing shot in a low-budget movie about a ghost town. Most of her memories of Harborville remained stubbornly colorless, like an old newsreel or those stark black-and-white photographs shot during the Great Depression. This was the town Iris had expected to show Frank and Logan. She thought they would be congratulating her on her clean getaway. Instead, now it only seemed as if she had escaped from the aisles of *Restoration Hardware*.

Like everything else, *Thibedeaux's* had been renovated to the point of shock and awe. The aluminum siding on the old Victorian-style structure had been replaced with eco-friendly wooden clapboards. Decorative trellises had been added to the wraparound porch, where numerous Adirondack chairs (made from recycled materials!) were artfully strewn about. The entire structure was painted a comforting robin's egg blue.

"Christ," said Iris. "A quaint funeral home. It looks like it should be called The *Dew Drop Inn*."

"Or *The Body Shoppe*," said Frank as he maneuvered the car into a parking space.

The first thing you noticed about *Thibedeaux's* as you entered the spacious foyer was its oppressive good taste. The dark rec room paneling of yesteryear was nowhere to be seen. Now it looked like the reception area of a fancy law firm. Fine Turner and Gainsborough reproductions lined the cream-colored walls. Where there was wood, it was polished oak. There were several exquisite chairs along one wall and an elegant sofa the color of raspberry sorbet. In the public areas, flowers were noticeably absent. The atmosphere was appropriately subdued. It made you want to whisper.

They were met by an older man in a sedate but attractive charcoal gray suit. This was Lincoln Thibedeaux, the proprietor, with whom Iris had gone to high school. He shuffled up to her with a charged expression on his face and took her hands into his own as if they had once been good friends. They had not.

"It is I, Lincoln," he said. "Celeste told me you would be attending, but one never knows what to expect. One can only hope. As you can see, I am falling apart before your eyes, but you, dear lady, are a vision, a vision of eternal loveliness."

"Hello, Lincoln," said Iris.

She would have known him anywhere, not because of his appearance but because of his familiar line of bullshit and the pain-in-the-ass way that he talked as if he'd just stepped out of a nineteenth-century novel.

"This is my son, Frank," said Iris, gesturing. "This is Mr. Thibedeaux."

"Hello, Mr. Thibedeaux," said Frank, extending his hand.

"Please call me Lincoln," said the funeral director, smiling broadly at her son.

She could not remember the word Logan wanted her to use

to describe his relationship to Frank. Paramour? Concubine? But before she could remember, Logan had stepped up himself.

"I'm Logan," he said quite pleasantly. "I'm with Frank."

At least he didn't say, *Nice place you've got here.*

If Frank had elicited a heated appraisal from Lincoln, his reaction to Logan was as if he had stuck his finger in a light socket.

Lincoln had been a theatrical and flamboyant kid in school, but Iris had not fully processed his sexual orientation back then. The fact that he was probably gay was something that came to her in hindsight, once she had broken out of her depressed little town and had relocated to the free-and-easy California of the 1960s. Iris did not have any memories of Lincoln being bullied in school, though *he* probably had plenty of those. He would have been called a pansy back then or a queer. It was interesting to her that the word *queer* had been so reclaimed and repurposed over the past half century, that it was now an emblem of pride and self-determination. However, as an elderly, straight woman, she figured this was an observation best kept to herself. She didn't need Logan telling her how the writers on his show had addressed issues of cultural appropriation on a recent episode of *Windsor Valley High*.

Lincoln might have been bullied for being gay but being the son of the town undertaker provided richer material. *Here Comes the Grim Reaper*, she remembered her idiot classmates hollering at him when he walked down the hallways. Or sometimes they would refer to him as *Doug Graves* or *Barry M. Deep*. Whenever the poor kid entered the cafeteria, half the student body made ghost noises or hummed the theme from *The Twilight Zone*. It must have been tough to be Lincoln Thibedeaux back then. And yet Lincoln had stayed in town and taken over the family business. Was this paternal pressure, diminished expectations, or simple bravery? Iris couldn't say. She wondered if he had ever really come out or met anyone? Did he have a husband in the basement in charge of the embalming?

Suddenly, when she realized she was being discussed, Iris willed herself back to the conversation.

"What's that, now?" she asked.

Lincoln turned to look at her. His jowly face was flushed. The expression in his milky blue eyes was rather animated.

"I was just telling your young men here that we always knew your spellbinding appearance would be the pass key to any number of opportunities. We used to gossip about your glittery potential on the open market."

"Who is *we*?" asked Iris.

"The other members of the drama club and me. We all had stars in our eyes in those days."

Lincoln blinked rapidly and looked briefly at one of the Gainsborough prints on the wall. Then he reached out and touched Frank's sleeve.

"But your mother would never join our club. She wouldn't even try out for the school plays. Can you imagine? Don't you find that interesting, considering her career path?"

"Not really," said Frank, shrugging his shoulders. "She's not much of a joiner."

Ignoring this, Lincoln went on.

"She no doubt already considered herself to be a professional. She must have felt we were all so far beneath her, what with our provincial productions of *Our Town* and *Arsenic and Old Lace*."

Lincoln sighed stoically after saying this and glanced toward the painting again. Frank and Logan were watching Iris with oddly expectant expressions on their faces. If they thought she should apologize for her behavior fifty years ago, they were going to have a long wait.

"Pardon me for asking, Lincoln," said Iris, "but isn't my mother located somewhere in this establishment?"

Lincoln immediately fell back into his obsequious funeral director mode.

"Of course, of course," he said.

Then he led them down a long, pale hallway, not unlike those described on daytime television by people who claim to have had near-death experiences. When they reached a high, elaborate arch with detailed molding, Lincoln stopped and nodded and extended his hand for them to enter.

"You are the first to arrive," he whispered. "Your mother has been laid to rest in our Santa Fe Room."

Iris was put in mind of Navajo blankets and tumbleweeds, but the room itself was just a large oblong space with the same pale-colored walls as in the foyer, except there were no paintings, just some crosses here and there, made of a glossy blond wood, as if they had been purchased from a Christianity sale at IKEA.

"Please let me know if I can be of any further assistance," said Lincoln.

Then he backed away from them deferentially and returned to the foyer.

The casket was at the far end of this long, narrow room. There were some flowers on either side of it, garish sprays of chrysanthemums and gladiolas and something else that looked like small red bugles, which Iris couldn't have named if she'd had a gun to her head.

CHAPTER NINETEEN

Most of the same folks who had come to the funeral home were now standing around the farmhouse kitchen eating rolled up slices of luncheon meat from the trays Celeste had picked up earlier at the local Hannaford. Frank had to be introduced to these strangers all over again. Most of these people were interchangeable, elderly friends of the family, a shuffling, geriatric convention. Celeste and Joe looked youthful in this crowd, thought Frank. Celeste was careening around the house, handing out beers and cans of soda, smiling tightly. Joe stood in the kitchen by the sink, staring into his phone, picking his fantasy line up for Sunday. Frank stood next to him, collecting his thoughts. Logan was making himself useful to Celeste, seeing that everyone was being taken care of. It was Logan, oddly enough, who remembered everyone's names from earlier, and now as he wandered around the house, he touched these old people on their shoulders and greeted them, like a sunny cruise director. Even the old folks who would never see *Windsor Valley High* fussed and clucked over Frank's handsome boyfriend. Opal and her friends were huddled in a corner of the kitchen waiting for Logan to reappear. One of the girls was quite bluntly filming him with her phone as he came and went. Back at *Thibedeaux's*, a few of these young friends had crowded around Logan, literally wanting him to make a TikTok video then and there. Frank had to nix this idea and move the kids along, like a weary publicist at a press conference. It was nice to see that Opal's circle of friends were a diverse bunch. Amelia, Opal's *bestie*, as she'd been described, announced on introduction that she'd been adopted from South Korea. Perhaps the girl was used to stupid ethnicity inquiries from annoying white strangers and wanted to cut to the chase. Two of the girls, he learned, had been born in West Africa, another in Mumbai. Though Harborville was hardly Silicon Valley, Frank had been told the tech company was luring talent far and wide.

"So much for your theory that this place is the epicenter for the Aryan nation," Iris had whispered to him when she had noticed the girls at the funeral home.

"That's not exactly what I said," Frank responded, "but it's encouraging nonetheless."

After Lincoln had escorted them to the Santa Fe Room, Frank had taken Iris by the arm and led her toward the casket. But when she reached the folding chairs, she had pulled away from him and took a seat in the third row. She was apparently not going to approach her mother. She sat there as if waiting for a performance to start.

"What are you doing?" asked Frank, standing over her. "Aren't you going up there to pay your respects?"

He realized this was a rather stupid way to put it, as respect probably didn't figure into Iris's relationship with her mother—but still.

"I'm good," said Iris as if she was passing up a soda refill.

"I guess I'm good, too," said Logan as he took the seat next to her.

Frank glared at his mother. He felt like stamping his foot.

"It's just that we've flown across the country and driven half a day," said Frank, "and now you're going to stop twenty feet short . . . of your destination. I can't quite wrap my mind around that."

"That would appear to be a personal problem," said Iris, "but feel free. You can go up there and pretend it's the Wailing Wall if you want. I'm not stopping you."

"Mother!"

"I can see perfectly fine from here. I have the proverbial front-row seat," said Iris.

"It's actually the third row," said Logan.

Frank sighed and turned away from them. What else was he going to do? He walked the rest of the way until he was standing in front of his grandmother. Then he knelt on the little cushioned step, which was meant for prayer, but he was using it now so he could see this woman up close and personal. But she wasn't really a person anymore, was she? Her personhood had vanished, departed; her soul had left the building. Frank knew this was a spiritual notion, not that he'd ever been particularly religious. As a child, his parents had occasionally taken him to a Unitarian church in El Segundo, which wasn't a church at all, but more like someone's finished basement. There was no actual minister and no sermons, just some smiling parishioners, like the greeters at Home Depot. They would raise their hands to share, as if it were one of Frank's NA meetings. He'd had this feeling about souls before, at the hospital, as he had identified Keith's battered body. There was a theory that souls had a measurable weight. Twenty-one grams to be exact. Some scientist had done an experiment, weighing bodies at the moment of death. The scientist theorized that this weight discrepancy was the result of the soul ascending to heaven—or something like that. There had even been a movie called *21 Grams* some years back. Frank had gone to see it thinking it was about cocaine trafficking. This was long before his own drug troubles, long before he would have chosen to avoid a movie like that. The film had nothing to do with drugs. It was about this rising souls thing, told through a sad but contrived plot involving grief and loss and children in peril. That Australian actress was in it. Not Nicole Kidman. The other one. Iris would probably know, as she kept track of these things.

He focused again on his grandmother. He was struck by how tiny she was, shrunken and frail, like a doll or a child. A child in peril. But did anyone make it to ninety-six and remain tall and imposing? She was wizened, of course, and very pale and wearing an ordinary dress, a house dress. Something she might have worn every day. This was probably an example of the old woman's frugality and thrift. Celeste had chosen what she was to wear. Frank doubted it was because she had refused to dress her mother up in anything nice. Even after only twenty-four hours, it was hard to imagine his affable aunt being so petty. The woman sitting behind him in the third row might have dressed her mother in army boots. But that wasn't true either. Iris wasn't so much petty as simply unbending. Had he really expected that she would race through the Santa Fe Room and throw herself across the casket weeping, confessing to fifty years of regrets? Who was he to judge anyway? He hadn't even made it to Keith's funeral—a memory that choked him up momentarily.

"I wish you hadn't been so terrible to my mom," Frank leaned over and whispered to his grandmother. "I know how she can be, but she didn't deserve it."

He stared at this lifeless old woman he never knew and imagined her response, some rant about his mother making love to the camera and spilling out of her costumes.

Then he got up and returned to sit with Iris and Logan.

"Closed casket," said Iris.

"I beg your pardon?"

"When the time comes, I want a closed casket. I don't want to be sprawled out there looking like a desiccated moth."

"Fine, Mother," said Frank. "I'll make sure to nail it shut."

Then there were the sounds of voices behind them. The others had arrived.

Now at the farmhouse, Frank wolfed down some smoked turkey and swigged ginger ale from a dented can. Joe looked up from his phone and waved it in Frank's face. He mentioned a star wide receiver who was much in the news recently for a string of ugly incidents—a couple of DUIs, getting kicked off a plane for disorderly conduct, waving a machete at some people in a strip club.

"That latest story is really blowing up," said Joe. "What an asshole."

"Sounds like a troubled guy," said Frank.

"Yeah, the trouble is he's an asshole. And to think he was my number one draft pick."

"I guess he can kiss those days goodbye," said Frank.

"Hardly," laughed Joe. "Once these headlines die down, somebody else will bite. Next season he'll be offered an insane contract with a signing bonus that could float a small country and we'll have to hear about how he's been all rehabilitated."

"People do get rehabilitated," said Frank.

"I'm not so sure about that," said Joe. "No offense. I know Celeste said you worked in one of those . . . places. Mostly I think when people get caught, they'll do whatever they have to, you know, to make things right."

"Sure, it can happen like that, but that doesn't mean people *can't* be rehabilitated. People do get better."

"That's what I'd call a West Coast sentiment."

"Really," said Frank. "I'd prefer to think of it as a human one."

Frank expected Joe to smirk at this retort or break into "Kumbaya" or something, but all he said was, "I don't think people ever really change."

He wasn't chuckling now.

"People can change their behaviors," said Frank.

"People *are* their behaviors," said Joe. He sounded a little defeated.

It wasn't appropriate, Frank decided, in this post-funeral atmosphere, to discuss his own personal journey through rehabilitation and self-discovery. And Iris wouldn't like it. Besides, he basically agreed with Joe. People might not change, but their responses to certain situations could be examined and modified. In his own case, he'd gotten sober, not only because it had been Erik's last wish, but because he'd grown sick and tired of being sick and tired. Or maybe his grieving for Keith had simply expired, reached its sell-by date. But he certainly wasn't going to get into any of this over the Hannaford platters with an uncle he'd only met yesterday.

Logan rushed into the kitchen just then with a determined look on his face. He smiled at them both and began putting meat and cheese into Tupperware containers.

"What are you doing?" said Frank.

"People are starting to leave and we have so much food left over. Celeste thought it might be nice to send people off with a little something."

"Like goody bags," said Frank.

"Or door prizes," Joe added.

"Jeez, guys, it's just a little hospitality," said Logan.

"Just a little hospitality," repeated Joe.

Logan grinned at them some more and waved to the girl filming him from the corner, before turning to leave the kitchen with a few containers tucked under his arm.

"Anybody ever tell you that boyfriend of yours is pretty as a picture," said Joe, smirking.

"Yeah," sighed Frank as he watched Logan's beautiful backside as it left the room, "I've heard that said—from time to time."

CHAPTER TWENTY

Celeste stood in the doorway to the sunroom as blue-haired Peggy Stickney was telling Iris about watching her on an episode of *Marcus Welby, M.D.*, in 1974. Iris sat, as if holding court, on one of the wicker chairs. She had *received* other admirers back at the funeral home as well—former classmates and neighbors eager to have an audience with the girl who had left town and gone to Hollywood. It was as if they considered Iris to be a pathway to their own lost youth. In the brief conversations, Iris had shared a few well-chosen narratives about her brushes with fame, all of them slightly generalized and possibly embellished. She delivered these memories in a crisp, tolerant fashion, all of which had put Celeste's teeth on edge when she overheard them. Iris had not participated in the funeral service or joined Celeste and Joe as they greeted mourners or thanked them as they departed. Not that any of these people were truly mourning Deb. She had been ninety-six, after all, and could hardly be described as universally loved. People simply showed up because that's what you did around here. Somebody died and then you went to the funeral home to say the standard things and sit through the service where some young minister delivered a eulogy for the person in the casket he'd never actually met before, cobbling together a tribute from a few hastily shared anecdotes from the relative who had arranged his presence over a phone. The deceased would be described as stalwart or enduring or, in Deb's case, *a real character*, and then everyone would nod somberly or smile ironically to themselves.

"You were wearing a red chiffon dress with a plunging neckline," Peggy was saying now.

She was standing in front of Iris, fidgeting like a child. Peggy was seventy-seven, skinny as could be and for some reason wearing a wine red beret.

"I remember you asked Dr. Welby about your husband's chances of survival," she continued. "He'd been in a plane crash. You were an ex-showgirl, see, a gold-digger, and you didn't really want your husband to survive. Dr. Welby had you figured out from the start, of course, so by the end of the show he had patched up your husband and convinced him to dump you. Oh, you were so angry!"

Iris smiled thinly.

"Do you still have that dress?"

"Do I still have . . . what?" said Iris.

"The dress."

"Not that I'm aware of," said Iris. "They tended to discourage us from walking off with the costumes."

"Oh," said Peggy. "Anyway, you never looked lovelier."

Iris grew very still. Peggy's time was up whether she realized it or not, but apparently she had figured it out, because a moment or two later, she practically curtsied and turned to go. When Peggy saw Celeste standing in the doorway, she greeted her pleasantly. She praised the service and this post-funeral *assemblage*, which was how she referred to the crowd of townspeople who had been milling about the house eating cold cuts.

"Your mother would have enjoyed this so much!" she said.

Celeste nodded reluctantly.

Why do people say such moronic things? Celeste thought. Deb didn't *enjoy* much of anything and who would write a rave review of their own funeral?

"It's been nice to see her again," said Peggy in a stage whisper, motioning to Iris, who sat six feet away. "Do you remember how pretty she was?"

Celeste looked over at her sister. Iris had turned slightly in the wicker chair and was watching them both, with an indecipherable expression on her face.

"Yes, in fact, I do," said Celeste. "Thank you for coming, Peggy. I don't want to keep you. You're almost the last one here."

Celeste's tone was sharp and somewhat dismissive. She had never much liked Peggy, who had grown up on a neighboring farm and was a few years older. She was known for her vague and condescending manner and had barely acknowledged the Flynn family while Iris and Celeste were girls. It was not until after Iris had left for California and started appearing on television that Peggy would greet the family extravagantly whenever she saw them. She began dropping off cookies at Christmas and pies on the Fourth of July, as if she had never been anything other than kind and neighborly to them. There had been a lot of unwanted attention like this in response to Iris and her Hollywood life, something that Jasper and Deb particularly despised. Practical strangers would ask random questions on the street about the direction of Iris's career. Blunt appraisals of her performances would be handed down at the dentist office. A local plumber once showed up with a screenplay he wanted Iris to read.

After Peggy had left the sunroom, Celeste crossed to the daybed and sat down.

"So how was that?" she asked her sister.

"That woman has always been a pill," said Iris.

"Yes, and a hard one to swallow at that," said Celeste.

"She told me her son is on television, just like I was."

"He makes commercials," said Celeste. "He owns a car dealership in Augusta. He dresses up as the Statue of Liberty or Santa Claus depending on the season and shrieks his holiday deals at the camera."

"I gathered it was something like that."

"It must be strange for you to be here," said Celeste, "facing people like this, asking you strange questions, making . . . remarks."

"You mean asking me to discuss a career that's long gone and being told how pretty I *used* to be?"

"I guess that's what I mean," said Celeste.

"I will admit there is some cruelty to the past tense," said Iris.

Celeste was surprised by this comment, which sounded like the most honest thing her sister had said since she had arrived.

"I guess it's the way these folks can claim a connection to you," Celeste said pleasantly, "considering they never even knew you."

"I came into their living rooms periodically, so for them it *is* like they knew me," said Iris.

"It's an odd familiarity, though," said Celeste. "It's sort of the way the girls have been falling over Logan."

"Imagine what it must be like for Brad Pitt."

"I can't even imagine that," said Celeste. "Not really."

"That makes two of us," said Iris.

There was a long pause as the sisters watched each other. They were almost smiling, but there was something tired about it.

Celeste smoothed the cover on the daybed.

"I hope the boys were comfortable here last night," she

said. "The bed's a bit small for them and it gets so damp in here."

"I'm sure it was fine," Iris sniffed. "Neither of them are particularly, what is the word, fussy. And compared to how Frank was living in New York . . ."

Celeste waited for Iris to finish this sentence, since she knew nothing of Frank's life in New York, but Iris let the comment trail off and then glanced, rather sternly, out the sunroom windows.

"I like Frank," said Celeste. "You've done a very nice job there."

"He's done a nice job on himself."

"And Logan, too," said Celeste. "He's been so sweet to Opal."

"I can take no credit for Logan," said Iris.

She shifted in her chair.

"Can I ask you something?" said Celeste.

Iris nodded and motioned for her to go ahead.

"Was it awfully hard to give up?"

"Give what up?" said Iris.

"Your career. Your acting . . . life."

Iris smiled tightly.

"No. Not really. It was a long time coming. When it was finally over, it was like I had given away a closet full of clothes long out of style, things kept only out of habit or sentiment. After the initial tug, it felt good to be free of the burden."

Celeste didn't trust this answer. It felt practiced, like dialogue, something Iris had invented to shut people up.

"So you enjoy real estate, then?"

"I enjoy paying my bills."

California real estate must be a lucrative business, thought Celeste. Iris had told them she'd been doing it for thirty years. She'd had two successful careers, one on top of the other. She apparently lived not far from the ocean, in Santa Monica. Logan said he spent his mornings swimming in her pool. Iris had done more than simply pay her bills.

"No plans to retire?" Celeste asked now.

"Not as such."

It must be nice to have the option, thought Celeste. She and Joe didn't have that luxury. Retirement was a privilege they didn't allow themselves to even think about. They'd have to work 'til they dropped.

Iris leaned in.

"Now may I ask *you* something?"

She didn't wait for Celeste to respond. She went on anyway.

"I'm wondering why Mother was cremated. I suddenly had a clear memory while I was sitting in the funeral home of her telling us when we were teenagers that she hated the idea of being burnt to a crisp. Why didn't she want to be buried with Father?"

"Mother's ashes *are* to be buried with Father. I told you this yesterday. I think I even texted it before you got here."

"Yes, but why the cremation?" asked Iris. "Did she have a change of heart?"

"Yes, you could say that," said Celeste.

The change of heart had been Celeste's. The cremation option was a full $8,000 less than the standard burial. But why should Iris care? Iris of all people.

"I don't really care," said Iris, as if reading her sister's mind. "I'm just curious. And I'd like to pay you for half the funeral costs, whatever they are. I'd be pleased to write you a check."

"That's not necessary."

"Why not?" said Iris, stiffening slightly in the wicker chair.

"For one thing, the three of you have flown across the country to be here," said Celeste, as politely as she could muster. "That's enough. That's more than enough."

"Nonsense. I'll write you a check."

"We won't accept it."

"Well, you must."

It was late afternoon. The drizzle had stopped and the clouds were lifting. There was a shaft of light coming through the windows, dancing across the room between them. Specks of dust were trapped in that light, thousands of them, swirling, glittering like jewels. Iris brushed her hand through the air, waving it about, stirring up the whole universe.

"And I'd also like to pay for any appraisals of the land and the house as we move forward with the division of the estate."

Now Celeste leaned forward.

"What do you mean, *division of the estate*?" she said.

"It's quite simple," said Iris. "You told me Mother did not draft a will. As her children, as her closest surviving relatives, we are the obvious beneficiaries."

"*We*, as in you and me?" said Celeste.

"Yes, of course. Any lawyer will tell you that. We shouldn't dally either, what with all the changes in town, this unexpected lollapalooza you've got going on here. The farms being bought up. It's probably an ideal time to see what we can get for the property."

Celeste attempted to keep her facial expression as neutral as possible. She doubted it was wise to reveal what she was feeling, which at the moment was a cloudy soup of indignation, anger, and fear. What she was not feeling was surprise. This was exactly what she had worried would happen, ever since Iris had announced she was coming to the funeral, and before that, too—since Deb had died in her sleep.

Now, running parallel to that prediction, in the breakdown lane of her thoughts, she was fuming at Joe, for believing that Iris would simply sign away any claim to their property, for implying that Celeste was paranoid for thinking that she wouldn't, for soothing her about it, for practically patting her on the head as if she were a fretful child. He had said various stupid, platitudinous things in his attempts to dissuade her from trusting her own instincts.

Iris sat across from her now, slowly blinking her eyes in a bloodless way, as if she were some kind of lizard, thought Celeste. Iris was displaying the same steely manner that no doubt helped her navigate the cruel and complicated world of Hollywood.

Celeste took a deep breath, so deep, in fact, that she felt a twinge of pain in her lungs. She had no choice. She would have to reason with her.

"Iris," she said, "you can't believe that Mother would have wanted you to be a beneficiary."

"Is that a question or a statement?" said Iris.

"Call it an observation," said Celeste. *Call it a scientific fact*, she wanted to say.

"I don't dispute the observation," said Iris. "But what is your point?"

Celeste took another breath, this time a less painful one.

"My point is that there would never have been a provision made for you."

She smiled encouragingly as she said this, as if coaxing a dim student through an algebra equation.

"You don't think so?" said Iris.

"No," said Celeste. "I do not."

"You mean if Mother had written a will," said Iris.

"Exactly," said Celeste.

"But Mother did not write a will."

Celeste heard herself gasp. It was a high-pitched noise, like a tire leak. She ran a hand through her hair and silently counted backward from 10 before responding.

"But that's merely a technicality, isn't it?" said Celeste.

She noticed her voice was fluttering. This was a worse sound than the gasp.

"Is it?" said Iris. She sat up even straighter in her chair. "A technicality is a small detail. I would say that the absence of a will is the opposite of a small detail."

I must appear calm, thought Celeste. She smiled again, gently, idiotically.

"Now, Iris, if you want something from here, some furniture, a memento, we can certainly discuss it."

Iris slowly scanned the room in a disinterested way and then she returned her focus to her sister.

"There is nothing I want from here," said the lizard queen. "I have no interest in keepsakes."

"Then what is this about?"

"What do you mean, Celeste? Are you being deliberately dense? This is about our inheritance, of course."

"But you can't, after all these lost years, expect to share equally in that."

"I think I'll leave that to the State of Maine to decide."

"You could sign a release," Celeste replied.

Her voice was no longer fluttering. There was a desperate quality to it now, as if she were standing in rising flood waters.

"I think it is safe to assume that I could do a lot of things," said Iris.

Celeste swallowed hard.

"Okay, okay. Look, Joe and I have had some personal setbacks. Deb took out a second mortgage and has been selling off bits of land for years, to keep us all going. There really isn't all that much left. We're not talking a grand sum here. We only want to keep the house and a couple of acres. Joe's had three heart attacks. With whatever is left over after paying his medical bills, we thought we'd get the house in shape and maybe renovate the barn. I thought I could expand the flea market idea and open a gift shop out there."

"A gift shop? In the barn? This far from town?" Iris scoffed.

Celeste ignored this.

"What I'm telling you," said Celeste, "is that the inheritance has already been earmarked and the only fair and reasonable thing for you to do is to make no claim on it."

"Fair and reasonable for whom?" said Iris. "It sounds as if you have already benefitted."

"How do you mean that?"

"Didn't you just say that Deb was selling off parcels of land to keep you all going?"

"I said there have been setbacks. Joe's health . . . and Opal coming to live with us."

Celeste's voice had morphed again. There was a pleading, apologetic tone to it now, which embarrassed her—until it made her angry.

"We weren't exactly freeloading these past fifty years!" Celeste snapped. The anger felt good, like receiving a gift, after all this restraint. "We were, after all, working the farm and then we were taking care of Mother. It was not the other way around. We had these fixed daily responsibilities for years and years, while you were out basking in your sunshine and canned laughter. Mother was not like some quiet, placid boarder either. These last years she hovered over this house like bad weather. She was a demanding, uneasy individual."

"So now you tell me," said Iris.

Celeste stared at Iris and could see the rigid teenager who sat across from her at the dinner table a hundred years ago.

"Let me repeat," she said. "It would have not been Mother's intention to leave you anything!"

"I know nothing of the woman's intentions," said Iris. "But if she wanted to avoid confusion, she might simply have drafted a will, if only to leave me out of it. But she did not do that, did she? It makes me wonder . . ."

"It makes you wonder what?"

"It's hardly a secret that the woman despised me, but perhaps she wasn't a big fan of yours either."

"That's ridiculous. She didn't write a will because she didn't trust lawyers or the government in particular. That describes half the county. You know that. But she would have done it if she thought you would come back here to make trouble . . . I'm certain of that."

Iris shrugged.

"Let me ask you," said Celeste, "do you have any moral hesitation about wanting us to split the estate, I mean whatever is left of it?"

"Oh, are we back to fair and reasonable again?" said Iris. "Because it seems to me that I left this house because of an absence of those qualities."

"You left this house because you were conceited and selfish . . . and dizzy with ambition."

There were voices outside in the driveway, Peggy and the others, the sounds of guests departing.

"Well, I won't apologize for my ambition," said Iris. "My ambition belonged to me. It was something that Mother and Father could not destroy."

"Oh, spare me!" hooted Celeste. "Despite your unhappy memories of growing up here, no one was chasing you around with a meat cleaver. Lord knows our parents were cold and flawed—and not very nice people. Funny how you've turned out exactly like them."

CHAPTER TWENTY-ONE

When Joe walked into the sunroom a few moments later, he could tell something had happened. The atmosphere was off. Celeste's eyes flashed in his direction. She was holding herself in such a taut and inflexible way that it seemed like she would crack in half if he tapped her on the shoulder. Iris, on the other hand, sat composed in one of the wicker chairs, with the same neutral expression she had worn since her arrival.

"Hello," he greeted them. "Here you are."

"Here we are," said Celeste. "Where is everyone else?"

"You mean our guests?" said Joe. "They're gone. The last of them snuck out of here a few minutes ago, smuggling leftovers."

"Good!" said Celeste.

Her tone was cold and worrisome. Joe wondered if he could stall whatever was coming.

"Frank and Logan have started cleaning up," he said. "Opal is pretending to supervise. I've sent the other girls home. I thought they might hit Logan over the head and drag him out of here."

The joke fell flat.

The vein in Celeste's neck was throbbing in the fading sunlight. He had noticed it at various junctures during the most stressful times in their marriage. It was like her poker tell. He looked from one sister to the other. There was no point in stalling.

"What's going on here?" he asked.

"Ask her," said Celeste. "I'd like to hear her explanation."

Iris sighed extravagantly.

"Your wife thinks it's somehow morally reprehensible of me to point out the legal realities of family inheritance."

"What she means is that she's decided to come back here for reparations," said Celeste.

"Huh?" said Joe.

"Her lousy childhood, her cold, miserable parents," explained Celeste. "She wants to cash in and take Deb's inheritance—as if she didn't resolve her issues with Mother and Father fifty years ago when she got the hell out of here."

"Celeste does not understand," said Iris, "that hightailing it out of Harborville and relocating elsewhere does not impede or obstruct one's legal rights."

"Listen to her," said Celeste. "*Impede or obstruct*. Like she's playing a lawyer in one of her terrible TV movies."

"Does that make you the unreliable witness?" said Iris.

"Now, now," said Joe rather stupidly.

"She wasn't coming back to set things straight after all," said Celeste, "or to reunite the family before it was too late."

"I never implied such a thing!" said Iris.

"No. I realize you didn't. Those were my husband's theories."

Joe took a seat next to Celeste on the daybed. He yanked the tie off his neck and threw it in a corner. It had been choking him all afternoon.

"You're not really serious, Iris, are you?" said Joe. "I mean about challenging the will."

"There is no will to challenge, Joseph. Only the fact of my existence. I am a legal beneficiary. It is as simple as that. I don't know why either of you are having trouble understanding that concept."

Joe paused and looked at his scuffed dress shoes. He could feel Celeste's prickly energy next to him, like a downed power line. He looked up again, into Iris's eyes.

"I guess the reason we're having trouble with the idea," he said gently, "is because Celeste and I have, I don't know, put our time in. We've lived our lives here and made sacrifices. We're the ones who took care of the farm and of Deb . . ."

"Don't waste your breath," hissed Celeste. "I've already gone down that road. It doesn't matter to her."

It had to matter to her, thought Joe, because otherwise it would amount to ruthlessly tossing them out of their home.

Celeste turned back to Iris.

"It's almost perfect," she said, "to be having this conversation here in the sunroom, the scene of the last time your selfishness threatened to wreck our future."

"Are you referring to the time I refused you that loan?" said Iris.

"Yes. That is exactly what I am referring to," said Celeste. "If you had lent us the money, we could have paid off our debts and modernized. We could have gotten upgraded storage facilities and had the start-up money to partner with that barley farm in Limestone. You could have changed our lives."

"How do you figure that?" said Iris. "You came to me because the bank thought you were a bad risk. How do you know my loan wouldn't have been like throwing money down a rat hole?"

"Well, we never got the chance to find out," said Celeste.

"It's interesting that your memory is so clear about some things," said Iris. "Do you also happen to recall how you lured me back here?"

Celeste exhaled loudly but said nothing.

"It was by telling me it was Father's dying wish?" Iris continued.

"We were drowning at the time," replied Celeste. "I would have said anything,"

"But you did not drown," said Iris. "It is forty years later and you are sitting in roughly the same spot as you were then, rehashing an old story. You have survived."

"I can't deny that we're still breathing, if that's what you mean," said Celeste.

"I never knew why you thought I was in a position to bail you out in the first place," Iris said now.

She made a strange, exasperated gesture with her hands.

"Are you joking?' said Celeste. "You were on television all the time, commercials, guest appearances."

This was true, thought Joe. He remembered those evenings when Deb or Jasper was always getting up to change the TV channel.

"I was working for scale on most of those jobs," said Iris. "You shouldn't have assumed."

"Well, you did nothing to downplay your achievements that weekend you were here. And I remember your husband going on and on about what a success you were and how you were on the verge of becoming a big, big star."

"I can't speak to Erik's misplaced optimism," said Iris, "or how you interpreted it so long ago, though it seems rather beside the point now."

Celeste was right about that, too, thought Joe. Erik's peppy appraisal of Iris's career and his descriptions of their fancy life *on the coast* did nothing to dampen their plan of asking for the loan. Joe hadn't liked Erik—at all. His hair was too long for one thing and his voice too mellow. He was altogether too *Californian*. It was not clear if Erik even had a job. He'd been vague on that subject and Joe had wondered if he might be a bit of a scam artist. But they seemed happy enough together, Iris and Erik—and affectionate, too. Frank had been a toddler then. Joe remembered Erik chasing him all over the farm that visit. He appeared to be just wild about his son. The term for it these days was *a hands-on dad*. Maybe this was an admirable trait, but it hadn't changed Joe's opinion of the guy. When it came right down to it, he couldn't imagine warming up to anybody whom Iris might have brought home. He recalled stealing peeks at Erik that weekend, wondering how the hell he had cracked the code and won her heart.

"You're right," Joe said suddenly.

Both women turned to look at him.

"You're right," he repeated, staring at Iris. "There *was* no guarantee that your loan would have changed anything for us. We might still be in the same spot now."

"Why tell her that?" said Celeste, slapping his arm with the back of her hand.

"Because it's true, Cee," said Joe, turning to his wife. "We don't know what might have happened. There's no way to guess, but it honestly doesn't matter forty years later. Today's situation is a whole other kettle of fish."

Joe turned back to face Iris. He leaned forward, putting his elbows on his knees.

"Look, Iris. This is important. I want us to stay in our home and raise Opal here," he told her. "If you're suggesting we divide the estate evenly, then that can't happen. We just wouldn't have enough money to buy you out and cover all our other expenses."

"I think you are painting a rather bleak picture," said Iris. "This is why we need to speak to a lawyer and to appraisers, to get the facts straight about the overall value of things before we get into any doomsday predictions."

The timbre of Iris's voice did not waver, but for the first time in the discussion, Joe noticed that she broke eye contact. She studied a water stain on the wall above the door.

"Don't you think we already have a general idea about the value of the estate?" said Joe. "I'm asking you to think about the fallout. Have you ever considered that we might have special responsibilities? Like Opal, for instance."

He paused for a moment.

"Her mother is not in the picture, because, you see, our daughter Cheryl . . ."

Joe then stopped speaking. He sat straight up again. He hadn't spoken of what had happened with his daughter for many years. He knew it would be painful now to say out loud.

"Don't tell her anything," said Celeste, sensing his discomfort. "We're not going to beg."

Joe turned to look at his wife. He reached over and gripped her hand.

"I'm sorry," he whispered.

He meant it as a blanket apology, one size fits all. Celeste could have plugged it in anywhere, for his heart attacks, for the state of the farm, for his infatuation with Iris. However, he could tell by the way she was staring back at him that she had already forgiven him or perhaps forgiveness had never even been required. Cee's true gift, after all, was her unconditional love.

"I already know about your daughter," said Iris, shifting her gaze away from the ceiling.

"What do you know?" said Celeste.

"Only what Opal told Logan—her incarceration for trying to blow up a ship and how she's been unable to settle down since prison and has no fixed address. I can understand that this must be difficult for the little girl."

"She shouldn't have told you. It's not your business," said Celeste.

"In fact, she didn't tell me," said Iris. "I just said, she told Logan, who told Frank, who told me."

"It's Opal's story to tell," said Joe quietly. "She should be able to share it with whoever she wants. Haven't we told her not to be ashamed, Cee?"

"I can understand it must be difficult for the little girl," Iris said again.

"You just said that," said Celeste. "And *the little girl* is our granddaughter."

"And I can understand that it must be difficult for you as well," said Iris, but somewhat flatly.

"So then maybe you *will* see it our way," said Joe. "We had these enormous legal fees and expenses after Cheryl's arrest and during her trial in Seattle. That's where our girl was . . . imprisoned. There were two failed appeals. It flattened us financially."

"I don't know what you want me to say by telling me these things," said Iris. "You are putting me in a difficult position."

"How do you figure that?" said Joe.

"You are asking me to play the villain," said Iris.

"No. That's not true," said Joe. "I'm actually asking you to do the opposite."

"You are forcing me to be blunt."

"No one has ever needed to twist your arm to do that," said Celeste.

"Okay, then," said Iris. "I am sorry about your daughter, but—"

"Her name is Cheryl," said Celeste.

"I'm sorry about Cheryl, but I don't see how her circumstances, or the choices you have made because of them, are my problem. No more than whatever issues you were dealing with forty years ago."

"Choices!" said Joe. "These weren't choices. They were the times when life . . . just lets you down."

"Yes," said Iris. "Life has a tendency to do that. You are an old man, Joseph. You should have figured that out by now. I'm simply saying I don't believe it is my responsibility to pick up the tab for your disappointments."

"We're not handing you an invoice," said Joe. "We were just hoping you would realize that you are not entitled to share in any inheritance. You might want to ask yourself if you really need it."

Iris sighed again and raised her chin theatrically in the air, as if waiting for the lighting to be reset. She was rather mesmerizing sitting in that chair, the late afternoon sun coursing through the windows, spilling across her. Joe had to push this thought out of his mind.

"Need it?" said Iris. "How would you know what I need? Do you have access to my bank statements? Have you been analyzing my portfolio?"

"That's the difference between us," said Celeste. "We're talking about keeping a roof over our heads. We don't have a fucking *portfolio*."

Joe stared at his wife and raised his eyebrows. He couldn't remember the last time she'd used that particular curse word.

"I am glad Mother was there to pitch in when your Cheryl had her . . . troubles," said Iris. "As a grandmother who was in a position to help, her response was perhaps appropriate. But let's not forget that Deb had another grandchild. He is in the kitchen right now putting the meat trays away. And now *he's* the one needing a roof over his head. We told you that he lost his home not three weeks ago in the wildfires. I might be able to wrap my mind around the fact that Mother wouldn't want me to benefit from her passing, but I will not forfeit the option of seeing what the old girl's death could do for my son."

"Mother did not even know your son!" said Celeste. "She saw Frank that one weekend when he was two years old. She had an actual relationship with Cheryl. She helped raise the girl. They got on. It's not the same thing at all."

"And why not?" asked Iris.

"Frank wasn't part of her life," said Celeste.

"And whose fault was that?" said Iris. "Certainly not Frank's."

"This is not a helpful discussion," said Joe.

He felt the situation slipping away from him, like a rope through his hands.

"It's rough about Frank and the fire," said Joe. "But Frank must have had insurance."

"He did not," said Iris. "It was a tiny rental home."

"But he's a grown man with a job," he said. "He doesn't need our help. Didn't you just say it wasn't your responsibility to pick up the tab for life's disappointments? Why should it be ours?"

"Please stop making assumptions about things you know nothing about," said Iris. "Simply put, my son should benefit from the estate. He's needs to get back on his feet as soon as possible."

"He's young. He'll bounce back," said Joe.

"My son is not that young. And he has lost everything in a fire, which was beyond his control. Many would even call it an Act of God. He is not a criminal trying to blow up some ship."

"Iris!" said Joe.

"That's enough!" shouted Celeste, jumping to her feet.

"Yes, it is!"

This comment was from Frank, who was standing in the doorway to the sunroom. They all turned in his direction. The look on his face was a mix of fury and mortification.

Celeste sat back down, landing next to Joe in an angry heap.

Joe knew he had been naive to hope that the visit would be peaceful, but he supposed there were worse qualities than trying not to anticipate disaster at every turn. He shifted his weight on the daybed. He felt some tightness in his chest and rotated his shoulder to relieve it, while gazing again at Iris. She didn't seem surprised by her son's sudden appearance. She looked confident and slightly irritated. This reminded Joe of that day in front of the movie theater in Caribou when she had scuttled his hopes and sent him away. He realized he was so old now that everything had the potential to remind him of something else. If anything, he had too many memories, too many associations. What was the opposite of Alzheimer's? he wondered. If he lived long enough, Joe would be reminded of this day, too, the whole afternoon in shards and flashes—Deb laid out at the funeral home, Opal and the girls fawning over Logan, Celeste and Iris poised for battle, and now Frank standing there with his sleeves rolled up after rinsing dishes at the sink, fairly busting to speak.

CHAPTER TWENTY-TWO

Frank took a few steps into the room.

"I need to apologize for my mother," he said.

Joe and Celeste stared up at him from the daybed.

"You do *not* need to apologize for me," said Iris.

"Well, someone does," said Frank. "Is this really why we're here? For you to make a cash grab on my account?"

"I'm hardly robbing a bank," said Iris.

"You don't think so?" said Frank.

"No," said Iris. "I do not."

Great, thought Frank, *she's digging herself in*, but he would not be deflected.

"So what you said on the plane about finding closure, that was never part of coming here, was it?" he said. "It wasn't exactly on brand for you, but I wanted to believe it."

"I think when you receive an inheritance from your grandmother," replied Iris, "something to make you whole again, as a lawyer might say, it actually *will* provide a measure of closure for me."

"I don't want their money," said Frank. He motioned helplessly in his aunt and uncle's direction. "I've already applied for those FEMA loans," he said.

"Loans need to be paid back, with interest," said Iris. "An inheritance does not."

Frank looked to Joe and Celeste.

"I hope you realize I didn't even know there was any inheritance," he told them.

"Yes," said Joe. "We can see that."

They all sat silently. A slight breeze picked up outside; a branch or something was making a dull scraping sound against the windows. Celeste smiled weakly in Frank's direction.

"I think your mother is being unfair about all this," she said, "and I'm relieved that you think so, too. But I don't fault her for trying to help you. I don't. Not that it changes anything, but I wish she'd have been more up front about it from the start."

"We only arrived yesterday," said Iris. "I'm not sure how much more up front you expected me to be."

"But it's more complicated than that," Frank responded. "This matter of being up front. Isn't that right, Mother?"

"I don't know what you mean," said Iris. She reached up to smooth her hair, but nothing was out of place. "But if you have something to say, then you should say it."

Frank stood very still and began to speak.

"I heard what Joe said, about how Opal should be allowed to share her story with anyone she wants, and I think that's exactly right. I think that's terrific, in fact. Because, you see, we're all only as sick as our secrets. This is something I have learned and that I believe, but I have not always put into practice."

He directed his next comments to his aunt and uncle.

"I have a secret, too. It is not particularly shocking or unusual, but I know it is one my mother would prefer I keep to myself. It was strange to hear her make such a snide comment about Cheryl—because she knows that I am a bit of a criminal myself. I am an opioid addict, and when I was in active addiction, I sometimes lied and I even stole from my friends to get painkillers. I didn't get caught or thrown in jail. That's the only difference. I'm in recovery now, but I suppose on somebody's scale, my past is right up there with trying to blow up a ship. And it's not even like Cheryl really blew it up. I told you I worked in a rehab facility and that's true, but I didn't tell you that I'd been a client there. That's how I found the job in the first place. I became an addict when I was living in New York City. A man I loved was killed in an accident and I could not cope. My father convinced me to get help. He was dying at the time. I am grateful to both my parents for arranging my treatment, but my mother has never been a fan of people who cannot cope. I think she would have preferred it if my partying had simply gotten out of hand and not that I couldn't handle my grief without drugs. Being a party boy would have been less of a character flaw. I have been a disappointment to her, you see, and I am afraid she imagines failure lurking for me around every corner. She wants that inheritance as preparation for my next wrong turn, I suppose, whether it be a relapse or getting caught in a mudslide. It's an insurance policy to cover my blown potential, my snakebit existence. This is probably easier than having any faith in me to adequately take care of myself."

Frank stopped talking then. His aunt and uncle looked uneasy; as well they might after watching this relative stranger air his dirty laundry. That's exactly what Frank was to them, too, an unknown person who had shown up on their farm after all these years. *Relative. Stranger.* The thought almost amused him, even in these unhappy circumstances.

Iris had been observing her son carefully while he spoke. "Did that feel good to get off your chest?" she asked now.

Yes, there was a certain satisfaction, Frank wanted to say, but he did not say this. He stared at his mother and waited for her to go on, which after a moment, she did.

"It's pointless to defend myself here," she said, "but it

seems like that's what you are asking me to do. All of you, with your accusations and finger-pointing."

"Something needed to be said," murmured Frank.

"Did *all of that* need to be said?" replied Iris. "You say I have no faith in you! You accuse me with such authority, as if you know me better than I know myself. How do you want me to respond exactly—with shouted denials and a stamp of my foot? You'll have a long wait for that, I'm afraid. I can't justify every notion that's ever passed through my head. And neither can you, by the way, and neither can those two."

Iris gestured in the direction of Celeste and Joe as she said this, who were sitting quite close to each other on the daybed, as if joined at the hip. She stood then, with some effort. Her back must be bothering her, Frank assumed, after sitting so long in one spot, not that she would admit to it, any more than she would admit to any other weakness.

"How tiresome all this is," Iris said, gazing from one of them to the other.

She stared at Frank for another moment after she said this and then she moved past him and out of the room.

CHAPTER TWENTY-THREE

Iris left the farmhouse and crossed the peeling, slanted porch. She walked down the steps carefully, gripping the handrail. Her back was bothering her. The last thing she needed was to take a tumble and break a hip. She did not want to end up like *The Man Who Came to Dinner*. Ah, that was another old movie she could show Logan once they got back to California. It was a fast-paced comedy about a famous, egotistical journalist who injures himself in the home of an ordinary American family and then wreaks havoc on his hosts and everyone else during his recovery. It was another Bette Davis film, but only technically, because she had a flat, thankless part in it. The movie was really a vehicle for its star, Monty Woolley, who'd had a huge success with the play on Broadway. It pleased Iris to think about this movie and its long-dead luminaries, even for a moment, especially after what had just happened in the sunroom. That had been her habit when she was a teenager, too, after her parents had infuriated her. She would storm out of the house and try to lose herself in some memory of a film. Movies had been therapeutic for Iris—and aspirational. It was not the same now, of course, because the film career she'd dreamt of had never materialized, so when she thought of movies, it was sometimes through the scrim of her own professional anticlimax. And today she had not stormed out of the farmhouse because she was infuriated, or not exactly. Joe and Celeste were simply being unreasonable, and Frank was overreacting. They were taking everything so personally and egging her on with talk of reparations and disappointments, dragging the past into it. Iris refused to indulge them or let them see that these exchanges had honestly distressed her. She didn't want to look too closely at her distress. She didn't want to think about the alarm on her sister's face either or Joe's vulnerability as they pleaded with her in the sunroom or the look of sorrow in her son's eyes when he'd leveled those assessments of their relationship. It was certainly easier to think about movie characters with all their finite goals and grievances condensed into ninety minutes, than flesh-and-blood people with all their messy complications, people who were impossible to please.

Iris walked along the driveway and then took a gravel path that led away from the house. She walked under a pergola she did not remember, though she could imagine wisteria attractively hanging from it in season. It was so strangely mild for this late in October—not at all as Iris remembered this time of year growing up, where snowdrifts on Halloween were not uncommon. Opal had cited some climate change statistics over breakfast. Perhaps something she'd picked up from her activist, ex-con mother in their FaceTime chats. It was a raw deal for the kid, that trouble with her mother. Opal could have done worse than getting Celeste and Joe as her grandparents. Her sister and brother-in-law were presumptuous and pigheaded, but at least they were trying to do right by the child.

The enormous old barn was now looming in front of her. Iris gazed up at it. Up close it appeared to be as unsound as the porch, tilted and wobbly, like it needed to be propped up with a giant matchbook. Iris wondered if the structure would make it through another winter. It might collapse before Celeste got the chance to remodel it and turn it into a gift shop. Isn't that what she said she wanted to do? An unrealistic idea, given that the trendy, overblown shopping district downtown probably already had the market covered when it came to pricey antiques and useless curios. The barn door was slightly ajar. She could see that the space was packed full of assorted furniture, clothes and dishes, and a bunch of other miscellaneous crap. Iris wondered if Celeste ever sold anything at the flea markets. Perhaps she just kept coming back here with more and more inventory for the prospective store, cramming it all in. Iris stared at these precarious hoarder-like stacks and she imagined her father spinning in his grave, rotisserie style. *A place for everything and everything in its place* was something he literally said while they were growing up, but it was delivered more as a threat than some quaint homespun motto. Though Iris had to admit that the cluttered barn sent a chill up her own spine. She thought of her empty cupboards at home, the vacant counter space. She pictured Marie Kondo frowning at all this with her eyes squeezed shut. There were two overturned barrels next to the barn, probably because they could not fit inside. Their surfaces were damp from the drizzle earlier, but she took a seat on one of them anyway. She was suddenly quite tired. It was exhausting to be misunderstood and reprimanded all in one afternoon. She must have dozed off for a moment, because when she opened her eyes, Logan was standing there in front of her. He looked strangely serious. His trademark grin was nowhere to be seen.

"I've been looking for you. I talked to Frank," he said. "I think you could use a friend right about now."

He took a seat on the barrel next to her and tilted his head at her.

"Is that what we are?" said Iris. "Friends?"

"Yes. I'd like to think so," said Logan.

Iris looked past him, past the low fence and out into the field.

"I always wanted a gazebo," she said.

"Excuse me?" said Logan.

"When I was little, I used to pester Father and Mother about building a gazebo out there in the field. I must have seen one in a movie and thought it would be like a sophisticated clubhouse or something."

"I take it the idea didn't go over too well," said Logan.

"That's right, to say the least. The thing is, this was a working farm back then, and there were potatoes right up to that fence. I might as well have asked them to torch an acre. What really troubled them, I suppose, was the frivolousness of the request. These were people who believed that even the time it took to go to the bathroom was an extravagance. Nothing got in the way of completing your chores. Where had I come from, they must have wondered. Was I some alien spore who had landed here to confuse and antagonize them?"

"So no gazebo?" said Logan.

"No gazebo."

"Who's to say?" said Logan. "Maybe they did you a favor. Maybe by, like, depriving you, it helped fuel your dreams."

"You mean if they had built me the gazebo, I would have been satisfied and stopped there?" said Iris, turning to look at him.

"Something like that," said Logan.

"I don't think so, sweetie," said Iris. "That was just one item from a long list."

Logan seemed to be expecting her to go on, but when she remained quiet, he cleared his throat.

"But you got the last laugh, didn't you?" he said. "You got out of this little town and it worked out just the way you planned."

"Is that what you think?" said Iris. "Look, kid, When I was imagining my future, it wasn't cattle call auditions I was thinking about. I wasn't dreaming about doing the pony behind Nancy Sinatra or landing an under-five on a soap. I didn't aspire to be the window dressing on forgettable television shows."

It occurred to her that she might have offended him.

"No offense," said Iris.

"None taken," said Logan. "I'm just an innocent bystander in that world anyway. And you weren't just *window dressing*; you were a working actor. That has to count for something."

"I was only a working actor until I couldn't find any more work," said Iris. "Does that count for something, too?"

Logan looked out over the field then, as Iris had done, putting his hand to his forehead and scanning the horizon.

"It really is lovely here," he said. "I'm glad I came."

"I'm pleased that our family dramas have not gotten in the way of your little holiday," said Iris.

Logan ignored this comment.

"You know. It's pretty much how I pictured it," he said.

"The farm?" asked Iris.

"No," he said, turning to face her. "Maine. New England. When I was kid, I figured that this part of the country must be the exact opposite of Las Vegas."

"I imagine Vegas is the opposite of almost anywhere that doesn't have casinos in the desert," said Iris.

Logan sighed.

"What is it?" she said.

"You know, you do that a lot," he replied.

"What do I do?"

"Disagree with me."

"I'm not disagreeing. I was only pointing something out."

"Okay then. You point things out a lot . . . in a disagreeable way."

Iris shifted on the barrel. She realized she was suddenly free of pain. Sitting on this old barrel had, oddly enough, soothed her sore back.

"I've had quite enough criticism for one day, Logan," said Iris, her tone rather defeated. "I thought you came out here in the spirit of *friendship*."

"So I did," said Logan. "I also thought you might appreciate the company."

Iris batted a fly away.

"I've never much minded being on my own."

"Oh," said Logan. "Well then, I guess I can leave."

He began to scoot off the barrel.

"No," said Iris. "You're here now. You should stay. Please stay."

"Neighborly of you," Logan smiled.

"Sorry if you were expecting an engraved invitation."

Logan laughed softly.

Some birds were making squawking noises above them.

"Crows," observed Iris.

A murder of crows, they were called.

"Look, Iris," said Logan, leaning closer to her. ""Frank gave me a rundown of your conversation. He mentioned this issue about the inheritance. Just for the record, I told him that I didn't think it was such a terrible thing . . . you wanting to help him."

"And what did he say to that?"

"He said I didn't know what I was talking about."

"Perhaps you don't. Perhaps—"

"You do want to help him, don't you?" said Logan. "Or did I get that part wrong?"

"Of course I want to help him. What he doesn't know,

and what I prefer you not tell him, is that my options are limited without that inheritance."

"What options?"

"The helping options."

"How so?" asked Logan.

"I mean that things are not exactly thriving for me in the financial department," said Iris. "We didn't have much when Frank was growing up. Being a *working actor* wasn't going to land us on *Lifestyles of the Rich and Famous* and then it took a while for me to make a living selling real estate. Eventually I had a few good years during the housing boom. That's when Erik and I bought the house in Santa Monica, but then came the 2008 crash and we almost lost everything. Frank never knew how badly we were hit. It took years for the real estate business to bounce back and then Erik was diagnosed. Insurance didn't cover some of the more experimental procedures or most of his medications. He fought hard for a long time. The medical bills piled up. We took out a second mortgage on the house and I had to stop working at one point to nurse him. That's when Frank came to us in a spiral and we had to get him into rehab. He had no insurance himself. We paid for that, too. Money well spent, but I don't have any more rainy-day funds lying around . . ."

Her voice trailed off.

"Don't you see?" said Logan. "That's why Frank's so upset. He doesn't want you to bail him out again."

"That's what he says now. But none of us can predict the future. Maybe he'll need help down the road and then what do I do? And it's not like he's totally above accepting my assistance. I'm sorry to mention it, but he did show up on my doorstep three weeks ago with his boyfriend."

"That was an emergency, Iris. It's only temporary."

"Everything in life is temporary until you make a habit of it."

"Wow."

"What?

"Frank says you like to be contrary because it gives you the last word," said Logan.

Iris raised her chin in the air.

"Is that what he says?" she replied. "I don't know. Maybe it's true. Then again, Frank's opinion of me is none of my business."

"That's strange," said Logan, "because Frank's opinion of me is the one I value most."

He glanced away, out to the field again.

"What is it, Logan?" Iris asked.

He turned back to her. His face had clouded over and his eyes were wet. *Something else is going on here*, she thought.

"Come on. You might as well tell me," said Iris.

"Yeah," he said. "I might as well."

CHAPTER TWENTY-FOUR

Iris was watching Logan as if anything he told her now would not come as a surprise. This should have been reassuring, but in the weeks since he had known her, Logan tended to distrust Iris's facial expressions. It was as if she considered it bad form to lose her footing in a conversation or to even give the impression that she might. Perhaps this was part of her acting training, he thought. Or maybe it was simply how Iris had always made her way in the world. Logan knew a little bit about presenting attitudes for public consumption. He'd used his grin like ten thousand times to defuse certain situations. The smile would be no help to him now. They were sitting, kind of stupidly, thought Logan, on pickle barrels, between an old barn and a barren potato field. The barn, though it was listing like a ship taking on water, was attractively weathered and oddly beautiful. Logan felt it would make a nice Maine postcard. The trees on the property were all blazing with color.

Iris suddenly snapped her fingers at him, as if he were back bussing tables at *The Atrium*.

"Am I supposed to guess what you were planning to tell me, Logan?" she asked.

"I'm sorry," he said. "I'm not sure where to start."

"Most people would say *start at the beginning,*" said Iris, "but I'd settle for a little free association."

"Okay, okay," said Logan.

He looked away from her then, squinting into the middle distance, and began to speak.

"When I left home," he said, "when I left Las Vegas and came to California, I moved into a house not far from Venice. A bunch of us lived there. A bunch of young people. A man named Oliver Lash was the owner of this house. He wasn't only our landlord. He hooked us up with various jobs and kept track of our schedules and assigned us our rooms. He kind of arranged everything for us, looked after us."

"He sounds like a concierge," said Iris. "Or perhaps a cult leader."

"We weren't exactly brainwashed," said Logan, "but he definitely controlled everything. He had his fingers everywhere."

"Do I want to know where he had his fingers, Logan?" said Iris.

"What? No. Gross. I just mean he had a lot of fancy connections for jobs and such. He found me work at a nice restaurant near the ocean, where he was a silent partner."

"Forgive my cynicism."

Logan sighed deeply.

"What is it?" asked Iris.

"Maybe you're right to be cynical."

"And why is that?"

"Because I wasn't making much money at the restaurant and Oliver told me he knew of other opportunities that might provide some extra income."

"What kind of opportunities?" asked Iris.

Logan hesitated. He was at one of those dreaded *before and after* moments where your world changes as soon as you say something out loud. People told you about these moments all the time and quite often they happened in the scripts for *Windsor Valley High*. He gulped and went on.

"There was this photographer in the Valley," he said.

Iris raised her eyebrows at him.

Logan wondered how many other sordid confessions had begun with just those particular words.

"He was a legitimate photographer," he added quickly, "with a nice studio in West Hollywood. He was very professional. When I got there, to the studio, he described the photos he wanted to take. He gave me a rundown of lighting options, but what it amounted to, what he wanted me to do, as you may have already guessed, was to strip down . . . and pleasure myself on camera."

"I don't know if that would have been my *first* guess," said Iris.

Logan stared off into the distance some more, remembering how the photographer had him sit on a sofa and had put a laptop in front of him with a compilation of porno clips to get him in the mood. There was a mix of gay and straight scenarios, so as not to make any assumptions about his viewing preferences, he supposed. This was probably what passed for a generous impulse in the photographer's world. The sofa was a worn-out shade of lime green. Logan had tried not to think of its long, frenzied history in the line of duty.

"It turned out the photo he was after," he told Iris now, "was a close-up of my face at the moment of . . . release. He'd apparently taken all sorts of pictures like that, of guys from different walks of life with their features all distorted in passion. He said he envisioned this project as a comment on the patriarchy and the need for men to relinquish control . . . or some shit like that. I don't really remember."

"Lofty goals," said Iris.

"The money was good," said Logan. "I guess that's what I was thinking at the time anyway."

"Money does tend to complicate our decisions," said Iris, "as we were discussing earlier."

Her voice sounded nice and normal when she said this.

"He was planning to publish the photos in a coffee table book," said Logan.

"A coffee table book?" said Iris. "You mean like *The Lakes of Minnesota*? I can just imagine the title."

"It wasn't so arty," said Logan. "It was—"

"I wasn't really asking!" Iris squirmed slightly on the pickle barrel. She offered him an uneasy smile.

Logan felt embarrassed and wretched. It didn't always make you feel better to unburden yourself. That was another lie depicted on *Windsor Valley High*, where the lead characters were usually confiding their heads off to various second bananas, like it was the most normal thing in the world to do.

"I'm not judging you, Logan," Iris said after a long pause. "Remember, I danced in a cage for a living."

"But there's something else," Logan replied.

"More photos?" asked Iris.

"No. Oliver also ran a side business where he arranged . . . dates for older gentlemen."

"You mean like an escort service?" said Iris.

"I guess that's what most people would call it, except Oliver liked to say we were just dinner companions. He told me that these old guys were so lonely and shy that they only wanted to eat a meal at some fancy restaurant across from a good-looking dude. Otherwise, these guys would have been on Grindr or Scruff or some other hookup site. I wasn't expected to have sex with any of them. I mean, it wasn't *required*. I was just supposed to be good company, Oliver said—with the option of *negotiation*. He told me to think of it as community outreach."

"Like meals on wheels?" said Iris.

"I know how it sounds," said Logan.

"Do you, though?"

"I didn't actually sleep with any of those old men, if that counts for anything."

"Who's counting?" said Iris.

"I did get groped under the table some."

"That would appear to be an occupational hazard."

"It was not an occupation, Iris!"

"Don't take offense. How long did you do this for anyway?"

"A few months."

"And what made you stop?" asked Iris.

"Well, one of my dates had a heart attack."

"Over dinner?"

"It was after dinner. We'd gone for a walk on the beach."

"He had a heart attack while you walked on the beach?"

"Not exactly. He was otherwise, ummh, occupied at the time."

"How do you mean?" asked Iris.

"He was giving me a . . . giving me a . . ."

Logan did not finish this sentence but motioned vaguely in the direction of his crotch.

"I thought you said you never slept with any of them!"

"I didn't. We weren't . . . sleeping."

"I see," said Iris. "Some Bill Clinton semantics."

Logan cringed but continued.

"If you must know, I didn't usually let any of the guys get that far. But he was very persuasive—a district court judge from Modesto."

"I don't need all the details, Logan. I'm happy for you to retain some mystery."

"Anyway, I took it as a sign."

"A sign of what?

"A sign for me to stop what I was doing. I mean the guy could have died. Right? I might have killed him."

"So he did survive?"

"Yes. It was only a minor heart attack. I rode with him in the ambulance. But when Oliver heard about it, he was furious. He said I should have left him on the beach."

"He really said that?"

"He was afraid that if there was a lot of fuss or a police report or something that he might have been exposed or even sued."

"Sued for what exactly?" asked Iris.

"I don't know. Renting me out as a deadly weapon, I guess. I told Oliver I wouldn't go out on any more dates after that. I told him I was quitting the restaurant, too, and moving out of the crappy house where I lived with all those other . . . accidental people. When I went to tell him this—he lived in this beautiful condo by the beach—he was sitting in a big peacock chair in the center of his living room, where he liked to receive his visitors, staring at me and sort of wringing his hands."

"Who does this guy think he is? A Mafia don?" said Iris.

"Sort of. Anyway, he told me I was making this huge mistake by walking out on him because he had all these big plans for me. He was pissed off."

"Big plans," said Iris. "What else did he have in mind? A snuff film?"

"I know, right?" said Logan. "That creeped me out, too. I couldn't imagine where he thought all this was leading. When I had left Vegas, all I had wanted was to change my life a bit, but then I'd gone about it all wrong and made a mess of things. I was glad to be getting away from the guy, even though I had zero in the way of backup plans."

"But what's the problem now? I don't understand. Has something happened?"

"Yes. Oliver started texting me a few weeks ago. Now he is leaving me voicemails. They're sort of threatening. I think he's blackmailing me."

"About the escort work and the dirty photos?"

"It was art photography!" said Logan.

"Okay. Art photography. I only mean that it all seems pretty tame compared to anything the Kardashians do on a minute-by-minute basis. Doesn't a teen show like yours thrive on social media scandals and naughty little tidbits? This would seem to be right up their alley."

"There's more," said Logan.

"Now what?" asked Iris.

"He owed me money. That's the real reason I went up to see him, instead of just clearing out. I wanted to get my security deposit back and I hadn't been paid for my last three . . . dates. Even with the extra gigs, I was nearly broke. I had paid my rent a few days before this and my car had been in for major repairs twice that month. I didn't even have enough gas money to get back to Vegas. My mother would have to wire me some cash and this was a miserable idea. But after I finished talking, Oliver told me he had no intention of paying me a cent. He said I hadn't given him sufficient notice. He wasn't having any of it. He said his hands were tied, even though he was still sitting there rubbing them together."

"A real prince above men, that one," said Iris.

"I stood there trying to form another sentence in my head, something smart and perfect, something to make him change his mind, but before I could say anything, Oliver got a call.

"Anyway, before he took it, he just dismissed me, motioned me away like a bug. I didn't know what else I could do. On my way out of the room, I had to walk by these bookcases that were filled with odds and ends. Oliver was this collector. I should have mentioned that part. He had all these crystal pieces and china. It took only a second to reach up and swipe a small crystal egg from one of the shelves and slip it into my pocket. I'd never stolen or shoplifted anything in my whole life. I knew it was a stupid move. It wasn't even about getting reimbursed, taking this little thing, but it seemed like absolutely the right thing to do in that moment. It made me feel better anyway. I looked over my shoulder. Oliver was still on the phone. He was standing now and facing the windows. He hadn't noticed what I'd done. He had probably already forgotten I was there. Suddenly, though, he turned around and our eyes met. He smiled at me, one of those thin, victorious smiles, before shooing me away again. That's when I smiled back, very broadly, like a maniac, and I could see this baffled him. I stuck my hand in my pocket and felt the glass egg and then I got the hell out of there."

"Is that the gist of it?" asked Iris.

"Yes, except now he wants the egg back."

"I see. When was this anyway, the taking of the egg?"

"About a year ago."

"Why is he contacting you now? I thought he didn't even see you take it."

"He didn't. Maybe he just discovered it missing and put two and two together or maybe there was a security camera somewhere. He could have been looking for me all this time. He thought I'd moved back to Las Vegas. I didn't stay in touch with anyone from the house, including my friend Hugo, who probably always knew more about Oliver than he was willing to tell me, and I jumped off all social media and got a new cell phone. I figured that was the end of it, until a few weeks ago. Somehow, he got ahold of my new number.

Maybe he saw me on *Windsor Valley High* and tracked me down that way."

"My," said Iris, "that little TV show of yours has sure given you a lot of exposure. What's its demographic anyway? Middle-schoolers from rural Maine and power-hungry scam artists?"

Logan shrugged.

"Can't you just send him back the egg? Did you keep it?"

"No. I pawned it."

"Pawned it? Was it worth anything?"

"Well, there's this pawn shop in the Valley—Zinnemann's. The guy who runs it is fair and honest and it occurred to me that maybe I could at least get enough for gas money to leave town. I had no idea what it was worth. Honestly."

"And what was it worth?"

"Ten thousand dollars. It's this rare kind of Russian amethyst, a poma something."

"Is that how much you got for it?" asked Iris.

"No," said Logan, "that's not how pawn shops work at all. I got seven grand for it, but it meant I didn't need to go back to Vegas. I found a cheap motel that charged monthly rates and right across the street was that Starbucks I told you about, the one where that casting guy for the show discovered me. That was literally the day after I'd pawned the egg. It felt like divine intervention or whatever they call it when your life bursts open before your eyes."

"Dumb luck?" said Iris.

"But now Oliver is back in my life and he's going to mess everything up for me."

"I still don't see how. These are unpleasant stories, make no mistake, but he probably doesn't have any evidence of the theft and I really don't think the show will fire you."

"I don't care about the show," said Logan.

Iris watched him closely for a while and then reached over to touch his hand, a surprising gesture.

"It's Frank you're worried about, isn't it?" she said. "You haven't told him any of this?"

"I meant to, in the beginning, but it didn't seem . . . necessary."

"And now?"

"Now it seems unavoidable."

"How do you think he'll react?" asked Iris.

"That's what I'm asking you. That's why I've told you."

"What is it that concerns you exactly?" asked Iris.

"That he'll be disgusted and toss me out. Frank can be very . . . proper and dignified," said Logan.

"Frank!" said Iris. "I would hardly describe my son in that way. He was a musician playing in crummy dives for years and then basically living on the streets of New York. He was a busker in subway stations, begging for coins. He is a recovering drug addict. This is not what I would call the biography of someone who is proper and dignified."

"Maybe I don't mean proper. Maybe I just mean reserved," said Logan. "Frank has had a lot of experiences, but not a lot of *experience*, if you know what I mean."

"No. I have no idea what you mean."

"He can be shy. He still blushes at dirty jokes. He even gets embarrassed talking about your Nancy Sinatra video."

"He's supposed to be mortified by his mother dancing up a storm in her underwear."

"All I'm saying is he hasn't exactly *been around*."

"Oh, I see," said Iris, finally comprehending.

She looked slightly embarrassed herself.

"He's led a very PG kind of life when it comes to his . . . personal affairs," said Logan. "And I clearly haven't."

"Clearly," said Iris.

"I don't want to lose him. If this all comes out, about the guys, and everything. He's going think I'm a hustler and a thief and I'm none of those things. I don't want him to doubt what we have together, Iris, because I really do believe it's real. I'm in love with him, you know."

"No big surprise there, Logan."

Iris nodded pleasantly enough when she said this, but then quite quickly he noticed she was frowning.

"What is it?" he asked.

"I was thinking of what you just said. I don't know everything about my son's life and some things I don't really want to know, but I suppose he has always had trouble connecting with people. And he has that rather inflexible, judgmental side, too. I wonder if he's been a bit closed off because of the haphazard way he was raised."

"Or it could be simple genetics," Logan said with some emphasis.

Iris shot him a look, but there was no real anger attached to it.

"Anyway," she said. "I don't know how he'll react. You have been around us long enough to know that I don't have some inside track when it comes to my son's thoughts and feelings. We are not always in sync, as they say."

"I'm not so sure about that. You two are a lot closer than you think."

"We are?" said Iris.

"Of course. He showed up at your house after the fire, didn't he? I wouldn't have gone back to *my* mother's and I figure, under the same circumstances, you wouldn't have gone back to yours. I'd call that progress, wouldn't you, generationally speaking. Look, he gets a kick out of you, Iris. He loves you. I think you've done a much better job than you think. And if Opal is any indication, it looks like your family is only getting better and better as time goes on."

Iris turned her face from him. Was she wiping away a tear?

"When did you get so wise?" she sniffed.

Logan didn't respond.

After a while she turned back to him.

"Logan," she said.

"Yes?"

"I'm sorry if returning to your mother was not an option. If your situation was anything like my own, then I know how terrible that feels."

She paused for a moment before adding, "I'm glad Frank brought you home."

Logan stared into her eyes.

"I am, too," he said, his voice cracking.

"And I wish you luck now," she said.

"With what?"

"With Frank."

"I wish I knew what to do next."

"I think perhaps you know exactly what you should do," said Iris.

"And what would that be?" asked Logan.

"You just need to tell him and get it over with."

"You mean feel the fear and do it anyway."

"I hate that stupid phrase."

They smiled at each other as a pleasant breeze washed over them. Some leaves from a nearby tree were released in the wind and drifted down. Logan closed his eyes. When he opened them again, he saw that a scarlet-colored maple leaf had landed behind Iris's ear, as if she'd pinned it there, but before he could comment on it, she had reached up, snatched it away with efficiency, and cradled it in the palm of her hand.

It had been a comfort to tell Iris, after all, to say the words out loud. She had received the news with her cool restraint, despite looking a little queasy once or twice. Logan tried to imagine her as she was when she was young, striving to get away from the farm. He could almost do it. He could almost make out her youthful beauty and bubbling ambition. He certainly understood the need to flee a place. Most people probably could. He supposed he was still fleeing, but now he and Frank were fleeing together—sort of. It was a relief to feel so far away from Vegas and from Tanner Van Dean and that business with Oliver, not to mention the fire that had taken so much. Maine had worked some sort of magic over him, what with all the backdrops reminding him of that children's book he loved and the fall foliage and the super-quaint downtown. Then there was Frank's sudden family and their laidback, ordinary charm. For the first time, Logan felt that he had the courage to tell Frank everything. This feeling came to him as if from outside himself, as if it clung to the trees. He and Iris sat quietly together for a few more minutes, until they heard someone racing toward them down the path. It was Frank. When he came into view, Logan thought he looked as he had the night of the fire, after he had been turned back by the firefighters from trying to reach the house to save Bertram. He was wild-eyed when he spotted Logan and Iris, a mixture of alarm and surprise flickering across his face.

"There you are," Frank said breathlessly. "I've been looking for you. Don't you have your phones? It's Joe. He's having chest pains. Celeste has called an ambulance."

Logan reached out and helped Iris off the barrel and then the three of them moved as quickly as possible back to the house.

CHAPTER TWENTY-FIVE

An old man with a formal demeanor and lavish white sideburns ambled up to Frank on the sidewalk.

"I think you are to be congratulated," he said.

Frank stared at the man blankly. He looked familiar, but he could not place him, something that the man himself seemed to understand. A flicker of disappointment floated across his careworn face.

"Lincoln Thibedeaux," the man added helpfully, gesturing to himself. "I don't believe we have seen each other since the funeral."

And then Frank remembered. The flirtatious mortician!

"Of course, how have you been?" said Frank.

"I'm fine," said Lincoln, "but again, let me congratulate you. What would Celeste have done without you these last months?"

The man smiled somberly when he said this, though perhaps there was no other way for an undertaker to smile.

Celeste would have certainly done something, Frank felt like saying.

But he did not say this. He simply looked away and glanced up at the April sky, which was the color of faded denim.

"Not everyone would have been so magnanimous as to drop everything and relocate," Lincoln continued.

Frank had just left a craft shop and was carrying two large

shopping bags packed with carefully wrapped mason jars. He felt weighed down and awkward. Lincoln's praise, sincere as it was, carried its own weight and he felt rather unworthy of it.

"Well, I was needed, you see," he replied. "And things sort of came together in that regard. Plus, they *are* my family, after all."

Lincoln offered up another somber smile.

"And yet family obligation does not always guarantee generosity, does it?" he said. "Sometimes it can trigger the opposite."

Perhaps, thought Frank, but the fact remained that he felt no such obligation and he was uncomfortable being congratulated for doing something that simply felt human. The decision to change his life was also easier to make in the aftermath of the wildfire and everything else that had happened.

"I just saw Celeste and young Opal outside *All You Knit Is Love*," Lincoln said now. "That's where I got my intel. They told me that *The Potato Barn* will be opening soon. They both seemed so excited about it, but they didn't offer many details. Enlighten me, what kind of establishment is this to be?"

"I think that remains to be seen," laughed Frank.

"Opal said something about it being like a New York coffeehouse with posters and comfy chairs. But Celeste described a place with knickknacks and some furniture for sale."

"Yeah, well . . . again, it's hard to say," said Frank.

Opal had been binge-watching *Friends* of late, so she had become obsessed with the idea of turning the barn into a Maine version of *Central Perk*, and Celeste had never let go of her original notion of the space being set up as a shop for her odds and ends—so she would no longer have to lug her inventory to various flea markets across the state. But now that the barn had been renovated with reclaimed wood, its roof raised and rafters blown out, the space was so streamlined and large that it was possible to accommodate any number of ideas.

"And Opal told me the news about your handsome television friend. That must have been a blow."

"Not really," said Frank. "Nothing lasts forever."

"Ahh," said Lincoln. "That is an uncomplicated attitude."

"Do you think so?" said Frank. "Sometimes you have no other choice. You can't wallow. You have to move on."

"It looks like you have done just that," the old man said, "staying on to help out, getting this business off the ground. It's funny that I should bump into you all this afternoon after so many months, though I tend to hibernate during our miserable winters, like a brown bear. I don't see much of anyone, except my customers, of course."

The old man's eyes flickered. *Mortician humor*, thought Frank.

He smiled encouragingly and said, "Well, we're all in town today running errands for the grand opening."

"So I see," said Lincoln.

He motioned over Frank's shoulder, in the direction of the craft shop, where just then Logan and Joe were coming out the door, carrying their own bags, more mason jars for *The Potato Barn*. They were an all-purpose acquisition. They could be used as coffee mugs, flower vases, or candle holders. Opal had seen this idea on some hipster website.

"Joe!" shouted Lincoln as the men drew near. "It's good to see you up and around."

"Better than down and out," said Joe.

It was Joe's first trip to town since his heart attack last fall. It had been touch-and-go through two surgeries. He'd recently been fitted with a new pacemaker. The first one had given him an infection. After months of rehabilitation, he was home, shockingly thin (Celeste said he looked like a deflated Mylar balloon), but he was getting stronger every day and his wise-ass tendencies had remained intact.

"How are you feeling?" asked Lincoln.

"Is that professional curiosity?" said Joe.

"I'm not booking your viewing hours, if that's what you think," said Lincoln.

Joe laughed out loud.

"I'm just screwing with you, Lincoln. I'm feeling good. I keep telling these guys I'm in great shape for the shape I'm in."

"That's true," said Logan. "He does keep saying that."

"Logan, you remember Lincoln," said Frank. "He arranged Deb's funeral last fall."

"Of course I do," said Logan.

He grinned at the old man, who blushed and twitched.

"I was just telling Frank that I was sorry to hear the news about your television program."

"*Windsor Valley?*" said Logan. "That seems such a long time ago now. Anyway, it happens. Cancellation is a symptom of the business."

"That's what I told him," said Frank.

"Still, it's unhappy news, isn't it?" frowned Lincoln.

"I'm not so sure," said Logan. He turned his grin on Frank. "Good news, bad news, who can tell?"

That phrase was as close to anything Iris had used as a philosophy when she was acting and didn't get a job; a slightly less generic version of *When one door closes, another opens*. She'd told it to Logan when he had gotten the message from his agent about the show being canceled as they waited in the hospital that first night for any word on Joe. That had been quite an evening. They had all followed Joe and Celeste in the ambulance. Frank still remembered the walls of the waiting room in the hospital. They were painted a sickly green and there were framed poems hanging everywhere, written out in large, cursive lettering, strange poems about suffering and mortality. It was as if whoever designed this room had decided that the families of the maimed and ill should just lean into their depression as they waited. The sudden news about *Windsor Valley* had given Opal another reason to cry that night. Logan had sat with his arm around the girl as she alternated between weeping on his shoulder and typing furiously into her phone. Celeste, however, would not sit. She stood at the edge of this room, waiting to intercept anyone who came back to offer news of her husband. Frank sat next to Iris. He was furious with her.

"I feel we're responsible for this, coming back here and all this business about the will. I can't even speak to you right now," he'd said.

"You're doing a pretty good impersonation of it," said Iris.

"So you don't feel responsible, then?"

"The man's already had three heart attacks, Frank. Flossing his teeth too hard could have done this."

"That's harsh."

"It is honest. I won't say something untrue just to make you feel better."

"And that's supposed to be news?"

"I know you want to think that I've been unfeeling and unsupportive your whole life, because it fits a narrative that makes sense to you. But I've always loved you enough to be honest with you."

"When it suits you, you mean."

"Will you stop for a moment?" she said. "You need

to hear something. You said today that I consider you a disappointment. I do not consider you a *disappointment*, certainly not in some fixed and sweeping way, not in the way people might refer to someone as a *deadbeat* or a *cheat,* as a means to convey their entire character. Perhaps your decisions have, at times, upset me, or maybe I was simply frustrated by the bad luck you have encountered or maybe it's just how the whole wide world keeps letting us down, as Joseph and I were discussing before you walked into the sunroom earlier. Maybe that is where everyone's disappointment stems from. Let's blame the world. The point is I have no way of breaking it down for you or explaining it any better than that. I think the real reason for the distance between us is that it's *me* you see as the disappointment. Not the other way around. I was never who you wanted me to be, but I have, at least, been true to myself. I'm sorry, but I'm afraid at this juncture this will have to be enough for you."

"Ma . . ." Frank began, but he didn't know what else to say.

"And I need to tell you something else," Iris continued. "Logan is very much in love with you, and since the first time I saw you look in his direction, I have known that you feel the same way. So my advice here, my *honest* advice, is to make peace with the past and don't let anything get in the way of your future. I didn't know your Keith, but if you loved him and he loved you, I believe he would want you to move on as well. Just don't screw it up. Okay?"

"Where's this coming from?" said Frank. "What's brought this on?"

But Iris said nothing. She stood up, rather regally from her chair, the result of her sore back again or maybe it was just her natural poise. She kissed the top of Frank's head and then crossed the waiting room, to where Celeste stood staring down the long, dark hallway. Frank watched her place her hand quite gently on her sister's arm. Celeste turned around to face her. Iris then leaned in to say something. Celeste dropped her head as Iris spoke. Frank half rose from his chair, worried that they might be a sentence or two away from a septuagenarian cat fight. But when Celeste raised her head again, Frank could see that her cheeks were tearstained and she was falling into Iris's arms.

Frank was pulled out of the memory of that night at the hospital as Opal hollered a greeting from across the street. She and Celeste were carrying their own bundles, looking pleased with themselves. They'd been on the hunt for linens, folk-art tablecloths and napkins. The barn project had been a great distraction for everyone during Joe's illness, and now as the opening grew nearer, it was the cause for high spirits and expectations. When Celeste and Opal crossed the street and joined them, everyone except Frank began to speak excitedly at once. Celeste grabbed Joe's hand and asked how he was feeling. In response, he pecked her on the cheek and then they fell into their usual banter. Opal began making more small talk with Lincoln, perhaps to defrost the undertaker's odd formality, but what more this thirteen-year-old could find to say to the old man, Frank could not imagine. Their chatty group had created a glut on the sidewalk, so that other townspeople had to weave around them, though most appeared to suffer this detour well enough, nodding good-naturedly at the little crowd as they passed. Logan moved next to Frank then and put his head on his shoulder. They observed this rather sweet scene for a while until Logan pinched Frank's backside and whispered huskily, "And a fine time was had by all."

CHAPTER TWENTY-SIX

Iris sat at a sidewalk café near Venice Beach. It was called *La Chaussette Perdue*, which from her high school French she translated as *The Lost Sock*. A better name for a laundromat, she thought. There was an awning, but it was insufficient, and did not completely shelter the outdoor tables. Luckily, she was not seated directly in the sun. The summer sky was swabbed and cloudless, the color of blue steel. In the distance she could just make out the busy boardwalk and the Santa Monica Mountains rising up as a backdrop to the sea. Iris noticed a middle-aged couple at a nearby table. They sat in a companionable silence. She could remember no time during her life with Erik when they had ever sat at a sidewalk café. This thought did not trouble her or make her feel wistful. It was simply an observation. There were many things she and Erik had not done together, given their conflicting schedules, different natures, and varied interests. They were also not known for their silences, companionable or otherwise. Iris checked the time on her phone. The man was late. She wondered if he would show up at all. He had seemed curious enough when she'd contacted him. Being affiliated with several businesses, his phone number had been easy enough to track down. Iris had explained that she wanted to return something of value that belonged to him. She had not told him what it was. Her instinct was to not give him too much information. The man told her she could drop off the item at his home, but she dismissed this idea. She had decided it was best not to travel to the man's home because of vague safety concerns and she wouldn't have suggested they meet at a park bench somewhere because that scene would have felt too nefarious, like a drug transaction. A sidewalk café was public and respectable. She had told him a day and time and given him the name of the café, a place she'd scoped out online.

Luckily, Iris remembered the name of the pawn shop. Zinnemann's. Fred Zinnemann had been a director she admired. He'd directed *The Nun's Story*, one of her favorites. When she visited the shop, the egg was no longer there. It had been purchased by someone in Ventura County. Logan had said that the owner of the shop had a reputation for fairness. He was a pleasant old man with the twinkly charm of Barry Fitzgerald in *Going My Way*. He had remembered Logan and the crystal egg quite well. Iris told him that Logan was her nephew and that he had been given permission to pawn the egg, a family heirloom, but she was now having regrets. When she mentioned that she was willing to pay one thousand dollars over the original asking price, the pawnbroker had twinkled some more and said he would do what he could to get it back. A few days later he'd phoned to say that the return of the egg had been arranged.

This was when Iris had contacted Oliver Lash.

As she waited at the café, she spotted several men approaching on the sidewalk whom she thought might be the man, or what she imagined he would look like from Logan's recollections. She was picturing someone brutal and sneering, a petty tyrant. But when Oliver did arrive, from somewhere behind her, she did such an obvious double take; it was as if she was back in sitcom land. He was standing next to the table, hovering and staring down at her. He had the round, pinkish face and squinty eyes of a newborn. His hair was cut so close to his head that it was difficult to determine its color, and his chin was weak to the point of being undetectable. He was short and squat and wore a white linen suit that looked to be a few sizes too large for him, as if he had recently lost a good deal of weight. There was something soft and infantile about the whole package, thought Iris, though the man no longer had any claim on youth.

"I am Oliver Lash," he was telling her. His voice had a peculiar, ironic quality. "Are you the woman who contacted me?"

When Iris nodded at him, he scooted into the seat opposite her, as if they were old friends about to catch up over lunch.

"What's this all about?' said Oliver, neither pleasantly nor unpleasantly.

Iris paused to collect her thoughts. She noticed the silent middle-aged couple at the next table had turned to watch her.

Oliver, too, was studying her face. "I know you?" he said.

He was staring at her with that familiar look of half recognition, that reminder to quasi-celebrities that they had never really made it.

"No," she said. "You do not know me."

A professionally breezy waitress came up to take Oliver's drink order just then. Iris had already been delivered a sparkling water, which sat untouched in front of her. Oliver glanced disapprovingly at the water and then somewhat defiantly ordered a glass of white wine.

"So we don't know each other," he said as the waitress walked away. "Yet you have something of mine. How does that happen exactly?"

Iris said nothing. She reached into her purse and retrieved a small white box, which she pushed across the table. Oliver did not look at the box. He kept staring into her eyes.

"Is it ticking?" he said.

"You tell me," said Iris. "Do you know anyone who wants to blow you up?"

He ignored this, took the lid off the box, and peered inside.

"Ah," he said. "I had a feeling."

"Did you, now?" said Iris.

"Are you the boy's . . . relative?"

Iris figured he was probably about to say *grandmother*, but some accidental sense of chivalry had persuaded him to go with a less age-defining label.

"I never said there was a boy," said Iris.

"Oh, there was a boy, all right," said Oliver. "A handsome one. Logan. He came to my home and stole my property."

"Can you prove that?" said Iris.

Oliver squinted disparagingly at her.

"Perhaps," he said as he picked the egg up to examine it.

He was weighing his options, thought Iris.

"At any rate, your property is not stolen," she said. "You are holding it in your hands."

The waitress returned with Oliver's wine.

Oliver carefully placed the egg back in the box.

"Are you ready to order?" the waitress asked.

"I think not," said Iris.

The waitress lost her breezy appeal at this point. She smiled tightly but rolled her eyes, which Iris assumed was the young woman's standard response to procrastinating customers. When she told them she would return in a few minutes, it sounded like a death threat.

"So why couldn't Logan drop this off for himself?" said Oliver.

"I never said I was acquainted with anyone named Logan."

"Lady, don't bullshit me. I could still make a fuss."

His eyes widened for the first time as they flashed with anger. Iris was not intimidated. She suddenly remembered another acting exercise from her time at the Actors Studio. It was called *Pursuing Your Objective*, where you had to mime a small bit of stage business, like ironing a shirt or scrubbing a floor, as if it were the most important thing in the world to you. It came back to her now. She swept her table setting out of the way, leaned as far forward as she possibly could, and whispered lethally, "I don't think that would be advisable for any of us, do you?"

This, she was pleased to note, wiped the arrogant expression off Oliver's face.

"I was only asking a question," he said. "Where's the kid now?"

"What does it matter?" said Iris. "He could be residing in another country for all you know."

Maine might as well be another country as far as someone like Oliver Lash was concerned, she thought.

"So you do know him?" he asked.

"I didn't say that."

"But he's left the country?"

"Sure. If you like. In any event, your business with him is now completed. Is it not?"

"It would appear so," said Oliver, touching the top of the box, while still looking at her. "I don't know what he told you about me, but I was only trying to help the kid. Truth be told, he wasn't the sharpest tool in the shed."

Oliver picked up his glass and took a swig of wine, but some of it spilled, trickling down his nonexistent chin.

"Is that so?" said Iris. "That's quite an observation coming from a Renaissance man like you. I think we're done here."

Oliver bristled at this.

Then he said, "Hey, I *do* know you. Weren't you on

television? Am I right? Guest spots. Dumb blondes. Chorus girls. *Love Boat* and so forth. I watched lots of TV in my youth."

"I never did a *Love Boat*," Iris said contemptuously.

"You were a knockout, as I remember it. Looks fade, though, don't they? Especially for glamour gals like you. What's that saying, *Old age is a shipwreck*?"

He sneered at her then, resembling at last the petty bully Logan had described, the one she'd been expecting all along. She had no intention of letting him get the last word.

"You know," Iris told him as she stood up from the table, "another old phrase comes to mind after meeting you. Beauty might be only skin deep, but ugly goes straight to the bone."

Then before walking away without a backward glance, she reached into her purse, tossed a twenty on the table, and slapped the wineglass out of Oliver's hand, where it shattered noisily on the sidewalk, finally giving that silent couple something to talk about.

Iris did not think it necessary to tell Frank and Logan about returning the egg. She only hoped they would now remain undisturbed as they went about their new lives in Maine. It wouldn't have happened at all if Celeste had not sent her the check. The money was a surprise. Celeste included a letter along with it, telling her she was sending the windfall for several reasons. For one, they had sold a chunk of farmland after the estate probated and the profit was much more than they'd expected. For another, she didn't know what they would have done without Frank and Logan these past months. She and Joe felt Iris should be acknowledged for raising such a kind and generous person, a feat, Celeste wrote, worthy of reward.

However, Celeste said, she was mostly sending the money to make something right from their past. She then explained in the letter how Father and Mother had paid a judge to fix that beauty contest in Augusta when Iris was nineteen. Given that she was due some prize money and a plane ticket, Celeste had adjusted for inflation and arrived at this figure. She wrote that she hoped this knowledge would not fuel any more bitterness, but Iris felt none. Indeed, it was so long ago, it was as if that pageant had taken place in someone else's past life. Losing the contest had provided her with more motivation to succeed in Hollywood than if she had won the thing outright—and she *had* succeeded. Iris was able to acknowledge that now. She had supported herself and her husband and her son, for years and years in an unforgiving business, against impossible odds. Spending this found money to buy back the crystal egg and neutralize someone like Oliver Lash felt like the perfect postscript to all of that.

Iris was pleased to have patched things up with Celeste. That night in the hospital, after Joe's heart attack, with Frank indignant beside her and Logan stealing worried glances at them as he comforted a weeping Opal (whose resiliency had cracked), Iris had the strongest desire to make things right for everyone. It was, she had to admit, because of what Logan had said about family progress and all the rest of it while they sat on the pickle barrels. That conversation had released something in her. Compassion perhaps. She'd told Frank in the waiting room what she should have told him years before and she had given him a warning, too, a simple plea not to throw away love. Celeste was standing alone at the end of the corridor looking inconsolable. Watching her reminded Iris of her last days with Erik in hospice. It also reminded her that she and her sister had never been close. What a shame that was, because otherwise she might have been a real help to her in this very sad moment. She walked over to Celeste then, unsure at first of what she intended to say, but it all became clear to her as soon as they were face-to-face.

"Joseph will come through this," Iris had said. "I feel it quite strongly, deep in my bones, in fact. He is a stubborn old coot, and he will come through, if only for you, the woman he has always loved—and you must tell him something as soon as you can. The farm is all yours. You will have no more trouble from me in that regard."

Celeste had begun to cry then, and as Iris held her, she had nearly cried herself. Iris wasn't sure, of course, that Joe would survive, but people weren't always candid in such situations. Even when Erik was on his deathbed, some folks had tried to pump Iris full of false hope. There were worse things, she thought. She was quite happy for Celeste and Opal when Joe pulled through. He *was* a stubborn old coot. And by giving up any claim on the farm that night, she had pleased everyone in one fell swoop, including Frank, who stopped staring at her like she was a Bond villain. Frank and Logan had decided to stay in Maine for another week, to look after Opal while Celeste was at the hospital round the clock. This was understandable, but Iris had gone back home as planned. She hardly thought three extra adults were necessary to watch over Opal, who was the most self-sufficient person in the house. And what could Iris have done to help? Reorganize the kitchen cabinets? This was something that Celeste would certainly not appreciate when she came home to shower and change clothes between hospital visits. Iris had seen enough Marie Kondo to know that decluttering provoked mixed emotions in people.

Later, when Frank called to inform her that he and Logan were not coming back to California at all, that he'd given up his job and they were staying in Maine to help out indefinitely, she was strangely unsurprised. She could see how the circumstances (the wildfire, Deb's death, Joe's heart attack, *Windsor Valley* being canceled) had presented them all with opportunities. For once in her life, Iris did not second-guess her son. She did not ask how he planned to support himself or what he planned to do about health insurance or what was going to happen with his sobriety or his whole goddamn future. Perhaps it was because he was a middle-aged man now and she had grown tired of these questions long ago. It already was the future. Or maybe it was because there was such happy confidence in his voice, as he spoke to her about the move and the plans for the barn, that she no longer felt his survival was in question. She attributed some of that to Logan, of course, whose newsy FaceTime installments kept her up to date.

When she had asked him what Frank's reaction had been when he'd confessed everything, Logan had said cheerfully, "I'm here, aren't I?"

"But what about that?" she said. "You're really on board with all this? Aren't you going to miss your . . . career?"

It was the first time Iris had ever referred to what Logan had been doing on *Windsor Valley* so charitably.

"My accidental career, you mean? Nope. Not as much as I'd miss Frank," he said. "And I told you I loved this place. It speaks to me. It really does. Besides, this was a good time to pivot. I'm teaching now."

"What do you mean you're teaching?"

"Like acting classes. In the barn. Opal and her friends. Some grown-ups, too. I'm a big hit."

Of course, he is, thought Iris.

The renovated barn housed not only the café and the secondhand shop, but a space for Logan's classes and Frank's twelve-step meetings, too. It was unclear if any of the business ventures were breaking even, though Iris refrained from asking these questions. Logan told her there was a talent night at the café once a month and Frank had begun performing again.

"Don't say anything, though," he'd said. "Can you wait until Frank mentions it?"

Recently, Logan had sent her a video. *This is Frank doing a song by Tracy Chapman*, he had written in the accompanying text, as if Iris were such a dinosaur, she wouldn't recognize "Fast Car" when she heard it. She watched the video while sitting on the sofa—Frank on a raised platform in the dimly lit café, strumming a guitar and singing as sweetly as she remembered. She would do as Logan asked and not tell Frank she'd seen the video until after he brought it up, but after she watched it, she'd gone to the sideboard and stood in front of the photo of Erik where he was rappelling down the rock ledge.

"Our boy's singing again," she had said out loud.

The 101 was a crawl on the way back home from Venice. Driving in the middle of the day in Southern California was the one factor more than any other pushing Iris into retirement. She called work to see if someone could cover a showing she had in Glendale the next morning. She would give herself a day off, a prize for dispatching Oliver Lash from all their lives. She checked her voicemails. Frank was inviting her again to come to Maine that summer for a visit. She played the message twice, enjoying the buoyancy in his voice. She wasn't sure why she was putting off the trip. She would make the arrangements tonight. At home, she went straight into the kitchen and poured herself a tall glass of water, which she drank thirstily at the sink.

Bertram was sitting on the tile floor, ignoring her and looking out the French doors toward the pool in a wistful, penitent way. Frank's landlord had found the cat wandering about the neighborhood a month after the fire. He had somehow escaped, jumping through a broken window perhaps, as the home was destroyed. Despite his advanced age and one badly scorched ear, he had survived. It seemed Bertram's life had been dictated by drama. Frank had told her that Keith's aunt had found him as a kitten after someone had dumped him from a moving car. Then when the aunt had died, he'd passed through various relatives until Keith had taken him in. Then, of course, Keith had been killed and Frank had relocated to California, where his home had burned to the ground. Perhaps this vagabond existence was what the old cat thought of as he peered out the French doors. Frank was thrilled by the news that Bertram had been found alive, but since he was in Maine (and Opal had allergies), he had asked Iris if she might hold on to the animal for a while longer, at least until he and Logan could get a place of their own. It sounded like there would be more disruption for the cat down the road, but what Iris said, in her new style of agreeableness, was, "Of course I'll take him. We'll make the best of it."

In truth, she liked the animal. She admired his survivor status and how he mostly kept to himself while not exhibiting signs of feline manipulation. He slept at the foot of her bed and rose with her in the morning. If she were going to Maine, she thought now, would she need to get a cat sitter? Clearly the animal was resilient enough (with his track record!) to make it on his own for a week, as long she left enough food and water. She would not overthink this, she told herself. She refused to become some crazy cat lady at this late stage. Iris crossed the kitchen then and stood next to the animal. Bertram looked up at her briefly with his watery, disinterested eyes. She reached down to pat his head, which he tolerated, until he slowly shifted his gaze back toward the pool. Iris remembered that last scene from *Breakfast at Tiffany's* again, when Audrey Hepburn and George Peppard found the cat in the rainstorm. That was not the ending from Truman Capote's novella. She'd read somewhere that Capote had hated the whole movie and the cat business in particular. Iris could understand that, of course, though she herself was still susceptible to those Hollywood endings—not always, but now and again.

ACKNOWLEDGMENTS

My writing life would likely not exist if I hadn't joined Katherine Mosby's amazing workshop at the 92nd Street Y some years back. I am grateful to Katherine for her immense talent, her wise counsel, and her steadfast encouragement since the first day we met.

My heartfelt thanks to Lori Milken and Joseph Olshan for giving *Underburn* a home at Delphinium Books. I have long admired Joe as a writer, but now that admiration extends to his great skills and patience as an editor. Thanks to Jennifer Ankner-Edelstein at Delphinium and to Colin Dockrill for his beautiful cover design. I am most fortunate to have Mitchell Waters as my agent. His warm guidance, good humor, sharp reader's eye, and overall persistence made this book possible. I am so grateful to him. Thank you to the remarkable Natalie Jenner for her early and ongoing support of this book and to David Leavitt for his inspiration.

Sincere thanks to Judd Stark for his *turbulent brilliance* and for the text exchange in 2018 that jumpstarted *Underburn*. A big thank you to Miriam Clark for her friendship, invaluable feedback, and sharing her wonderful work with me during our writing sessions through the years. I am grateful to her and to Christina Burz for their comments on the early drafts of this novel. Thank you to Denise Tolan, whose consummate gifts as a writer and friend help to motivate me on a daily basis and to Simon Donovan and Meg Loftus Suchan, for their artistic example and for their support, literary and otherwise. Special thanks to Martha Gaythwaite and John Tebbetts for their endless avenues of generosity, too numerous to name—and for the lake.

I wish to thank the following for their love and friendship while I was writing this book: Susan and John Loftus, Jack and Juliana Tebbetts, Bill Tebbetts, Shaun Suchan, Denise and Matthew Price, Donald Albrecht, Burt Brody, Michael Fishman, Regina McFadden, Kevin Meade, Veronique Jeanmarie, Elaine Stenson, and Jeremy Walker.

I will be forever grateful to Thomas Westburgh for not taking no for an answer and for listening with his heart. Thank you to Zach for a million games of catch and for so much more. And finally, to my parents, William Oxley Gaythwaite and Julia Catherine Leavitt, storytellers supreme.

ABOUT THE AUTHOR

Bill Gaythwaite's short fiction has appeared in *Subtropics*, *Chicago Quarterly Review*, *Puerto Del Sol*, *Willow Springs*, *Solstice*, and many other publications. Bill's work can also be found in the anthologies *Mudville Diaries: A Book of Baseball Memories* and *Hashtag Queer: LGBTQ+ Creative Anthology, vols. 1 and 2.* Bill has worked at Columbia University since 2006, where he was on the staff of the Committee on Asia and the Middle East. He is currently the Assistant Director of Special Populations at Columbia Law School. Bill grew up in Boston and raised his son in New York City and its suburbs. An avid swimmer, movie aficionado and football fan, he lives in New Jersey with his partner, Tom. He has been writing stories since he was six years old. *Underburn* is Bill's debut novel.

Printed in the USA
CPSIA information can be obtained
at www.ICGtesting.com
JSHW020046011024
70848JS00001B/1

9 781953 002440